THE BLEAK AND EMPTY SEA

THE TRISTRAM AND ISOLDE STORY

THE BLEAK AND EMPTY SEA

THE TRISTRAM AND ISOLDE STORY

JAY RUUD

To Jim –
Hope you enjoy!

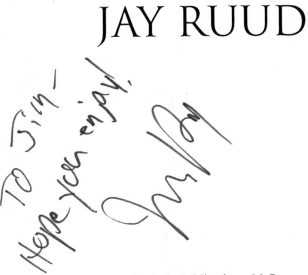

Encircle Publications, LLC
Farmington, Maine U.S.A.

Paperback ISBN 13: 978-1-893035-73-7
E-book ISBN 13: 978-1-893035-75-1

Library of Congress Control Number: 2017951278

Book design: Eddie Vincent
Cover design: Eddie Vincent
Cover images © Dmytro Zinkevych/Shutterstock

Published by: Encircle Publications, LLC
PO Box 187
Farmington, ME 04938

Visit: http://encirclepub.com

Printed in U.S.A.

Publisher's Cataloging-in-Publication data

Names: Ruud, Jay, author.
Title: The Bleak and empty sea : the Tristram and Isolde story / Jay Ruud.
Series: A Merlin Mystery
Description: Farmington, ME: Encircle Publications, LLC, 2017.
Identifiers: ISBN 978-1-893035-73-7 (pbk.) | 978-1-893035-75-1 (ebook) | LCCN 2017951278
Subjects: LCSH Tristan (Legendary character)--Romances--Adaptations. | Iseult (Legendary character)--Romances--Adaptations. | Arthurian romances--Adaptations. | Merlin (Legendary character)--Fiction.
Arthur, King (Legendary character)--Fiction. | Great Britain--History--Medieval period, 1066-1485--Fiction. | Historical fiction. | Mystery fiction. | BISAC FICTION / Mystery & Detective / Historical.
FICTION / Mystery & Detective / General.
Classification: LCC PS3618.U88 B54 2017 | DDC 813.6--dc23

DEDICATION

For Lucas and Elijah

Öd und leer das Meer!
Wagner, Tristan und Isolde (Act III, scene 1)

ACKNOWLEDGEMENTS

The basic source for modern versions of the Arthurian legend is Thomas Mallory's fifteenth-century compilation *Le Morte Darthur*, an amalgam of mainly French sources from the earlier Middle Ages. The stories of Arthur and Morded, of Gawain and Lamorak, of Lancelot and Guinevere, come essentially from this source. The text of the Whitsunday oath recited by Knights of the Round Table in the fourth chapter is modernized from Malory. The character of Merlin and his infatuation with the nymph Nimue is also from Malory, but Merlin himself is introduced as a character in Geoffrey of Monmouth's twelfth-century *History of the Kings of Britain*, which first describes Merlin and the moving of Stonehenge, and more importantly depicts Merlin as a soothsayer who utters inscrutable prophecies from a kind of trance. The story of Arthur on Saint Michael's Mount also comes from Geoffrey.

The story of Tristram and Isolde (and the faithful Brangwen) is told most famously in Gottfried von Strassburg's early thirteenth-century verse romance *Tristan*. Gottfried's poem lacks an ending, however, and it is usually assumed that the end would have followed the story as told in the twelfth-century version by Thomas of Britain, which describes the wound, the black sail, and Isolde's death. The story is also told in a more modern version in Wagner's opera *Tristan und Isolde* (from which the novel's title and headnote come). Malory includes tales of Tristram as well (Tristram is the English spelling), and the character of the rival knight Sir Palomides in my text comes from Malory.

Gildas is the name of a sixth-century monk whose text *De Excidio et Conquestu Britanniae* first introduces a depiction of Arthurian-era battles into written European history. Nennius was a Welsh monk whose *Historia Brittonum* names Arthur as the leader of the British in their battles against the Saxons, although Nennius lived in the ninth century and was not contemporary with Gildas.

Saint-Malo is the setting of Marie de France's twelfth-century Breton lay *Laustic*, or "The Nightingale," the story told by Captain Jacques in the novel. The monastery attached to the Cathedral of Saint Vincent in Saint-Malo was founded in 1108. The Cistercian abbey at Beaulieu was founded in 1204. Its first abbot was Abbot Hugh. Saint Dunstan's Abbey in Hereford is fictional.

I should probably say a word about canonical hours, and the keeping of time in the novel. Before the development of accurate clocks, medieval people often thought of the day as broken up by the established times for divine office as set by monastic communities. There were eight of these hours or offices, and the bells of churches, monasteries, and convents rang out to call their members to do the work of God, to sing the holy offices, at those times. Assuming a day in spring or fall, with approximately equal twelve-hour periods of day and night, the office of *prime* would occur around sunrise, about six A.M. according to modern notions of time. The next office, *terce*, would be sung around nine A.M., *sext* would be around noon, *none* at about three P.M., *vespers* at six P.M., *compline* about nine P.M., *matins* at midnight and *lauds* around three A.M. These are the approximate times for events in the novel.

Information on sea travel in medieval England, especially on the single-sail Cog ships common around 1200, can be found in Richard Gorski's *Roles of the Sea in Medieval England* (2012) and in N.A.M. Rodger's *The Safeguard of the Sea: A Naval History of Britain, 660-1649* (1997).

The chess match in chapter three is actually drawn from the compilation of games on the "Best Chess Games of All Time" web site http://www.chessgames.com/perl/chesscollection?cid=1001601

CHAPTER ONE
UNWELCOME NEWS

Tristram was dead.

Sir Dinadan had interrupted us in the king's private chamber to bring us the news immediately upon his return from Brittany. And Dinadan had been there to see it.

We had been talking about Camelot's two newest arrivals, Perceval and Mordred. Or, to be fair, I was in the room to wait upon the knights who were discussing them. There was Sir Gareth, his older brother Sir Gawain, Sir Lancelot, Lancelot's kinsman Sir Bors, and of course King Arthur himself. I was asked to attend as Gareth's squire, since they naturally needed somebody to pour their wine. So I stood on one side of the table holding a bottle of claret, while Lovel, Sir Gawain's new squire, stood across from me, holding a bowl of fruit, just in case the king or any of his closest counselors should get a craving for something cool to munch on during their debate, a debate that was becoming more heated by the moment. Lovel seemed a bit out of his element: he was trying hard to stay awake, since we'd been standing mute for a good hour and the council seemed no closer to reaching any kind of decision. I couldn't blame him; he was new, chosen to replace Sir Florent, who not long before had been invested himself as a Knight of the Round Table, only to leave the table almost immediately to marry Nimue, one of the chief retainers of the Lady of the Lake. Sir Florent himself had replaced the murdered Sir Lamorak, and his departure had left a vacancy among the hundred and fifty knights of the table, one that the king sought to fill at the great feast of Pentecost, just a week hence. Florent, Gawain's eldest son, had now also been replaced as his father's squire by the great courtier's second son, and Lovel had a steep learning curve. I say that myself as one whose curve had once been the steepest of any squire in Camelot.

"Look here," Sir Gawain was saying. "This Perceval does not deserve to be made a knight of the table before your own nephew, Sire. Think how that puts our family to shame. Especially when he is the brother of that same Lamorak who shamed our mother in such a vile fashion. Your own sister, milord…"

"That same Lamorak that you and your brothers ambushed and killed in recreant fashion?" Sir Bors jumped in. "Saving your honor," he added with a glance toward Gareth.

My lord Gareth nodded, though his scowl betrayed a suppressed anger. Sir Gawain's red face suggested no such suppression. He sputtered, "Recreant? You say so, do you? If we were not in the presence of the king, I would throw my gauntlet in your face and see whether a foot of steel in your gullet will seem recreant to you!"

"Cousin, you go too far," Sir Lancelot spoke calmly, relishing the role of peacemaker. "No knight of King Arthur's table can be called recreant. We do not know all of the circumstances behind that rumored ambush, but I daresay you might have a different perspective if the ambushed knight had indeed been defiling your father's bed."

"Your dead father's bed," Gareth added. "Of course, let us not forget that my brother Gaheris killed our mother. I can't see that either side is without blame here." I had never heard him defend his brothers' actions in the matter of Lamorak's murder, but if it were a question of loyalty to family or to the fellowship of King Arthur's knights, he would always choose the latter. Still, I could see that he was feeling some strain in this situation, but wanted to join Lancelot as a peacemaker. If Lancelot could restrain Bors, then Gareth seemed determined to assuage Sir Gawain's ire. "It's true I was not present at the ambush, but I can't condemn outright what Gawain, Agravain, and Mordred did there."

"This relates directly to what I was just saying," Lancelot began, his square jaw jutting forth like a rock. "Mordred has performed no knightly services. The only action we know him to have taken part in is this…this thing with Sir Lamorak. Sir Perceval, on the other hand, has been out seeking adventures. He killed the Red Knight and took his arms, an encounter I witnessed myself, and knighted him instantly on the field, for the Red Knight had just insulted you, your grace, in your own court before riding off."

Arthur rolled his eyes at this. "Yes, yes, he was a young man with a hot temper and bad judgment. Not unlike some people in this room," at which he glanced surreptitiously at Sir Gawain. "But I'm not sure the insult deserved instant death at the hands of a raw country boy…"

"Which Perceval, or I should say Sir Perceval, certainly was at the time. But raw as he was, he came from good lineage: son of your ally King Pelinor, brother of Sir Aglovale and Sir Lamorak, both of whom have been knights of your table. And he followed that first adventure with a number of feats in which he defeated knights who were breaking the laws of your land, sending them to Camelot to kneel before you for judgment."

"The son of Pelinor will receive no welcome from me!" Gawain exclaimed, shaking his red hair vigorously. "The knight who killed our father? Gareth, this is intolerable!"

"King Lot was killed in a fair fight, and he was a rebel against my lord Arthur," Bors stated matter-of-factly.

"Yes, yes," Arthur admitted, waving away Lancelot's arguments as if he had heard them a hundred times—as, in fact I'm pretty sure he had, at least half of them in the past hour since I'd been standing there—and essentially ignoring Gawain's outburst, since he had doubtlessly heard it a thousand times. I know I had. "We are going in circles here and not reaching any kind of agreement. Does anyone have anything to say that has not already been said a dozen times in this counsel? I would welcome a new point of view."

Silence fell over the group. Gawain shook his long red locks, his green eyes burning with wounded family pride. Golden-haired Gareth leaned his head on his hand, his thumb under his chin and his index finger pointed up along his cheek, and gave a bemused smirk as he surveyed the other faces in the room. Stolid, stone-faced Bors merely glowered in Gawain's direction, and my lord Lancelot, greatest of all Arthur's knights—rivaled only by Lamorak and Tristram in prowess—crossed his arms, raised his dark eyebrows toward his flowing brown hair, and looked around questioningly, blinking his pale blue eyes. Finally, someone spoke.

"Uh…I think there might be an easy way to fix all this…" came a small, squeaking voice from the opposite side of the table.

Sir Gawain glared at his son, who had clearly broken protocol. "Lovel!" he barked. "Squires are here to serve and be silent. How dare you presume—"

"He presumes because nobody else will," King Arthur interrupted. "Let the boy speak. You were saying, Lovel, something about an easy fix?"

"Well, yes, my…my lord, it…I mean, I guess it's obvious, but… why, um, why don't you just have a double-investiture, and install Perceval and Mordred as knights of the Round Table at the same time? Then nobody gets to say they were invested before the other. Nobody is disgraced by having the other ranked ahead of them…so, everybody is happy?"

Sir Gareth latched onto his nephew's suggestion immediately, though with his own sardonic flair. "Or at least everybody is equally unhappy, if our main goal is keeping the other fellow in his place. Why not, brother? It serves our purposes, does it not?"

Gawain was unconvinced as he turned his glare toward Gareth, but Sir Lancelot was ready to give up the quarrel and move on to other things. He had a life outside of the king's chamber, as I was well aware. "Done, for my part. As long as Sir Perceval gets his seat, I have no objection to your little brother having one as well."

"But Lamorak…" began Gawain, interrupting Sir Bors, who had started to grumble "What about Lamorak?"

"Lamorak is dead," King Arthur pronounced. "Nothing will bring him back. Nothing will undo what he did or what was done to him. We must move on in unity and in loyalty to the principles and ideals around which the Round Table was formed: A system of justice under the law, not one of revenge and more revenge. The commonwealth cannot survive that kind of worldview. I will not tolerate it in my realm. This must end here and now. As for the investiture, though, there may be some difficulty in putting young Lovel's suggestion into effect: there is but one vacancy among the Round Table knights, created by Sir Lamorak's demise—and, of course, Sir Florent's departure. Only one knight can join the brotherhood at this time."

"For my part," Lancelot intoned graciously, speaking through his beaked Roman nose, "I forswear any revenge for Lamorak. True, Lamorak was my dear friend. Between him and Sir Tristram, I saw our trio as the three pillars of the kingdom. Now, Tristram and I—"

In the midst of Lancelot's speech, Sir Ywain, Arthur's chamber guard for the day, stepped into the room and stood at attention. Startled by the interruption, Arthur looked up, questioning Ywain with his eyes.

"My lord," the knight began. "Sir Dinadan is outside. He begs immediate audience."

"Dinadan?" Sir Bors was surprised. "I thought he had been with Sir Tristram in Brittany."

"Obviously not anymore," King Arthur responded. "Let him come in, Sir Ywain. Let us see what is so pressing. Perhaps an urgent message from Sir Tristram."

"Yes, my liege," Ywain made a slight bow as he backed out of the chamber. The knights at the table looked at one another with curiosity, while Lovel scowled at me over their heads, shrugging his shoulders in bewilderment. And then Dinadan came in.

Dinadan fell to his knees and bowed his head, avoiding the king's eyes. His hair hung unkempt and unwashed around his shoulders. His habergeon was stained with rust and sweat. What I could see of his face looked haggard and begrimed, and there were lines along his cheeks that may have been the tracks of tears. "Your Grace," he began. "I come with distressing news."

"Is it news…of Tristram?" Lancelot prodded. "He is in danger? Does he need our help?"

"Not our help," Dinadan murmured. "Our prayers."

"Prayers?" The king's face turned a cloudy shade of gray, and I felt a cold hand tingling the back of my neck.

"Sir Tristram is dead," Dinadan said. And the room exploded.

Gawain and Gareth were shouting questions at Dinadan: How did it happen? Where? Was it in battle? Was it illness? Did Dinadan see Tristram's body? Sir Bors was moaning aloud while King Arthur made indignant sounds of wounded royalty, as if death had not shown him the proper respect. But worst of all was the deep cry that came from Lancelot—the wild animalistic wail of "Nooooo" that rose from his bowels to fill the chamber. Nothing in my experience with the great knight had prepared me for that kind of reaction. It was personal. It was profound. It was hopeless.

I couldn't help but feel for him. If, as he had just said, he and Lamorak and Tristram had been the three pillars on whom the weight of Camelot rested, then the loss of Tristram following hard upon Lamorak's death left him as the sole support of Arthur and all his ideals, as well as the whole realm and all the citizens within it.

Besides which I knew what few others did: that the Great Adulterer saw in Tristram as in a smoky glass the dim reflection of his own circumstances. How could he help but see in Tristram's death the presage of his own?

The king was the first to recover his composure. "Tell us how it happened," he said simply. "But first rise, Dinadan, you need not kneel there so long."

"My liege, please indulge me. I have not rested for several days; indeed it has been a week of constant rushing to come here with the news. Let me rest now on my knees as I give you the story as best I can. Know that I did not see him die, but I was with him when he took his wound. We were with Sir Kaherdin, his brother-in-law, and a posse of knights, including Kaherdin's cousin Sir Andred, his squire Melias, and a few others. We had ridden at the behest of Duke Hoel, Kaherdin's father, to put down a small band of marauding Norsemen that had been harassing the villages of eastern Brittany. We had pursued them to the coast off Mont St. Michel, where they turned to fight, their backs to the sea, and we slaughtered the main part of them and scattered the rest. But somehow, somewhere in the skirmish Tristram was wounded by somebody's spear. It had been an attack from behind and he was slashed in his upper thigh, but it did not promise to be fatal, and we bound up the wound and carried him back to Kaherdin's palace."

"If the wound was not judged to be mortal, how came he to die of it?" Sir Gareth voiced the question on everyone's mind.

Still looking down, Dinadan shook his greasy locks and continued his tale. "His wound grew more evil-looking every day, and soon the leech that attended him concluded that the point that had pierced him had been poisoned. Sir Tristram grew weaker as the poison coursed through his body, and he began to despair of his life. Finally Tristram admitted where his only hope must lie: La Belle Isolde, Queen of Cornwall, is known to be the most skillful of all physicians in the arts of healing, especially of healing poison."

"It's true," the now subsided Lancelot added. "Isolde of Ireland had cured him once before, when he nearly died from wounds received at the hand of her own brother, Marholt. She knows the healing arts better than any woman alive. If anyone could have cured him it had been her."

"King Mark's queen was his lover, though, was she not?" Sir Bors stated the obvious. "How did that request go down with his wife?"

Dinadan looked up at Bors and shrugged. "How would you think? To have her husband put his only hope for life on the woman who had been his lover for years before he married you: At the same time knowing that he married you only because of his friendship with your brother, and because by bizarre coincidence you shared the same name as his true love?"

"Women often have little voice in the choosing of their husbands," Lancelot acknowledged, his eyes darting toward Arthur as he said it.

"But they still have the unreasonable expectation of being loved," Sir Gareth chimed in, playing the innocent with his tongue in his cheek.

The king's chamber was decorated on three sides by enormous tapestries depicting scenes from the life of the classical hero Hercules. Behind me was a graphic portrayal of the great hero capturing Cerberus, the ferocious three-headed dog of Hades. On the wall to my left was another weaving depicting Hercules slaying the Nemean Lion, clubbing the great beast whose skin was impenetrable to arrows. On the wall across from me, behind Lovel, was a tapestry showing the infant Hercules, attacked in his cradle by two enormous serpents sent by Hera. As I recalled, the queen of the gods was jealous of Zeus's affair with Alcmene, and was bent on destroying the fruit of their union. But the tapestry showed the babe Hercules strangling a snake in each of his tiny hands. Another story, like this of Tristram and Isolde, full of love and jealousy. The door to the chamber opened through the fourth wall, and a large window let light into the room, which now slanted down toward the wall of the serpents.

Sir Dinadan now rose to his feet, moving into the light steaming down, and casting a shadow on the tapestry of Hercules and the serpents, and he continued his tale in a stronger voice. "Isolde of the White Hands," he began thoughtfully, measuring his words to present as fair an account as possible, "clearly felt resentment about the means Tristram sought to save his life, but she wanted her husband alive, and said nothing against it when Tristram gave Kaherdin his ring as a token for Queen Isolde, and asked him to sail to Cornwall to bring her back. And so Kaherdin left, with Tristram's request that he equip his ship with two sets of sails, one white and the other black. Upon his return to Brittany, Kaherdin was to fly the white sail if La Belle Isolde was on board, the black sail if he had failed to convince her to come. He wanted, you see," Dinadan added, looking around the room, "to know his fate immediately upon the ship's sighting, rather than wait for hours for the ship to dock."

"Might it not have been more prudent for Kaherdin to send someone else on the journey, rather than leave his friend in the care of a woman he knew to be jealous of the project itself?" Sir Bors asked. Reasonably, I thought.

"Sir Kaherdin did not abandon his friend," Dinadan continued. "I was still there. I was as close to Sir Tristram as any man. Jealous wife or not, I would have protected him from anything. But I could not protect him from the poison in his system or from the despair in his heart. Kaherdin left his castle and guard under the titular command of his sister Isolde, and Tristram in the care of me and his leech. The doctor, Master Oswald, saw Tristram several times a day. He warned me not to spend too much time in the chamber, for fear of wearing the patient out. His wife, of course, attended on him as well, though seldom in my presence and generally, it seemed to me, in a spirit of subdued resentment. As it happened, I was not with him when Kaherdin's ship was sighted on the horizon, returning some seven days later. When a call went out from the city walls that a ship was in sight, I ran to the ramparts and looked out. It was still tiny against the blue sky, but I could see it clearly: the sails were white. Kaherdin was bringing Isolde to heal her lover."

"Then she did come?" Sir Bors urged him on. "Were her arts not sufficient to defeat the poison?"

"She was never able to put them to the test," Sir Dinadan sighed. "Word went forth that the ship was seen, and Tristram heard it in his sickroom. His wife and Master Oswald were with him when the report came, and he begged her to tell him the color of the sail. She paused for a moment, the leech told me, and then she lied. 'Black. The sails are black,' she told him. And at that word…he died."

The silence that greeted this last revelation was profound. What, after all, could anyone say to that? The despair in which Sir Tristram must have ended his life was palpable to every one of us. At length, Sir Gareth pursued the questioning: "And what of La Belle Isolde? She had come all that way with Sir Kaherdin. What was her reaction when she learned she had come in vain?"

Sir Dinadan sighed again, even more deeply if that was possible. "She entered the sickroom an hour or so after her lover had expired, and his wife standing over him stony-faced. From what Master Oswald told me, La Belle Isolde fell to her knees, cradled Tristram's body in her arms, raised her eyes to the heavens, and collapsed. She was dead in seconds. Dead of a broken heart."

Lancelot was shaking his head. "It's all too convenient," he thought out loud. "Someone is to blame for this." He brought his fist down hard on the table. "Someone is behind this and should pay for it. How do we know that Mark is not culpable in this? If so this is murder."

For a moment the pallor faded from Dinadan's face, and I saw in that instant a flash of the old, sardonic Dinadan that I had known as Tristram's companion. With a slight uptwist of the left side of his mouth, he admitted "Mark is as likely to be behind this as not. He was subject to ridicule as a cuckold. I myself once wrote a song rhyming 'Cornwall' with 'Horn all,' and sent a troubadour to sing it to him. He was not amused."

"I remind you," the king's deep baritone chimed in, "that *King* Mark is still my vassal, and the sovereign lord of Cornwall. I will not have him made the object of ridicule in my own castle." It was the closest King Arthur ever came to showing anger, except on the battlefield. Lancelot nodded and sat back in his chair. There was little left to be said. Sir Tristram was gone and no one in that room had the power to bring him back. All we could do was bear our grief. The king dismissed Sir Dinadan with thanks, and the shaken knight left the chamber, to eat and to bathe and to get a good night's rest.

When he had gone, Sir Gareth called to me. "Well, that's unwelcome news. Gildas, come fill my glass. There is one thing we can say about this: Sir Tristram's death has solved our other problem: there are now two vacancies in the fellowship of the Round Table. We can now put our young squire's proposal into effect. We can induct both Mordred and Perceval into the fellowship next week at Pentecost."

"Yes," the king said distantly. "We can do that, I suppose."

CHAPTER TWO
AN IRRESISTIBLE REQUEST

The lists of Camelot were located behind the keep, where a door opened into a long, narrow field some twenty yards wide and perhaps a hundred long, between the crenelated outer wall with its guard posts overlooking the moat, and the narrower castle wall within. Here was where knights and squires trained several grueling hours a day: The knights to remain battle-ready, the squires, like me, to train for that day when we, too, like Mordred and Perceval in four days' time, would be ready to kneel as the king placed Excalibur on our shoulders and we rose Knights of the Round Table.

This morning I had spent two hours slashing and parrying with Sir Gawain's squire Lovel, trying to teach him the best way to defend himself as Florent had taught me in my first stumbling steps toward knighthood just a year or so past. But this afternoon Sir Palomides had set up a quintain so that the knights and their squires could practice their best jousting moves. He rode a great grey destrier, and I sat astride one of my master Gareth's brown beauties.

A war-horse like the one on which I was mounted was a knight's most expensive accoutrement, normally worth a knight's entire salary for at least a year. The fact that Sir Gareth had two such prize animals said something about the fortune he had inherited, with his four brothers, from King Lot of the house of Orkney, in addition to the fortune his wife Lyonesse had brought to the marriage. I sat my horse close by Palomides, waiting for a break in the knights who were practicing their skill with the quintain. Sir Bleoberis and Sir Lionel, and Sir Ywain's squire Thomas, were waiting in line, while Sir Safer, Palomides' younger brother, was set to charge the wooden jousting dummy. Safer sat on a lighter Arabic steed, the kind he preferred from his home country, and after staring momentarily at the target, he gripped his lance firmly, proffering it straight ahead while squeezing it snugly against his side, and pounded toward the dummy some fifty yards before him. He lunged at the quintain with all the weight of man and horse behind the thrust, and his horse reached its top speed just as Sir Safer walloped the target, which spun around on its post so swiftly that Safer had a devil of a time scooting through and out of the way before the weighted sack of the quintain swooped down to pommel the area that Safer had just evacuated.

"Well done, brother!" Sir Palomides called, the sweat glistening on the Moorish knight's dark features. Then he glanced at me out of the corner of his eye while Sir Bleoberis trotted up to take aim at the wooden jousting dummy. "Young Gildas," he murmured in low tones. "You are one that I think will understand this, and my heart is anguished, I must open it to someone."

I looked at the dark knight dumbfounded. He had never confided in me in this manner. It was true that I knew some personal things about him, as a result of investigations I had helped my lord Merlin to conduct in times past, but I had never considered my relationship with the Moor close enough to, as he said, open our hearts to one another. "My lord," I answered abashed, "I am nothing but a low squire. Surely your brother or another knight…"

Sir Palomides squeezed his eyes shut and shook his head as if fighting off great pain. "I cannot show weakness to the others. But you, you are a sensitive soul. I know this. I know that you understand a deep and hopeless love, for you too have experienced this with regard to the lady Rosemounde."

That slapped me in the face in a way I hadn't expected. I mean, I loved Rosemounde without reserve, but I wouldn't characterize my love as hopeless. Desperate, maybe, but hopeless? Wasn't I in training to be a knight just now precisely because I had a sincere hope that knighthood would make me worthy of her? "Look, my lord, I don't think that 'hopeless' is really—"

The painful wag of the head again. "I refer to the time when your beloved Rosemounde was betrothed to Sir Florent. That was indeed a hopeless time."

I had to nod in agreement.

"You, young Gildas, may be the best equipped in all Camelot to understand my plight. You know, do you not, of my love for La Belle Isolde?" Ah. Now I could understand where this was leading. I was not sure I wanted it or was comfortable with it, but Sir Palomides was about to share his grief with me. It was true, I knew that Palomides loved Isolde—loved her, indeed, hopelessly, since her body belonged to King Mark according to the bond of marriage, and her soul belonged exclusively to Sir Tristram, according to the bond of true love, that love that never wavered. The love of Sir Palomides, I believed in all faith, was just as true, and just as never-wavering. But for me, it was embarrassing to see the big man brought so low.

"My friend," he continued, his lower lip quivering with emotion, "she is gone. My Isolde has breathed her last. I suffered, it is true—no one knew how much—because her love was fixed only on Sir Tristram. I jousted with Tristram on many occasions, but he was a great knight. Fine. He deserved the most beautiful of ladies. I could resign myself to Tristram's having her, and I could love her from a distance. But this new rival I cannot brook. How can I live if Death is the one now claiming her? Over such a distance no one can love. I tell you, Gildas, I want to challenge Death itself, as I once challenged Sir Tristram."

"All the kingdoms of Arthur's realm mourn with you." I knew it was a ridiculous, and useless, thing to say to him. To the rest of us La Belle Isolde had been only a name, or a distant vision of regal beauty. No one, perhaps not even King Mark, felt her loss so personally as Sir Palomides. But there are no words in any human language that can console the inarticulate cry of the heart.

Palomides, though, as I knew from past experience, was a man of words. His deep feelings became poems, and this grief had moved him now to compose an elegy on the death of Isolde of Cornwall and Ireland.

"My friend," Sir Palomides began, and I knew what was coming.

"I have composed one last love poem for my dearest lady. Let me sing for you the last verses. It will help ease my heart."

And without a word from me he launched into a troubadour song in his deep baritone voice. The words, as I recall them, went something like this:

My Love, you do me wrong
When you do not heed my song
As you wait within your tower in empty silence.
Can it be you hear me not
As you lie upon your cot
For the life has left your limbs through wicked violence?
Oh God, take me away
I've no desire to stay
In this cruel world bereft of Beauty's charms.
Take me back to those sweet days
When I mourned her haughty ways
And dreamt someday I might be in her arms.
For now, her smile, her eyes, cannot be found,
All hope is buried with her in the ground.

I waited a moment after the last note, watching the tears streak his quivering cheeks, and reached out once more with empty consolation: "My lord, this hopeless love is painful. There is no consolation in this world. Life is suffering." I didn't really believe that. I mean, yes, life *is* suffering. But it is so much more than that. The more, at this point, would not be visible to Sir Palomides, and there was no sense talking about it.

"One more thing, young Gildas," Sir Palomides whispered, shaking off his grief momentarily. "It needs to be said. There is something that does not smell right in these fatalities. The manner of their deaths is all too neat, all too perfect. I swear there is something behind it."

"Behind it? You mean…"

"I mean that there were strong forces that wanted both Tristram and La Belle Isolde dead. King Mark for one. And the jealous wife. I cannot believe these deaths were accidents."

Before I had any real chance to process what Sir Palomides had said, Thomas was calling to me, "Gildas! Where's your head today, boy? It's your turn. You're keeping actual knights waiting, and that's not a good thing." I looked up to see a number of faces glowering at me, most notably Sir Lionel, who was due to run at the quintain after me, and was trying to be courteous and give me my chance at the dummy, but was clearly beginning to resent being kept waiting by a mere squib of a squire. "Sorry, sorry," I babbled as I maneuvered my horse into a position to charge the quintain. All the time my mind was racing. First Sir Lancelot, and now Palomides, both suggesting foul play involved in Tristram and Isolde's deaths. And both suspecting King Mark. Lancelot, of course, saw his own plight in Tristram's, and naturally looked to the husband, possibly reflecting his own inner uncertainties. Sir Palomides was in love with Isolde himself, and so also focused on that which had kept her unattainable. Without Tristram to blame, he needed to impugn King Mark. The fact was, though, that Mark was my king. He was Arthur's vassal, of course, and so I saw Arthur as my true lord, but Cornwall was my native land, and Mark was King of Cornwall. I did not want to believe he could be behind this. I did not want him to be so much of a villain.

My mind was still on what Sir Palomides had said as I readied my lance and kicked my horse, so I was a bit off balance when I struck the dummy, and the lance skirted off the edge of the wood rather than hitting it solidly. My instinct was to pull up and look back at the target as I passed through, and when I did I felt a heavy thump across my back, tumbling me in a somersault over the head of my horse so that I lay sprawled on my back in the dust, the horse dancing around me as he tried not to stomp me with his hooves.

"Hmmph," came a voice from above. "At this rate you'll never make a knight, Gildas of Cornwall."

I squinted upwards and put my hand over my eyes to shade them from the sun, and recognized Sir Gaheris's blond hair and blue eyes as he reached down to give me a lift up. He looked a good deal like his younger brother Gareth, but didn't have Gareth's playful smile or jocular disposition. "I'm sent by the queen," he told me. "You are summoned into the royal presence, lad. Let Peter here take your horse back to the stable." As I righted myself I noticed the thirteen-year-old page of the queen's chamber, holding my horse and looking at me with big, expectant brown eyes. It was like looking at myself four years ago, when I entered Camelot in the same position as this boy, as page to Guinevere. A pang of jealousy pinched my heart as I watched him take my horse away. Did she open her heart to him the way she used to with me? Did she tell him her inmost thoughts? Or was I somehow special? Her sending Sir Gaheris to bring me to her even now suggested that might be the case. Why the king's own nephew? Even if he was assigned as her personal guard this week, why send a knight at all? Couldn't young Peter have summoned me just as well? Sir Gaheris's involvement suggested something important was afoot that the queen wanted me to be part of. Or…perhaps I was just building myself up over nothing, and she just wanted to hear the latest gossip. Well, only one way to find out. “"Lead on, then, my lord," I said with a quick nod. "I am at my lady's bidding," and I fell in behind him as he walked.

"Bet your Cornish tuckas you are," Gaheris muttered. "Aren't we all?"

***

The queen's private chambers were off the castle's great hall beyond the throne room. There was a large outer chamber, where I expect her page Peter slept at night, as I had when I worked for her. It was separated from the inner chamber by a thick curtain, manned by the old clerk Master Holly, supervisor of the queen's household. He recognized me as I approached with Sir Gaheris and rose from a small desk to greet me. "Ah, Master Gildas," he said, squinting up at me, his welcoming countenance appearing no different from his most forbidding one: both were sour, pinched, and filled with suspicion. "I know that the queen is expecting you. Wait here and I will announce you."

After a moment, Master Holly stepped back out and waved me in, returning quickly to the papers and figures on his desk. Sir Gaheris turned on his heel to face outward, and relaxed into his guard position. I stepped behind the curtain into the inner chamber and found the queen sitting with her ladies in waiting: Lady Vivien, Lady Anna, and her newest, the fourteen-year-old Lady Constance, eldest daughter of King Bagdemagus, another of Arthur's vassals. On her right hand sat the lady Rosemounde, the Rose of the World and the bright star of my personal heaven. It had been more than a week since I had even glimpsed those deep brown eyes. Rosemounde's dark hair was clasped behind her head by a golden pin, and she held some embroidery in her lap. She was not working on it now, for her eyes were looking into mine, searching, and when she caught my gaze the corner of her mouth curled up in her signature smirk. Something was going on between her and the queen, I could feel it.

The inner chamber was only about twenty feet square, and four of the women were embroidering items from their wardrobes, while Lady Anna had a book of romances open in her lap from which she must have been reading before I appeared. Her eyes rose from the book for a quick look at me and then darted quickly to her left to see what Guinevere would do.

"Gildas!" She cried. "It's been far too long since I've seen you. No doubt your duties leave you little time to visit a poor lonely old queen." I glanced quickly at Rosemounde, who was rolling her eyes, which made *me* smirk as well. "Oh, you find that amusing, young Gildas of Cornwall? Perhaps Sir Gareth needs to work with you on your courtly manners. And aside from that, look at the state of your clothes! You come before your queen covered with the dust of some pigsty?"

"My lady," I stammered, as Rosemounde stifled a laugh. "I apologize for the state of my clothing." Quickly I began brushing the dust of the lists off my hose and doublet, causing Lady Anna to cough and try to fan away the small dust cloud with her book. "Sir Gaheris brought me straight form the lists, where I had had…some misfortune with my horse." I stopped brushing when Lady Vivian, too, started coughing. Then, regaining my poise, I added, "As for the smile, it was only the absurdity of your calling yourself 'old' that made me lose my composure for an instant. Your beauty is so ageless, your poise and charm so timeless, that I could think only that I had stumbled into someone else's chamber by mistake. But when I saw you, my lady, your visage took away my breath, and I knew I was in your glorious presence."

Now it was the queen's turn to roll her eyes. "Glib as always I see, lad," Guinevere answered. "But if you lost your breath, it was at the sight of the lady Rosemounde, I suspect, and not of me at all."

"Indeed my lady, her proximity is so close, that it is difficult to divide the radiance that surrounds the two of you."

"Oh, enough, Gildas, enough," the Queen grumbled. "Ladies," she announced, "my devoted servant Gildas has come to meet me in my private closet, with the lady Rosemounde in attendance. Continue your work. And your reading," she said to Anna as she rose with Rosemounde and started for the door that led into her private quarters. "I shall have to forego hearing about Sir Guy of Warwick again," she droned in a tired voice over her shoulder.

We entered the room, a rather small bedchamber of about fifteen feet square. The queen and Lady Rosemounde sat on the bed facing me, and I looked around the closet while they arranged their clothing in as seemly a manner as possible.

I had the honor only once before of being in this private room, and the furnishings looked familiar to me: floor-to-ceiling tapestries on three walls portraying, on the wall to my right, the martyrdom of Saint Agnes, tied naked to a stake and beheaded because she would not burn; on my left the story of St. Ursula, martyred with ten thousand virgins for her refusal to give up her chastity; and on the wall behind the bed a much more active heroine, Judith with the head of Holofernes.

On the wall behind me, above the fireplace that kept the small room warm no matter what the season, there hung a shield with the coat of arms of Leodegrance, King of Cameliard, Guinevere's father, and with it a two-edged short sword in its scabbard—for decoration or defense I couldn't say. But now that the ladies were comfortable side-by-side on the queen's bed, I nodded and posed the obvious question:

"My ladies, you have sent for me. How can I be of service?"

"The matter of Sir Tristram," the queen began without ceremony.

I shrugged. "Your Grace, I know no more of this matter than you do, probably less."

"We haven't brought you here to tell us what you know or don't know, you silly thing," Guinevere corrected me. "We want you to find Merlin."

I started at that. I hadn't seen the old man in months. And what could they want him for? "My lady," I protested. "My lord Merlin has gone into his cave. He hasn't been seen since the lady Nimue chose to marry Sir Florent, and took him away to live with her and the Lady of the Lake. The last thing he said to me was that he wanted to be left alone. Is it absolutely necessary…?"

My lady Rosemounde now spoke for the first time. "It may not be necessary but it is optimal," she said.

"My lady Rosemounde," I bowed to her. "I would gladly beard the lion in his den for you, which is not much different from bearding Merlin in his cave, but tell me why I need to rouse the old man. What has it to do with Sir Tristram?"

"We need Merlin's expertise," the queen answered. "And yours too, my boy, for I know you have been indispensable to him in the past. But he has helped us—helped me particularly—twice before in finding the truth in situations where someone has been falsely accused…"

"Yourself and Sir Florent, yes, your Grace. But who is it that has been falsely accused in this case?"

"My sister!" Lady Rosemounde stood up with some passion as she emphasized her point.

"The lady Rosemounde is anxious for her half-sister, the elder daughter of her father Duke Hoel," Guinevere explained.

"Oh, what an idiot I've been. Isolde!"

"Of the White Hands," Rosemounde added. "My older sister. She and my brother Kaherdin were the children of my father and his first mistress, Eleanor of Tours. She was nearly grown when I was born, and went off to serve as lady-in-waiting for Eleanor's brother's duchess. She later returned to live in Kaherdin's palace. That was where she met Sir Tristram."

"And where she married him," I completed the thought. "But my lady, what has she been accused of?"

"She has been accused of nothing…yet," the queen replied. "And it is important to keep it that way."

Rosemounde was still agitated, but now sat back on the bed and strove to keep her emotions in check. "Everyone is saying it. Saying that she killed Tristram, if not with the spear that pierced him then with her cruel words that pierced his heart. My own Gildas, do you see how this affects me? I have not spoken with my sister in years. We were never close because of the age difference between us, but she is still of my kindred. If she is tainted with the accusation of murder, I am shamed along with my whole family. Oh Gildas, you saved my reputation once before. Can you and Merlin find a way to do so again?"

I was too flabbergasted that she had actually used the words "My own Gildas" that I pretty much stopped listening after that. I could feel the blood rush into my face and babbled something to the effect that I would find Merlin and try to rouse him to action. But the queen wanted to get into some practical details that I had not had the time to consider at all.

"Of course, if you and the mage plan to truly investigate these deaths, you will have to travel to Brittany. That is where the deaths took place. That is where the lady Isolde of the White Hands resides, as well as her brother Kaherdin, and this doctor who cared for Sir Tristram. Are you up for a sea journey? It should not be difficult, just a short sail across the channel."

"Sail?" I glanced down, calculating the odds. It was going to be difficult enough just rousing Merlin from his melancholy. Getting him on board a ship seemed beyond imagining.

"The crown shall provide your transportation to and from Brittany," the queen went on. "All you have to do is get to the bottom of this."

"My lady," I replied automatically, "for you and for the lady Rosemounde I would cross a thousand channels. If I cannot rouse Merlin to this task, I shall go myself to Brittany. I will seek to exonerate Isolde of the White Hands, and for myself will look to clear the name of my own lord, King Mark."

Guinevere was taken slightly back. "I had forgotten, young Gildas of Cornwall, that you too have some stake in this. Your loyalty does you credit. But I urge you: get Merlin's help."

"Yes," Rosemounde agreed, rising from the bed again. "Merlin is vital to the investigation." She gave me her hand and I brushed my lips across it, catching a hint of rose petals as I kissed her skin that was softer than a baby's, and, with a slight upturn of the right side of her mouth and a quick raise of her left eyebrow, she passed out of the room, leaving me alone with the queen.

"Well, young Gildas of Cornwall, your little lady seems to be quite infatuated with you now. You're her hero on the great white horse, apparently. Don't botch it, my boy!" So she still felt the way she had when I was her page: comfortable dropping the formality while I was present and finding it easier to let her guard down with me than she was even with her own ladies, Rosemounde included.

"I still need to train myself into knighthood," I answered "Which would be a lot easier to do if I weren't running off to Brittany on a royal whim," I answered in the same vein. "I can never win Rosemounde's hand until I am ennobled by knighthood, since unlike you and she, my queen, I am not of noble birth."

"And yet have desires far beyond your station. Don't be a fool, Gildas. By sending you on this mission I am endearing you to the lady Rosemounde's heart. For that matter, her father the duke may himself be grateful to the young man who clears the name of his elder daughter, a name which, as Rosemounde is well aware, is now a hissing. Win over the daughter *and* the father, and your dream may come true."

I had not considered these possibilities, and naturally took great heart at the queen's words. "So you do think there is a chance after all that I may ultimately win her?"

"She will marry whomsoever her father and the king think will best undergird the stability and the security of the realm. I would not mislead you about that. The lady Rosemounde stands to inherit the duchy of Brittany: her half-brother and sister were not born to Duke Hoel's lawful wife, and even though he has legitimized them and provided for their living, Rosemounde is his heir. I will not deceive you, my young friend, there is but a slim chance of your being the lucky one. Sir Florent was an obvious choice, as Sir Gawain's heir and prince of Orkney. But that, as you know, fell through. Your only hope is to be the salvation of the house of Brittany, and win the girl through gratitude. At least this gives you a chance."

"A chance, yes," I answered. "But what if I find nothing? I hope to clear the name of King Mark as well, but what if I find that he and Isolde of Brittany are as guilty as everyone is saying? It's as likely I'll raise Lady Rosemounde's ire as her gratitude."

Guinevere shrugged. "The truth will out. The messenger often gets the blame. You might lie about what you find…come back with a story that exonerates both Isolde and Mark, and stand by it."

I didn't know whether she was testing me or making a serious suggestion. But I didn't like it. And I let her know that indirectly when I said, "Deception has never been my forte, my lady. I know for some it is second nature, and a great deal of deception was certainly wound up in this story of Tristram and Le Belle Isolde. Which reminds me, it was Sir Lancelot who first voiced suspicion of King Mark. I got the feeling he was reading his own story into the finale of Tristram's."

The queen's manner changed abruptly and her tone returned to the haughtiness of transcendent majesty: "Do you dare suggest, Gildas of Cornwall, that the king can be compared with a petty tyrant like your Mark? Or that Lancelot would engage in deception? Bring that up in his presence and you may well forfeit your life. You are to investigate this matter. You are to go to Brittany in the company of our servant Merlin, as his assistant. Neither the lady Rosemounde nor I believe that you have the maturity or the cunning to find the truth of this matter on your own. Go now. This interview is at an end." With that, she gathered her skirts and swept out of the room as I bowed after her.

"Yes, your Grace," I said to her retreating back. But mentally I kicked myself. Never learn, do you Gildas? I asked.

CHAPTER THREE
MERLIN

The bells of the convent of Saint Mary Magdalene just southeast of the castle were tolling sext when I exited the queen's chamber and stepped out into the courtyard of the castle. Since I was certainly likely to miss the midday meal if I were going to visit Merlin's cave, I got it in my head to stop by the kitchen and see if I might beg Roger, the chief cook, for a bit of bread and cheese to tide me over until I returned. The kitchen, a one-story structure along the castle wall with a covered passageway connecting it to the great hall, lay just across the lower bailey, the main courtyard of the castle. But if you didn't know where it was, you could always just follow your nose. Or your ears. The doors of the kitchen were wide open, as they were even on cold days, but on a warm spring morning so close to Whitsunday, the cooks and kitchen lads inside needed fresh air in those close quarters. Pigs were cooking on spits and the aroma of pork wafted across the courtyard along with the din of furious activity within. But other smells and sounds were coming from the pen to the left of the open doors as I approached, where four goats, three cows, a dozen sheep and some chickens were making their own rough din. I peeked through the doors and called to the back of the first cook I saw. When he turned, I saw he was not Roger, but one of the new kitchen lads, Jerome.

"Jerome!" I begged. "I've got to head out on the queen's business. Can you give me a bite to eat on the run?"

"Give us a minute," Jerome said through the greasy brown hair that hung in his face. He turned and ducked to his right, first opening the baking oven and grabbing a small piece of bread, and then picking up a large knife and walking over to one of the four fireplaces along the right wall, where two other kitchen boys were turning a whole hog on a spit. He used the knife to chop off a good piece of pork and handed it to me with the bread. The pork, coming from the crispy outer part of the meat, was quite well done, and I admit I made a comment to that effect.

"Well, like my father always used to say, when it's brown it's cooking, when it's black it's done. If we'd a' known you was coming, we'd 'ave 'ad better cuisine and a bottle of our best wine for the likes of Gildas, the most important squire in Camelot."

"Yes, yes, and Arthur's seneschal Sir Kay himself to wait on me, I suppose," I took the joking good naturedly, as it was intended. "Well, I see you're stocking up the animal pen for Whitsunday now. Expecting as big a crowd as usual at the feast are we?"

"Bigger, bigger, my lad. The great feast of Pentecost, and we've got more animals coming in every day. We'll be feeding all the knights of the Table, I understand, as well as visiting dignitaries; most of Arthur's vassals'll be 'ere to see Mordred and Perceval made knights of the Order. The king's sister, Morgan la Fay, might even be coming down, as well as the Lady of the Lake. Big doings, that."

"Ah," I replied. "Can't wait." Clearly preparations for a trip to Brittany could not be made so quickly that I would be leaving before the great feast four days hence. Besides, I really wanted to be there. It was the social event of the season, after all.

Merlin's cave was within walking distance and through a thickly wooded area, so I opted not to stop by the livery to get a mount from Taber, the stable keeper. Instead I strode toward the guardhouse and barbican, finishing my bread and meat along the way. But as I passed under the barbican to cross the drawbridge a familiar voice called out from the guard tower above the gate.

"Halt! Stop and justify yourself, you bloody dolt of a Cornishman!" It was Robin Kempe, captain of the King's Archers and devoted thorn in my side. I couldn't see him but I knew his voice anywhere.

"My errand needs no justification from you, Master Kempe," I called back. "You lowly, churlish villain. I'm on a mission from the queen. Can't you tell by the sanctified glow about my person?"

"No, it was obscured by the dullness of your stupid face. Get along then, I've got work to do."

"When did you ever do any work? Lying about all day in the guard towers napping?"

"Shows how much you know, Gildas my lad. The king's got me putting on extra guards for the big Pentecost induction. There'll be a crowd here and that's for sure. Not only all the knights. Petty kings and such like. I understand Duke Hoel is coming over from Brittany with a small retinue. And old Mark himself from your own neck of the woods. Be wearing black he will, I suppose, but he's agreed to come on Arthur's invite. This double-induction of Perceval and Mordred looks to be the biggest Feast Day in years."

"Duke Hoel is coming here? And King Mark?" That was pretty convenient. If I could get Merlin up and mobile, we could talk to Mark and maybe rule him out as a suspect right away. As for the duke, maybe I could ingratiate myself with him while he was here, if we could get to him and let him know we were on the case, looking to exonerate his older daughter. "That's great news," I muttered thoughtfully.

"What? You gonna ask them for a keepsake, are you? Move along, Gildas, your presence is distracting me from important things!"

"I'm off then," I called back as I moved at a quick walk onto the drawbridge. "I'll be back before nightfall."

"Unfortunately…" came the answering cry from the barbican.

Once across the moat I turned left, heading north. South of Camelot was the convent and then the capital city of Caerleon. Northward were the king's fields, the crops just starting to mature, and beyond those the woods that surrounded Lady Lake, on which, among other things, lay the realm of the mysterious Lady of the Lake and her companions, including, of course, Merlin's beloved Nimue and her consort Sir Florent. I plunged into the woods and, in a furlong's way, waded across the cool running brook whose water came halfway up my shins. I scrambled up the grassy bank on the other side of the brook and came to the vast white and brown wall of limestone and dolomite rock perforated with shallow caves formed by the stream and the lake waters. I knew which one of these was Merlin's, and I expected to see a red glow coming from the mouth of his cave, for though it was a warm spring day the cave was certainly chilly and damp. But there was no glow. That could only mean that he was in the deepest of melancholies, lying on his bed and dead to the world. With some reluctance I tiptoed to the cave mouth and gingerly poked my head in.

"White or black?" boomed the necromancer's voice as he looked up at me from his chessboard.

***

"Wha…? But…how'd you know I was coming?"

Merlin looked at me askance through the untamed bushes of his eyebrows as he sat cross legged on his small wooden chair. "Gildas, you're joking, right? Do you really imagine that you move through the woods with the grace and silence of a gazelle? I heard you a furlong off. Maybe if you'd stop cursing when you waded through the cold water you might be a little more stealthy."

"Well, all right, but how did you know it was *me*?" I challenged him.

The old mage shrugged. "Who else?"

"No one from the lady's palace ever visits?"

"If that's your subtle way of asking whether the lady Nimue deigns to drop in, the answer is no. I haven't seen the nymph since she rode off with Sir Florent at their glorious nuptials. Not that I'd have wanted to see her, you understand. Not her or anybody else," he finished meaningfully, with a glare in my direction.

"As I deduced myself,' I nodded back to him, pulling his other chair up to the chessboard. I noticed that his small fireplace was cold, and appeared to have been so for some time. But the cave was not completely frigid, since Merlin had long ago lined the walls with tapestries, mainly of knights fighting mythological beasts like dragons and basilisks. The straw bed against the wall was rumpled and unmade, and probably still warm. I assumed he had not been out of it long, since a few of the bound volumes from his bed's head lay open on the pallet as if he'd been perusing them shortly before I arrived. "Been up long?" I asked innocently.

"Not long," Merlin admitted. "The dark cloud has been hovering over me for weeks. Getting out of bed has, frankly, been a struggle I was not able to face. But you are here, and have, I suppose, some request from the queen to make of me. But first, more importantly, I'm asking you: white or black?"

"Ach, here, give me black. I'll give that a try for a change."

The old man raised his considerable eyebrows. "Overconfident, are we? Think because I've been a vegetable for two months that my mind's gone sluggish? Fine, boy, I'll take white and we'll see what you learn from it. So, pawn to king four. Tell me what the queen wants this time."

"Well," I answered, turning toward the board to answer his first move, "why do you think I have to be here on the queen's business? Pawn to queen's bishop four."

Merlin scoffed. "Why else would you be here? You didn't come on your own account. Oh, you probably wanted to, but you'd have kept away until you were sure I wanted company. King's knight to king's bishop three. The queen, of course, has no such compunction, or consideration, when it comes to the likes of you and me—the son of a Cornish blacksmith and the bastard son of a nun and an incubus."

I gave a short guffaw at his characterization of himself. I knew the incubus story as well as anybody else, but I also knew that Merlin really assumed simply that his mother had refused to identify his father, who had visited her secretly in her convent. But I corrected him regarding myself: "You know that my father is an armor-maker, old man, not a simple blacksmith. Pawn to queen three."

"An armor maker is just another name for a blacksmith who works for rich people. Queen's bishop to queen's knight five. So tell me what your queen wants of her devoted servant this time. How are the court magician and his trusty sidekick expected to save Camelot from today's disaster?"

"Look I just want to know, Merlin, if you are feeling up to the challenge of taking on this new assignment with me. Queen's bishop to queen two."

"Up to the…why you runt of a peasecod litter, the day I'm not able to keep up with you…" Yes, I knew that would get him. "Tell me what's aggravating the queen's nerves and I'll see if I'm interested. Oh, and bishop takes bishop," he cried triumphantly.

"Well, queen takes bishop, then," I replied. "And all right, if you're going to insist, I'll tell you. First…you've heard about Sir Tristram, I take it?"

"Heard about Sir Tristram? About as much as I've heard about the boils on your mother's backside, boy. How could I have heard anything about anything when I've been holed up in this cave for the seven ages of man? Pawn to queen's bishop four."

"No, sorry, of course not," I swallowed a smile. "Umm…queen to queen's knight five." I used to be apprehensive about the old man's tirades, but now that I knew him well I was more amused by them. But I knew he was not going to react well to the news I was about to give him. "Well, this is difficult to say…"

"Why? You're going to say it in Cornish? Out with it, boy, I'm not one of your dainty ladies-in-waiting that can't bear to hear about your great uncle stubbing his toe on a wine barrel."

"Tristram is dead."

"God's eyelashes, Gildas," he exploded. "Why didn't you say so? How did this happen?"

I sighed. "He was pierced by a poisoned spear in Brittany. It's a long story."

Merlin shrugged. "I've been here for months with no one to talk to. I have time for a long story. And as for your queen…" I steeled myself, anticipating a harangue about the moral and ethical qualities of Guinevere. "She looks like she could be vulnerable there," his eyes glanced down at the chessboard. "I'm going to castle here," and he moved his king to his right, jumping his rook over it.

"Queen takes king's pawn," I countered, and then launched into an account of what Sir Dinadan had told us in the king's council, with all the details I could remember, going over the battle with the Norsemen and the wounding in the skirmish, the slow decline from the poison, the request to Kaherdin to bring back La Belle Isolde, Isolde of the White Hands' heartless lie concerning the black sails, Tristram's death, Isolde's heartbreak and subsequent demise.

Merlin listened carefully to the entire account. Then he said thoughtfully, "Pawn to queen four."

I blinked. "That's all you have to say? Pawn takes queen's pawn."

"I'm thinking, you Cornish dolt. If I were inclined to wagering, I'd say the odds were fairly high that King Mark had a hand in Tristram's untimely end. He had the motive. He definitely had the means—his royal power could reach out to any place he desired. Rook to king one," he said. "Now your queen is really in trouble. Speaking of which, why does this so trouble Guinevere? What concern is it of hers if some knight and his tart die in a foreign land?"

"Queen to queen's bishop three," I retreated. "You know it's far more complex than that. Tristram is a knight of the Round Table. Brittany is not a foreign land, but a part of Arthur's realm. King Mark is Arthur's vassal. As is, for that matter, Duke Hoel. Hoel is the father of Isolde of the White Hands."

"And the father, as well, of the lady Rosemounde, the queen's favorite lady in waiting and your own hopeless love." Why did everybody think my love for her was hopeless? This was becoming annoying. But Merlin continued, "So in fact it is for Rosemounde that you want to undergo this investigation, because the way the story is circulating her sister comes across as the guilty party because of her cruel comments. Bah, sentimental drivel. King's knight to queen four, taking pawn," he said.

"Queen takes bishop's pawn," I said. "So what are you saying? Isolde of Brittany is not responsible? Because that's what the queen—and Rosemounde—want to establish, if you're willing to take it on. As for King Mark, I wish everyone wouldn't keep jumping to conclusions about him. How could he have had anything to do with it? He was in Cornwall. Tristram and Isolde were in Brittany, dying of broken hearts."

Merlin snorted. "No, no, no," he shook his head. "One thing I've learned in my endless years on this earth: No one actually dies of a broken heart. Trust me. I've been lying on that bed for two months trying my best. It just doesn't happen. Look, Gildas, when Nimue went off with Florent my own heart was torn from me. No physical pain could possibly equal the agony I suffered in that time. Certainly I wished I was dead. I waited. If it were possible to die of grief, I would have done so long ago. Sure, I could have jumped into Lady Lake and drowned myself, but the cause of my death would have been the water in my lungs, not the grief in my heart. Tristram died of poison from his wound. La Belle Isolde? She may have died there, but somebody helped her along. Queen's knight to queen's rook three," Merlin answered.

"So Isolde of the White Hands is not to blame?"

"Oh, she is very much to blame for her hardness of heart. But her words did not kill anyone. Was she somehow behind the poison that killed Tristram? That we cannot yet say. The spearing could have been inflicted by one of the Norsemen, though the poison suggests it may have been planned earlier and one of the Breton party inflicted the wound unnoticed in the battle. And as for La Belle Isolde—someone killed her, you can bet on that. And the manner of her death also suggests poison, does it not? The same person may have been behind both murders."

"Murders? So now you are certain these were murders? Queen to queen's bishop one," I countered. "But if you really think King Mark may be behind this, I still don't see how. Or why. If he wanted the two of them dead, he could have done it earlier, when they were carrying on in his own court."

"Queen's bishop to king's bishop four," Merlin responded. "Your loyalty to your native king is touching, I'm sure, but it may be misplaced. The first question you have to ask about this is, who hated the two of them enough to want them dead? Mark had the greatest motive. He was cuckolded by his nephew, and forced the culprit from his court. Living in Brittany, Tristram may have been out of sight, out of mind. But when he sent for his lover, La Belle Isolde apparently did not hesitate to leave her husband and sail across the channel to come to the aid of her lover. That may have been the final straw for Mark. It would have been so for many men. As for Tristram's wife, her motive was equally strong. Her husband was in love with another woman, and though she spent every day by his sickbed, he only wanted to see the rival that bore her name. Isolde of the White Hands was bitter enough to lie about the sails. Was she bitter enough to arrange her husband's death? Or that of his *lover*?"

"I know there was motive enough between the two of them," I countered. "But Tristram was wounded with the poison spear before he sent for Isolde, so the jealousy that you see flaring up as a result of that couldn't have been behind the poisoned weapon. And La Belle Isolde had just arrived. When would the wife have had time to poison her? Queen to queen two."

"You keep moving her around and not doing anything with her!" He said of my queen. Then, looking thoughtful he went on, "That might in fact have been Tristram's great error. His wife was there, he paraded her around for the look of the thing, but like you he did nothing with her. It was all for show. An unpleasant life she must have had. Anyway, if Sir Dinadan is still here, I'd like to talk to him about some details. Exactly how long had La Belle Isolde been in Brittany before she saw Tristram? Who had the opportunity to poison her? Where exactly were Tristram's wounds—was he struck from before or behind? What was his relationship with Kaherdin like? If Tristram was treating his sister with disrespect, then would he not also have a motive for murder? Queen's knight to queen's knight five," he said.

"Dinadan's still here. Everybody will be in Camelot over the next few days. It's nearly Pentecost, and Perceval and Mordred are due to be inducted into the fellowship of the Round Table. Pawn to king four," I tried.

"Bold move," he said sarcastically. "Bishop takes king's pawn. So I suppose that means we can't leave until after Sunday."

"Leave? What do you mean? Oh, and pawn takes bishop," I said triumphantly.

"Rook to king five, takes pawn," was Merlin's comeback. "And, by the way, check. Of course we're leaving. If we're really going to find out who is behind these killings, we're going to have to go to where they happened. We'll need to talk to the wife and to Kaherdin, and to the men who were along on that skirmish with the Norsemen. We'll certainly want to talk to this Master what's-its-name, Oswald.

Can't do that from here, boy."

"Oh, guess I didn't really notice that rook there," I said. "Uh... king's bishop to king two. So you don't mind picking up and taking a ship for Brittany just like that?"

"Boy, I've been here in this cave for months. It's time I did something. And now that I've thought about it, I really want to find out who did this. But I'll tell you from the start, if it proves to be your Cornish king or the lady Rosemounde's Breton sister, that's what I shall report to the world. Or at least, to anybody who'll listen to me. I don't care what your queen says about it. Rook to king five," he said.

"Attacking my queen. I mean, on the chess board. But I don't get it. The queen can just take the rook." Then I looked again. "And so you move the knight and check my king and I lose the queen. Okay, I'm not falling for that one. Queen to queen's bishop one."

"Knight to king's bishop five," he said.

"Whatever you find," I assured him now, "I give you my word the queen will not be displeased. She only wants to get to the truth." Maybe a little white lie on my part. What she really wanted, as far as I could tell, was to squelch the gossip regarding nobles related to her court. And I can't say that wasn't at least what I most hoped would happen. But I had to agree with Merlin, that if truth were not the goal, then the task would not be worth doing. We weren't going to go all the way to Brittany to pretend we agreed with a conclusion already drawn in the councils of Camelot. "King to king's bishop one."

"Knight to king two, takes bishop," he said. "We're going to need to start right away to make arrangements for the trip. The queen is paying for our transport, no doubt. It's been some time since I've been on a ship. I had pretty good sea legs at one time, as I recall," and with that he got up from the chair and did a few squats, limbering up his legs, before he seemed to pull something in his knee and sat back down again a little gingerly.

"King takes knight," I said, though I could feel the end was coming. "One more thing that I forgot, Merlin: King Mark is coming to the Pentecost feast to see the knighting ceremony. It's the perfect time to talk to him."

"Hmm. Yes, if he'll deign to talk with the likes of us. I suppose with Guinevere insisting upon it, he'll give us an audience. Whether we can believe anything he says without some kind of substantiation, I'm not sure. Rook to king five. Check again." With that Merlin got up again, looking anxious to be off somewhere, and prodded me, "Come on now! We need to strike while the iron's hot. Let's go see Sir Dinadan right now."

"Wait a minute, finish the game will you? King to king's bishop three. Want to lose that rook?"

"Oh for heaven's sake. Queen to queen six. Checkmate. Now let's go."

CHAPTER FOUR

THE TABLE ROUND

"I would rather have my daughter married to a knight of the Table Round than a petty knight or duke, for all their wealth," Duke Hoel was saying. "Of course my Isolde had her suitors from among the noblest families in Brittany, but when the chance came to marry her to one of King Arthur's three greatest knights, I never hesitated. These are men of great worship," he nodded to the scores of knights milling about in the great cathedral of Caerleon in preparation for the Whitsunday induction. "Any father would be mad to prefer wealth over honor. Isolde had enough wealth. What need had she of a little more land or another small castle when her marriage could bring her honor by association with the knights of Camelot?"

I blinked in some surprise, while Merlin cleared his throat and Sir Gareth elbowed me in the ribs. For after all, if Duke Hoel felt this way about his elder daughter, why should he not feel the same about his younger? And wasn't he saying in a most straightforward manner that if I were to be knighted, and further if I were to become a knight of the Round Table, he would consider me worthy of wedding the lady Rosemounde? Hopeless my eye. It seemed even the son of an armor-maker could be worthy of a duke's daughter if he attained an exalted position at the Table Round. Never mind that he was really talking about Tristram, and that Tristram had been of royal lineage after all and nephew to a king.

Duke Hoel was dressed all in black, and wore only a doublet and hose covered with a light woolen cloak, also black. His simple dress and rough good humor belied his aristocratic rank, but hearkened back to his youthful days when he was Arthur's close companion in his early wars against the Scots, the Irish, the Gauls, and the Roman Emperor Lucius—wars that had established the Arthurian empire. Hoel lacked the pretense and snobbery of some of the younger nobles I could name, and he kept his unflappable perspective despite the recent tragedy that had rocked his own family.

"Excuse me for asking, my lord," Merlin began. "But you wear black—this is in mourning for Sir Tristram?"

"For my son-in-law, yes. Cut down in the prime of his life. Oh, I know," he said, noting Gareth's quizzical expression, "People are saying he never loved my daughter. People say all kinds of insensitive things in times like these. But look at it my way: there is no evidence, no accusation from anyone, that Sir Tristram was ever unfaithful to my daughter during their marriage, Indeed, my son Kaherdin tells me, and others affirm it, that Tristram was ever the attentive husband, honoring my daughter as his wife while he protected and provided for her."

"He did send for La Belle Isolde, asking for her with his dying breath…" Sir Gareth offered.

The duke shrugged, his jowls quivering as he shook his head firmly. "He was dying of a poisoned wound. She had healed him of a similar wound years before, when he fought Marholt in Ireland. Why would he not send for her when he was in need this time? Oh, I'm not a complete fool. I know she had been his lover. I know he may very well have still loved her in the end. Who can probe the secret recesses of the heart? But did he act on those desires? He did not—not when he was married to my daughter. Therefore yes, I mourn for my son-in-law. What the man did before the marriage is his own affair. You may not think it to look at me now, but I too have loved… well, a number of women, before I was married. Isolde herself, and her brother Kaherdin, were the children of one of those women, the lady Eleanor of Tours. But I was a faithful husband once I married the duchess, the lady Rosemounde's mother. No, one cannot hold the boy's youthful exploits against him."

"Unless, perhaps, you were King Mark," Sir Gareth opined, not without a half smile.

"Well, there he is, you can ask him," the duke responded, nodding across the nave toward another figure dressed all in black. Mark, my own king, stood conversing in low tones with a few Cornish knights who had made the trip to Caerleon with him. Yes, we would definitely need to chat with him as well. But for the moment we were trying to pick Duke Hoel's brain. He was a pleasant veteran knight whose nobility sat on him like a comfortable old cloak. Stocky with a round face fringed with a salt and pepper beard, he had close-cropped hair and a head brown as a nut.

"But I do thank you gentlemen for being willing to come to my country and look into these deaths for the king. He has told me of your interest in finding the truth behind this tragedy. And I have offered to take you back to Brittany on my own ship when I leave on Wednesday next. I'll have my son Kaherdin arrange for your return to Logres once you have finished your investigation. I know," he lowered his voice now and spoke in a hoarse whisper, "what people are saying about my daughter. Perhaps it is true; Sir Dinadan and Master Oswald have no reason to lie. But if she was spiteful in telling Tristram that the sail was black, who are we to judge her? Most of us say things we regret when we are angry or jealous. But we don't have our words broadcast to the world by eavesdropping physicians. In any case, you have my support. I would like to see my daughter's name cleansed of its infamy, and you, old necromancer, are the one to do it, if anyone can."

Merlin tilted his head toward the duke. "Your confidence is inspiring, my lord. We will see you again to make arrangements for our passage to Brittany." The duke nodded and turned from us as knights and visiting dignitaries now began to take their seats in the small wooden chairs in the nave. I expected we would be standing, there being nowhere near enough chairs for the numbers crowded into the cathedral. Merlin, Gareth and I made our way to the other side of the nave, the better to waylay King Mark to interview him after the induction. Standing close to the back on the right side of the sanctuary, I spent some time looking about and taking in the full grandeur of this space that the nobles of Camelot had devoted to their Creator.

The vault of the great cathedral of Caerleon was tall, ribbed in the new Gothic style, and the side windows let in a rainbow of color, making the space seem open, light and airy. The windows of the left side of the nave featured scenes from the Old Testament: Adam and Eve, Noah's Flood, Abraham and Isaac, Abraham with the three heavenly visitors, Pharaoh and Moses. On the right side the windows depicted parallel typological scenes from the New: Christ as the Lamb of God directly across from and paralleling Abraham and Isaac, the holy Eucharist across from Abraham and the three angels, Christ's baptism from Noah's flood, Herod's slaughter of the innocents from Moses found in a basket among the bulrushes and, closest to the altar, Adam and Eve in the Garden of Eden across from the scene of the risen Christ with Mary Magdalene in Gethsemane, holding his own spade. In the apse itself was a grand fresco of the Christ Pantocrator, watching us from above, keeping his eye on all of us—Arthur, his knights, his realm, and all who sought to protect them, and all who sought to harm them.

The ceremony began promptly as the cathedral bells tolled sext, as William of Glastonbury, Archbishop of Caerleon, led the procession down the nave, crowned with the miter that proclaimed him a prince of the Church and dressed in his full bishop's regalia, including cope and chasuble, and carrying the crozier, the crook of his office. The king himself followed him, wearing his imperial crown and purple cloak edged with ermine, with Excalibur on his side. Behind the king on the right walked Sir Gawain, his flowing red locks framing his ruggedly handsome face, his green eyes staring rigidly ahead of him, underscoring the seriousness of the moment. He wore a finely woven olive-colored tunic with brown hose, and an Orkney-plaid cloak of red and green fastened at one shoulder. On the left Gawain was flanked by Sir Lancelot, whose tunic was a fine Bleu de France covered with a sable cloak edged with ermine. Lancelot and Gawain were to help arm the inductees, Perceval and Mordred, both of whom were currently on their knees at the altar, where they had been since Matins—that is, for twelve hours. Next in the procession walked Father Ambrose, the king's own chaplain, in his best vestments, followed by a dozen or so canons of the cathedral, whose task would be to help the archbishop with the mass that would take place before the induction ceremony.

Candles burned from dozens of candelabra in the choir and the apse as the procession reached the altar and the archbishop, facing the east with his back to the congregation, began the celebration of the mass. *In nomine Patris, et Filii, et Spiritus Sancti, amen*, he intoned, and then *Introibo ad altare Dei. Ad deum qui laetificat juventutem meam* ("I will go in to the altar of God. To God, Who gives joy to my youth"), and with that I began to daydream, thinking mainly about what our investigation had yielded so far.

When I had told Sir Gareth about the queen's command, he had grumbled a bit good naturedly, something about how her majesty was always using her royal prerogative to snatch the services of his only squire away from him, but then he had insisted on coming along with Merlin and me when we questioned people, at least in Camelot. He was interested in finding the truth behind Sir Tristram's death, having admired the Cornish knight for his skill at arms and pitied him for his poor judgment in matters of the heart. But he drew the line at sailing to Brittany with us. "There, I'm afraid, you're going to have to fend for yourselves," he'd admonished me.

We had started, of course, with Sir Dinadan, who had nothing to add to the report he had made to the king, which both Sir Gareth and I had heard previously. He could say no more about Tristram's or Isolde's death, since he had not been in the room where they died and had reported essentially what he'd been told by Master Oswald, the physician, and when Merlin pressed him, he had to admit that he had not seen Tristram take the wound in the skirmish with the Norsemen, so he was unable to hazard a guess as to where that spear thrust had come from. Dinadan did, however, plead with us to allow him to accompany us to Brittany for, as he put it, "I've got a score to settle with the bastards who did this, and I'll be buggered if I'm going to stay here and let you blokes track them down by yourselves."

As for Duke Hoel, he was a pleasant surprise, and his offer to take us across the channel on his own ship solved a transportation problem for the queen. His blessing of our investigation certainly promised to make our task easier once we got to Brittany. As for King Mark, it remained for us to question him. I watched him, sitting near the front of the sanctuary with his small retinue, and wondered what kind of heart might beat beneath his sable mourning weeds.

Sanctus, sanctus, sanctus Dominus Deus Sabaoth! Pleni sunt coeli et terra gloria tua. Hosanna in excelsis! The Archbishop droned on. "Holy, holy, holy Lord God of hosts! Heaven and earth are full of your glory. Hosanna in the highest!" I knew by this that we were getting near to the end of the mass itself, and soon the induction ceremony would begin. And my thoughts strayed again to Duke Hoel's comments about his daughter's marriage. If a knight of the Table Round was good enough to marry Isolde of the White Hands, would one not be equally good enough to wed the lady Rosemounde? And couldn't that knight be myself as easily as anyone else? I just needed to step up my training and reach the point that Perceval and Mordred had reached today. Sir Gareth, in one of his rare serious moments, had confided that he saw great promise in me, and said I only needed to master some of the more refined techniques of the arts of chivalry, having already attained the basics. It could not be long now—perhaps within another year I would stand where Perceval and Mordred stood today.

For in fact they were now standing. The mass had concluded and the ceremony moved seamlessly into the induction into the fellowship of the Table. King Arthur stood before the altar, and called the names of Perceval of Wales and Mordred of Orkney, bidding them to step forward. When they had done so, kneeling again and facing the king with their backs to the congregation, Sir Lancelot and Sir Gawain stepped up from behind the king, each holding a pair of golden spurs. Lancelot then fastened the spurs to the heels of Perceval's shoes, while Gawain affixed his to Mordred's.

King Arthur now lifted two newly forged short swords and held them high, one in each hand, while Archbishop William, now turned to face the inductees and the congregation, raised his hands for the blessing of the arms. Making the sign of the cross over each sword, he prayed in English:

"Oh thou, God of power and might, of justice and mercy, bestow we pray your blessing on these swords, with which your humble servants, Perceval and Mordred, wish to gird themselves. May they use these swords with skill and judgment in the defense of your Holy Church and people, of widows and orphans and of all in need of succor, and may they always strike with these swords only in a righteous cause. In the name of the Father, and of the Son, and of the Holy Ghost. Amen."

Now as the congregation echoed the Archbishop's "Amen," the king lowered the swords while Lancelot and Gawain stepped forward, each embracing his respective charge, and placing on the inductees' cheeks the kiss that symbolized the fraternity and loyalty that characterized the Order of the Table Round. The king now lifted one of the swords and delivered to Perceval the colée, striking him on the right shoulder with the flat of the sword, a blow hard enough to leave an indelible memory in the Welsh knight's mind. Perceval had already been knighted by Sir Lancelot himself on the field of battle, but in this ceremony that marked his entrance into the exclusive brotherhood of the Table, it was the king's blow that he would remember. When Mordred received a similar blow, there was no doubt that he too would remember being made knight by his liege lord, the king himself.

Now Sir Lancelot and Sir Gawain took the swords and handed them to Perceval and Mordred, to be girt on when they stood, at which point Arthur concluded the knighting itself with his acceptance of the two inductees into the order: "As King of Logres, Emperor of Ireland, Brittany, Normandy, and Gaul, and as sovereign of the order of chivalry known as the Knights of the Round Table, I hereby accept you into the order. Rise now, Sir Perceval and Sir Mordred, Knights of the Table Round." Now amid loud cheers from the congregation, the two new knights rose and Lancelot and Gawain girt on their new swords, upon which the Archbishop stepped forward and bade all of the knights of the Table to rise. "On the day of Pentecost," he intoned, "the Holy Spirit descended upon the Apostles of Christ, and the Church was born. In our own day, the Knights of the Table Round are descendants of those Apostles, and in this world God's work must be our own. The Spirit of God and His power inspire this fellowship, and we renew that relationship each year on Pentecost, as we repeat the oath that you all took when you became knights, and that Perceval of Wales and Mordred of Orkney join us in reciting now."

I had heard the oath once a year, every Whitsunday, since I had come to Camelot three years ago, and I now could recite it by heart along with the knights themselves. Each of the hundred and fifty knights, including Mordred and Perceval, raised his right hand and spoke the words that renewed the ideals of Camelot:

"We swear always to follow the commands of our king: never to do outrage or murder; always to flee treason; never to be cruel, but in all circumstances to grant mercy to him who pleads for mercy, or forfeit our own worship and the lordship of our lord King Arthur for evermore; and we swear always to give succor to ladies, damsels, and gentlewomen, on pain of death. And we further swear never to go to battle in a wrongful cause no matter what law may try to compel us to do so, and no matter what the worldly reward. All of this we swear, both old and young, the Knights of the Table Round."

***

The ceremony was over, and the hundreds of visitors to the cathedral waited impatiently for the dignitaries from the altar to file out down the long aisle of the nave, led by the archbishop and the king, in the same order by which they had proceeded in, but this time with Sir Perceval and Sir Mordred bringing up the rear. Sir Perceval was beaming as he sauntered down the aisle nodding and waving to compatriots and well-wishers among the congregation; Sir Mordred, on the other hand, stalked out of the sanctuary looking neither to the left nor the right, his face stony, his eyes fixed and lightless. I felt a chill as he passed.

Once the dignitaries had exited, the rest of the congregation began to push out as one great mob. "Not sure how we can grab King Mark in this crowd," I told Merlin.

"I'll try to catch him," Merlin replied, beginning to push his way through the jumble of bodies. "If we can't get hold of him here we'll still have a chance later at the feast." And off he went, leaving me and Sir Gareth behind.

Gareth was in no mood to rush. He held back and put a hand on my shoulder, so I relaxed and waited in order to leave with him after everyone had cleared the sanctuary. It gave me a chance to raise a question with him that had been bothering me throughout most of the ceremony. That had, in fact, been bothering me for quite some time.

"My lord," I began. "Your brother Sir Morded. He is, begging your pardon, a rather surly fellow. He seems to dislike everyone in Camelot and associates only with you, his brothers. I wonder…is there something that makes him this way? Or…" I quickly added when I saw Sir Gareth's brow knit, "if you think it isn't my business, then just forget I ever asked. I mean I…"

Gareth sighed, closed his blue eyes and brushed his long blond hair from his forehead. "You ask a good many questions, Gildas of Cornwall. I suppose that is why my lord Merlin uses your talents to help him make his inquiries. This is one question that is not easily answered. A difficulty the explanation of which only a few of us know. But as my trusted squire," he emphasized the word trusted noticeably, warning me that his trust had better not be misplaced, and that the story he was about to tell had better go no further, "I will tell it to you, but it is a story that must needs stay within the family. More than one disaster could follow if these things became widely known."

I looked about, and saw that we were the last of the congregation left inside that vast sanctuary, and Sir Gareth lowered his voice to a near whisper, so that I needed to lean in closely to hear him. "You know," he began, "that my mother's reputation for virtue was not, shall we say, impeccable?"

It seemed like the time for tact, though I couldn't deny having heard a good many rumors about his mother's licentiousness, in addition to the well-known fact that, when Sir Gaheris had caught her in bed with Sir Lamorak, he had beheaded his own mother, leaving the knight to escape only to be murdered later in ambush. But it didn't seem a good time to bring those details up either, so I merely managed to utter "Hmmph."

"Well, you know of course about the sordid affair with Sir Lamorak. Everybody in Camelot knows about that. But it was not, unfortunately, my mother's first illicit assignation. When I was about four years old, my mother came to Camelot as an ambassador from the court of my father, King Lot of Orkney. She had really been sent as a spy, of course, since my father and his allies were planning their rebellion against the newly-crowned boy king whose right to the throne was contested at the time. You know of course that Arthur became king through a device of Merlin's: a sword plunged through an anvil sitting on a great stone that, according to the mage, could only be removed by the rightfully born king of all Logres. When the upstart fifteen-year-old Arthur was able to do what none of the boldest and most nobly-born peers of the land could do, many of those very peers took umbrage and denied Arthur their support. Anyway, Queen Margause, my lovely mother—who was, by all accounts, the most beautiful woman in the kingdom—arrived in Camelot, the young king was besotted with her, even though she was trailing her whole brood of brats: Gawain was ten, Gaheris eight, Agravain six, and then me, the baby of the family. Of course I didn't realize it at the time, but while she was here Margause managed to seduce the young king (not, I'm sure, a difficult task for a mature and beautiful woman targeting an adolescent boy with raging hormones)."

"The king…and Margause?" I was taken aback by the revelation. "But wasn't she his…"

"His half-sister, yes. Now you understand why this must remain a secret. This liaison occurred around the beginning of August, and Margause returned with all of us to Orkney immediately afterwards. My brother Mordred was born nine months later."

"But…brother and sister…I can't understand what could have moved them to…"

"As I've already said, what moved Arthur was hormones. What moved my mother was much darker, I have no doubt. She certainly thought that her sexual favor would bind the boy king to her and enable her to supply Lot with information he would otherwise have no access to…or, in the event that Lot was ultimately defeated, would make the victorious king sympathetic to her and may even give her the opportunity to act as the power behind the throne—the older woman manipulating the young king through her carnal powers. In the long run, she might even be the mother of the king's only son, the likely heir to the throne, and someone she could continue to manipulate, and make her the power behind the throne over the reigns of two kings. Don't look skeptical, young Gildas, you did not know my mother. She was not only capable of thinking this way, she was exceedingly likely to think this way.

"But let your mind be at ease about the incest. Neither Arthur nor Margause knew of their relationship until after their encounter. Only Merlin knew at the time who Arthur's father was. As I said, after the incident with the sword in the stone, a number of the great barons of the country refused to recognize Arthur as their king. The sword was Merlin's test, and everybody knew that Merlin could have rigged the contest so that only his own candidate knew the secret of how to draw it from the anvil. My father was one of them. Who was this Arthur, anyway? Who was his father? Was he somebody's bastard, and if so, what right did he have to the throne of Logres? So Merlin had to come clean. He revealed the fact that Uther Pendragon had sired Arthur on Igraine, the Duchess of Cornwall, in the guise of her husband Gorlois. Since Gorlois himself was already dead, and since Uther married Igraine afterwards, Arthur was the only legitimate son of Uther, the last king. That knowledge satisfied some of the barons—not, I should say, King Lot—but it did mean that Margause was Arthur's half-sister, and it made Mordred not only a bastard but the child of incest."

"So…," I began, "I guess that explains why you and Sir Gaheris have blue eyes and blond hair…"

"Like my mother," Gareth agreed.

"Sir Gawain and Sir Agravain have red hair and green eyes…"

"Like my father," Gareth agreed.

"And Sir Mordred has dark hair and dark eyes…"

"Just like the king."

It gave me a lot to think about. "And Mordred knows where he came from? So his surliness is because he resents the king for not recognizing him? Not legitimatizing him?"

"No," Gareth told me. "Actually, I haven't really gotten to the bad part of the story."

"What? What could be worse than incest and adultery? What do you mean the bad part of the story?" I felt a cold hand squeezing the back of my neck as I shivered at the tale. This was my hero. This was Arthur, founder of the Round Table and creator of a new order of chivalry. How could he be behind these things?

Sir Gareth drew a deep breath. "Here's the thing. As I said, nobody but Merlin knew the truth about Arthur, and he hadn't even told Arthur. So when Arthur admitted to him what he'd done, Merlin blew up. He told him the fruit of that union could only bring destruction on his kingdom. Well Arthur, impressionable kid that he was, thought Merlin was making a prophecy that his son by Margause would grow up to kill his father and destroy Arthur's kingdom. When Arthur heard that Mordred had been born on May Day, he issued a command that all of the male babes in the kingdom born to noble families on that date must be surrendered to the crown. Not realizing what was coming, the nobles complied, and my mother dutifully allowed the agents of the king to take Mordred away."

"Well then, what was coming? What did Arthur do with the children?"

"He put them all into a ship," Gareth carefully explained. "A ship that had no captain or pilot or crew—that just contained the babies, all of them just a month old. The reasoning was this: if he set them adrift on a ship, he felt that nobody could claim that he had murdered the children. Whatever happened to them was God's will. If God wanted the babes saved, then He would do it. If He was willing to let them be slain, then He would not intervene. And who could say that it was Arthur's fault? Wouldn't it be blasphemy to blame the king for what God failed to do?"

"No, it would not. In fact, that line of reasoning is blasphemous in itself. It's an attempt to manipulate the people's faith and use it for personal advantage. I cannot believe that the king had any hand in this villainy."

Gareth gave a grim smile. "Your outrage is well placed, my friend. I will not say the king himself gave out this rationalization, but his advisers certainly did."

"But obviously Mordred survived. Did all of the babes live?"

Sir Gareth shook his head gravely. "The ship was cast adrift in the

Channel, and a storm drove it against the rocks near a remote castle on the shoreline, breaking the ship apart. Every child on board was drowned—every child but one. A good man, Lord Berwyn, came rushing from the castle when he saw the ship flounder, and found only one survivor cast up from the sea—the baby Mordred. Shortly thereafter, word came to the kindly fellow of the ship and its tragic cargo, and he realized that the babe was in danger if he was found to have survived. So he kept the child hidden and raised him as his own for fourteen years."

"I don't understand," I interrupted. I was breathing hard now, so distressed was I about this story that I couldn't digest it all at once. "The ship was full of children, all of the same age and all from noble families. How can anyone be sure that the child that survived is Mordred, and not one of the other noble children?"

"Ah," Sir Gareth answered. "Good question. And one, I might add, that nobody ever asks. But here is what happened. My mother had put a necklace around the boy's neck with a pendant that carried the crest of the House of Orkney. That pendant was on the child when Lord Berwyn found him, and when he sent the child back to his mother in Orkney fourteen years later, he brought her the pendant as evidence of his parentage. Besides that," Gareth added with a slight shrug, "Mordred at fourteen looked so much like his father the king had at that age—just about the same age as Arthur was when he conceived him—that Margause could have no doubt of his identity."

I began to feel dizzy, as if I were about to faint, and sick to my stomach as well. I felt as if all the pillars supporting my world were being knocked out from under me one by one. King Arthur? This sounded more like King Herod. How could I remain devoted to this man and his ideals—ideals that the Knights of the Table had just finished swearing to, but which now seemed as hollow as that broken ship's hull? "Well," I said after a fairly long pause. "I guess that would explain Mordred's bad temper. Knowing your father tried to kill you when you were a month old might cause you some resentment, especially if you were now grown and were a knight in his castle, without being acknowledged as his son. I mean, why go through this ritual? Why would Mordred play Arthur's game and join his order of knights?"

"I suppose because it's family. All of his brothers are here, right? Our parents are dead. Where else can he go?"

"Stay in Orkney? Rule there? Not have to face his bitterness every day? I don't know, but it would have to be a better life."

"Not if what you wanted most was to show your father he'd been wrong about you. To show him you were better than he expected, or better than the others that he'd placed ahead of you—worthy, in fact, to be the heir that he refused to name you."

"Also not if what you really wanted was to take revenge on him," I added, seeing the picture a little differently. "But what about you? You and Gawain know all of this, and yet here you are, among Arthur's most trusted knights. I have to admit, this news about the king makes me question my devotion to him, even question my allegiance to Camelot. Why do you stay? Why did you even come here to be a part of what you knew was a…a sham?"

Gareth gave me a fond half-smile and tilted his head slightly. "Gildas my lad, people are better than their worst acts. Yes, Arthur ordered the destruction of the children. Remember, though, that he was fifteen years old at the time…"

"Old enough to know right from wrong!"

"Perhaps," Sir Gareth admitted. "But old enough to measure one evil against another and clearly see which is the lesser? It takes a mature mind. And to make decisions that affect all the people of a kingdom and to appear to know beyond question which is the correct decision is a skill only learned through years of experience on a throne. Remember that Arthur had been raised far from court by old Sir Ector, and had never had the slightest suspicion that he was the rightful heir to the throne until Merlin set up that damned sword in the stone. I can't blame Arthur for what he did. He was doing nothing in those early days without the advice of his closest counselors. They are the ones who convinced him to pull that stunt with the ship."

"And who were they?" I demanded. "You're going to tell me that Merlin was one of them?"

Sir Gareth nodded slowly. "Merlin was the chief adviser to the throne, it's true. But before you get too riled up about that, let me assure you that he didn't have anything to do with the ship disaster. He had made the comment about Mordred growing up to destroy the kingdom, which did lead to that plan, but Merlin wasn't in on the plan. If he had been, none of us would be on friendly terms with the old necromancer even today. No, it was his other close counselors, chief of which was King Pelinor. He was most to blame."

"Pelinor?" I said in disbelief. "Pelinor who killed your father? Pelinor, the father of Lamorak, who bedded you mother? He was responsible for the murder of those children and the attempt on Mordred's life?"

"The same," Gareth said, chuckling at my bewilderment. "Now you see. All the stories turn out to be the same story in the end, don't they, Gildas?"

"That, or an endless cycle of blood and treachery. And yet out of all this Arthur tries to make a phony world based on false ideals? Isn't he a hypocrite? Why should we follow them? Why should we follow him?"

"Because the ideals aren't false. People are often false, but the ideal remains. The world of Camelot is not phony, it's a place in which we try to rise above the mundane world of falseness and incest and adultery and murder and revenge. If we can live by those ideals we can make a new world, a better world, and if we defend those ideals we can sustain that world. Gildas, Gildas, all men are sinners. What we have to do is try not to be. Arthur made a mistake when he was fifteen led on by the machinations of a scheming woman, and he compounded that mistake through the evil counsel of those whose task it was to set him on the right path. That was a long time ago. It will be thirty years, in fact, this coming May. I can forgive him, and I can applaud what he has done. People learn. They do the best they can, and when they know better, they do better. King Arthur has set a high standard to help them do better. That is what the Table Round is."

I wasn't completely convinced. But I was talked down. It would take a lot more ruminating on my part before I could assimilate everything Gareth had burdened me with that morning. The canons were returning to the sanctuary to clean up after the ceremony and to store the mass elements and put out the candles, and some looked our way with some curiosity, so we began to make our way slowly toward to west portal of the church, neither of us saying anything as we shuffled out. Trying to put this new knowledge out of my head for now, I forced myself to think about the lady Rosemounde. I was glad to be setting out on this task for her, and particularly glad because it would take me away from Camelot. I felt that being away from the castle and the direct circle of Arthur and his knights would allow me to think about all of these things more objectively. And indeed, I could find joy in the fact that I was serving my lady, the one person that I still had the utmost faith in, the one being in earth and heaven that would never let me down. Thank God I was not fifteen, that malleable gullible age the king had been when he had committed his heinous crimes. A seventeen-year old like myself was far too experienced to be so naïve.

CHAPTER FIVE

THE NARROW SEA

It was perhaps three hours after we had watched the harbor of Southampton disappear to our stern that Sir Dinadan and I stood on the port side of the deck, looking southwest with a salty sea-breeze blowing through our hair. I was tickled to have learned that the name of our vessel was the *Rosemounde*: the duke had named it after his younger daughter, and I loved it. I was fated to love anything with the name of Rosemounde. Merlin was in the wooden After Castle in the stern of the ship, where they had put our quarters along with those of the ship's captain and the five officers of the Duke's Guard, on board to protect the ship from pirates. The twelve members of the crew slept below deck, and six of them were there now, resting before taking over their shift at night. Our expected sailing time to cover the 170 nautical miles to Saint-Malo was a day and a half, assuming we could maintain an average speed of five knots.

Dinadan and I found it peaceful, leaning on the wooden railing and gazing out into what mariners called the Narrow Sea. Inwardly, I was brooding over the story Gareth had told me of King Arthur and the child Mordred. Despite Gareth's rationalizations, I had difficulty reconciling my devotion to the ideal of Arthur's Camelot with the reality of rottenness at that world's core. It did not sit right with me. But for now I was determined to complete the task at hand, the task that Rosemounde had given me. She, at least, was no fallen idol. She still deserved my devotion. And so I tried to put the king's malicious act out of my mind. It was something I could think about, and deal with, later on. Much later on.

Looking down, I contemplated the overlapping oak boards that formed the clinker-built hull of the large Cog ship we sailed on. Duke Hoel, as things worked out, was not on board. After a long private counsel with King Arthur he had decided to stay in Camelot for a few weeks to attend to some private matter. He did, however, follow through with his offer of transport to Brittany on board his personal ship. He needed to send some urgent messages to his son, Kaherdin, in any case, and would wait for our return on the same ship to make his own crossing back to Brittany. King Mark, on the other hand, had returned straightaway to Cornwall on the day following the induction ceremony.

Sir Dinadan had joined us for the crossing, and chiefly wanted to know how our interview with King Mark had gone. As Sir Tristram's closest companion, Dinadan had spent a good deal of time in Mark's court. But his scathing sense of humor and merciless satire of the king had made him persona non grata of late, especially now that Tristram was gone, and he had thought it wise not to join us in our questioning of the king. But he was intensely interested in what Mark had to say about the deaths of Tristram and Isolde, and pushed me to recount the interview for him as we stood on the deck of Duke Hoel's ship, looking out into the channel toward France, and I was quite willing to describe the meeting for him.

King Mark was of an age with King Arthur, perhaps a few years younger, but he had far more grey in his hair and beard, both of which were long and flowing. His bearing was kingly, but he was of slighter build than Arthur and a little more stooped, as if there were a great weight upon him. Indeed, in the interview his face had appeared strained and sallow, his pale grey eyes mournful. The expression perfectly matched his attire, which, though black, was made of the finest materials: a cloak of finely woven wool with sable trim, over a tunic of heavy samite in a twill weave, died black. It was a mourning fashion Merlin referred to later as "bleak chic." He wore inky black in his grief, but whom was he grieving? His wife, who had died trying to reach her fallen lover across the sea? His nephew, who had died crying for Mark's wife? For both of them? For his own life, whose closest relationships had proven unworthy, unfaithful, unsatisfying? What a sad life for a king. And a lonely one. He was lord of my own native land, but even if he were not, I could not but have felt some sympathy for Mark.

"Your Grace," Merlin had said as we were finally able to approach Mark at the feast in the great hall of Camelot following the induction ceremony three days earlier. "Please accept my most sincere condolences on the loss you have suffered." Leave it to Merlin to be as ambiguous as possible with regard to which particular loss Mark may have in fact been feeling most at the time.

Mark had nodded in response, and replied vaguely, "I appreciate your sentiments, my lord Merlin," as he began to turn away.

"And," Merlin had drawn the word out as Mark took a step away from us, then turned back with a mildly quizzical look to allow Merlin to finish. "Please allow me to introduce one of your own countrymen: Gildas of Cornwall, trusted squire to King Arthur's nephew, Sir Gareth of Orkney."

This news seemed to pique Mark's interest somewhat, and he turned to me, offering his hand to allow me to kiss his ring of office. "Indeed? I don't believe I am aware of your family, Gildas. Who is your father?"

I bowed slightly and, with a faintly stammering voice, reported that my father was an armor maker, the best in Launceston, providing mail, helmets, and weapons for several noble families in the area. It was through those connections that my father had been able to secure me a position in Camelot, beginning as page in the queen's household before obtaining my current status as Gareth's squire.

"Ah," Mark had said condescendingly. "Where would knights be without their little armor makers, after all? But your father must be proud, surely. For look at how far you have risen in the world! Have you been back to see him since you left Cornwall?"

"I have not, your Grace. I do write my parents often, however." If by often you mean twice a year or so. The gulf that had opened up between us was a problem, since the details of my world were so foreign to them. The fact that both my parents were illiterate was also a problem; when I did write them, they would have to find someone else to read them the letter. But how could I say this to the king? Their lives were as remote from his as mine was from theirs.

Merlin took advantage of the pause my awkwardness opened up by introducing the subject of our investigation. "You may have heard, my lord, that the queen has commanded Gildas and me to look into the deaths of your wife and nephew."

Mark's head snapped up with surprise and sudden interest. "She has done what? What does she expect you to find?"

"The truth, my lord. She only wants us to find the truth," I answered, looking up at Merlin, who lifted his left eyebrow at me. He didn't like to encourage my questioning of interviewees when he was the one conducting the investigations.

King Mark snorted. "The truth? The truth is that they're dead. I don't know what you can add to that. He died of a wound got in battle. She died of a broken heart. Why should there be any question?"

"We," Merlin looked down at me to keep me still, "have reason to believe that it is not that simple. But aside from that, many are blaming Sir Tristram's wife, Isolde of the White Hands, and saying she killed Tristram with her sharp tongue. Her father Duke Hoel is disturbed by this talk, and wants her exonerated. And finally, to be frank, your Grace…there is talk that you yourself may be behind these deaths."

I moved back a step or two. Only Merlin could have thought this was a good way to approach a king. But Mark only gave Merlin a grim kind of smile. "There have been times that I could have killed both of them. When I wanted to kill both of them. When I first learned of their betrayal, the rage I felt within was uncontrollable. I couldn't think straight. I wanted them to suffer as I was suffering. I put Isolde through the trial by ordeal of walking on hot coals—somehow she was not burned and the court was forced to find her innocent. When they fled my court into the wild I pursued them, but when I found them there in the woods in their love grotto, sleeping with Tristram's sword between them, the rage drained from me. Do you know what I finally realized?"

Still a bit cautious, I slowly shook my head. Merlin raised his considerable eyebrows.

"They were doing the best they could. I mean, why else was that sword there? Sometimes people's best is just not acceptable. But in this case, I felt that it was. As long as the affair ended there. I took Isolde back and Tristram went into exile. And married the Breton girl. That is where the story should have ended."

"But it didn't end there," Merlin stated the obvious. "So do you have any idea who might have wanted Tristram dead? Or La Belle Isolde?"

"You mean besides myself?" King Mark's smile became a bit more sardonic.

"I harbor no suspicions at to that," Merlin demurred . "But you must surely understand that others might. One of the things we are trying to do is belay any such rumors, and the only way to do that is to uncover the complete truth about the affair. Let me remind you that not long since, we found that the lady Elaine, one of the queen's ladies in waiting, was a spy of yours, and had conspired with others to implicate Sir Tristram in the rape of a peasant girl. Do you deny that?"

I winced at Merlin's word choice but watched Mark intently for his reaction. Finally, he shrugged and said, "Spy is your word. She was an agent of the Cornish crown, and would report to me the latest doings of King Arthur's court. Any plot against Sir Tristram she engaged in on her own authority, not mine."

"I daresay," said Merlin, sounding unconvinced.

"As for Tristram's enemies, there were probably dozens in my court who saw Tristram as a rival. He was my nephew, and so I made him one of my closest advisors. It was Tristram I sent to battle Marholt when the Irish refused to pay their tribute. It was Tristram I sent to sue for the hand of La Belle Isolde—that, of course, did not turn out so well." The sardonic smile again. "But these favors made him something of a prima donna in the court, and many were jealous of him, They railed against him to me behind his back. But that all ceased when he went to Brittany. I can't think that any of them would have had the courage or the ingenuity to arrange for a murder by long distance."

"Are there names you might give us? Anyone particularly fervent in his animosity toward Tristram?"

"How much time have we got? There are dozens I could probably name. But I can't think of anyone who particularly stands out in that respect. Suffice it to say that if a man was a member of my court, he harbored envy of and sometimes hatred for Sir Tristram. But there are too many to list here and now."

There was no more to be gotten from the king, and we had let him go. When I told all this to Dinadan, he nodded. "The old bird's right, I'll say that for him," he offered. "I was in that court dozens of times, and you could cut through the hatred with a knife. Gossips and backstabbers all over the place. Tristram couldn't stand it," Dinadan shuddered. "Even Sagramore, as it worked out, turned on the poor bugger."

"So he did," I muttered, thinking back to Sagramore's part in the plot to frame Sir Tristram in the case of Mistress Bess of Caerleon, now married to Colgrevaunce. "And you? Why did you stay with him?"

"Ah," Dinadan waved the question away. "Everybody needs a friend, right? Well he was mine. And he sure needed me, you know? Always a loner, which is not so bad in itself—I mean, Sir Lamorak was always something of a loner too, from what I hear. But Tristram brooded. His very name means sorrow, doesn't it? He needed somebody to cheer him up."

"As I recall, your constant jibes weren't always cheering," I told him.

"Purely for his own good. He took himself too seriously all the time. I liked to remind him of how absurd his whole situation was, right? 'Thought havin' a go at your uncle's wife was a good idea, did ya? How's that workin' out for you, then?' sort of thing, ya know? Anyway," Dinadan grew more serious. "Tristram was a great knight. He made me a much better knight by giving me an example of what that looked like. Of course," he added with a gleam in his eye, "he believed that his love for Isolde gave him his courage and his nobility. He was always talking about making himself 'worthy' of his beloved by performing great and noble deeds. Well, you can only take so much of that before you need some fresh air, if you know what I mean. Noble deeds are a good in themselves. I performed some of my own while I was with him. How else could I be worthy to be his companion?"

I felt myself turning a bit red since, of course, the only reason I wanted to be a knight at all was to be worthy of the lady Rosemounde. Not only to impress her and to win her love, but now also to impress her father and make him think me worthy. But I didn't say anything to Dinadan, whose motive for his own deeds did not seem so very different, after all. Though he didn't seem to recognize it. But at that point I glanced around and saw my lord Merlin approaching us from the After Castle.

"Ah, there you are!" He cried. He seemed in particularly high spirits, his long hair and beard stirring in the sea breeze. "Marvelous day, isn't it?" He took a deep breath. "Yes, the salt air in the lungs. It's good to be at sea again. I haven't been on board a ship since the days of the Irish wars, back at the beginning of Arthur's reign."

"Oh yes," Dinadan responded. "I wasn't a part of the Table yet, but I remember stories of those times." He winked at me surreptitiously. "They said you proved yourself the greatest magician in the world in Ireland, when you conjured the Giant's Circle aboard Arthur's fleet of ships and then brought it to Logres to set it up on Salisbury Plain. Greatest feat of magic in history, they all said."

Merlin snorted. "Stuff and nonsense, Dinadan. No magic was involved in that project. Now, greatest feat of mechanical engineering in history, that I might believe."

"You say what now?" Dinadan responded, somewhat lost.

"It wasn't wizardry but winches that moved those stones, you great lunkhead. Look," Merlin turned and pointed to the mast amidships, next to which stood a fairly large windlass. It was a device made up of a horizontal cylinder that sailors turned by a large crank. Rope was wound round the cylinder, or barrel, and a winch was attached to the rope. "Sailors use that windlass to raise and lower the sail, do they not?" The mast, some two feet wide where it intersected the deck, was as tall as the length of the ship itself, about forty-five feet or so, It supported a single large sail, roughly thirty-five feet square, which the seamen had raised that morning. Looking up, I couldn't help thinking about that white sail on Kaherdin's ship when he returned from Cornwall. The white sail that Isolde of the White Hands had claimed was black. Such a simple thing to have caused such anguish. Dinadan would say it was foolishness. But I think I might have died if I was in Tristram's position, and waiting for news of my lady Rosemounde.

"In the same way the crew of the *Rosemounde* raised the great sail this morning through use of that engine, Arthur's army raised the stones of the Giant's Ring and got them aboard our ships for transport back to Logres. I used giant engines that worked on the same principles as that windlass, both to lift them into the ships and to set them up on Salisbury Plain. Stonehenge was raised through science and mathematics, Dinadan, not by magic."

"I hear there was some good fighting in those Irish wars," Dinadan continued, drawing the old necromancer out a bit more. "A good number of reputations were made there, from what I've heard. King Mark would talk about it sometimes, I remember, when he was waxing lyrical about Isolde's homeland."

"He might well talk about it," Merlin replied. "The war there gave him his reputation and his throne. And his wife, for that matter. I suppose that's where all of this began."

"All of what?" I wanted to know. "Do you mean the Tristram and Isolde saga is connected with the Irish war?"

"I mean that, and much more." Merlin's eyes grew far away. "And it goes back long before the Irish wars. It goes back to a different war—the war that Uther Pendragon waged against Gorlois, Duke of Cornwall over the duke's wife. Uther had taken a great longing for the fair Igraine, and felt he would die if he could not have her."

"Another great recommendation for this 'courtly love' madness," Dinadan said. "Never mind that she's married. Just fight a war for her. That'll impress her. As for the men killed in the war, well, those are acceptable losses, since it was done for love. Right old man? You had something to do with that as well, or so I've heard."

Merlin did not deny it. "There was a madness on Uther. He would indeed have destroyed his kingdom, sacrificed all the men in his army—and Gorlois's as well—to win Igraine or die trying. I could not dissuade him. So I did the next best thing."

"Which in this case was disguising Uther as Gorlois and sneaking him into Tintagel castle," I added. As a Cornishman, I knew this history as well as my name.

"It ended the war," Merlin stated matter-of-factly. "It was a simple matter to dress Uther in Gorlois's arms and get him past the guards into Igraine's chamber. Once there, in the dark of her room, I cannot speak for her."

"What does that mean, you 'cannot speak for her'? What are you saying?" I bristled. This was, after all, a former duchess of my homeland.

Merlin sighed. "I mean, of course, that anyone who wants to believe her story that she thought it was the duke in bed with her is free to do so. For myself, I have difficulty believing that, darkness or no, she did not know her own husband."

I fumed a bit while Dinadan conceded, "She did marry King Uther pretty quickly afterwards, as I've heard. Convenient that Gorlois himself was killed in the battle about the same time little Arthur was being conceived."

"Yes, quite a stroke of luck, that. Well, who can really say what the timing was. It was important that people believed in that version of events, at least. But the important thing for my story here is that it was Cador, a cousin of Gorlois but one fighting on Uther's side, that slew Gorlois in battle and brought the body to the doors of Tintagel while Uther was still ensconced with Igraine. It came as a big surprise to all of Tintagel's defenders, but when Uther emerged from Igraine's chambers, they were less surprised. And the lady Igraine did not seem greatly perturbed. So Igraine married Uther, I took Arthur when he was born to be secretly fostered by Sir Ector, and Morgan and Margause, the daughters of Gorlois and Igraine, were sent north to marry King Lot and King Uriens and get out of Uther's hair. And Cador inherited the Duchy of Cornwall."

"And all of this has to do with the Irish War how?" I asked a bit impatiently, as I was losing track of relationships here.

"Duke Cador of Cornwall had two sons," Merlin went on patiently. "Constantine, the elder, was a bookish lad who was earmarked for the monastery from an early age. Cador's second son, born two years after Arthur, was Mark. Pretty much the opposite of his brother, Mark always preferred swords to books and a charging destrier to a spirited debate. By the time he was fifteen he could unhorse any knight in Cornwall. By that time, Arthur had been on the throne a little over two years, and had won his wars against King Lot and his allies. King Pelinor, Duke Hoel, and Duke Cador were young Arthur's closest advisors, along with myself, of course. All of us a good deal older and wiser than the brash young king."

"And then there was this war with Ireland?" I put in with some irony. Was the old man ever going to get to his point?

"And then there was war with Ireland," Merlin glowered at me, his eyebrows lowered like thunderclouds over his eyes. "King Rience of Ireland sent the young king a message: Rience had the unusual habit of trimming his cloak not with fur but with the beards of kings he had subdued, and he informed Arthur that unless the boy shaved his beard and sent it to him, Rience would come to Logres and take it, along with the head it was attached to. Well, you see, it was a double insult. Arthur had won his throne by force even though he'd inherited it by true bloodline…"

"More or less," Dinadan added.

Merlin shrugged, "More or less. But Rience refused to acknowledge any martial prowess in the lad, and figured he could bully him into submitting to Ireland's hegemony. But it was also an insult to Arthur personally, you see, because he was just seventeen at the time. He really had no beard at all. I offered to lend him mine if it would prevent a war, but he wouldn't have it, and we were off to Ireland."

"So how does Mark come into all of this?" I asked, for these were details even my Cornish roots had not supplied me.

"Old Mark was there as Cador's squire," Dinadan answered, sharing what he knew. "He was the great hero of the war, right? Or at least that's how he told it."

"He told it true," Merlin conceded. "He was in the war, originally as his father's squire. He was fifteen, but a full-grown lad and powerful, like Arthur himself at that age. We had battled the Irish in skirmishes for some weeks before we came to Dublin, which they had fortified against our coming. We besieged the city for days before

Rience decided it would be better to come out and face us in the open. A foolish mistake, because he was outnumbered and they had plenty of provisions within the city. They could have waited us out until we were forced to break camp with the coming winter. But Rience had removed that option when he sent Arthur the insulting note. He had to face him in the field or lose all honor. So out he came, with his thousand troops. We had probably sixteen-hundred, about two-hundred of those being mounted cavalry. Rience had maybe three hundred knights, so that helped even the odds for him. And he used the cavalry like a battering ram, charging through Arthur's assembled host and killing or wounding at least a hundred of our infantry before he'd run through the whole army and taken up a position on a hilltop behind us."

"Bad planning," Dinadan commented.

"Well, to be fair, Arthur was expecting a siege, the army was putting together siege engines, and Rience took us by surprise when he rode out of the city at full charge. Many knights were not able to get mounted at all, and the bowmen were lucky to be able to get off one shot before the army was through us. But there they were, atop that hill, forcing us to travel upward into a shower of their arrows to attack them. But Arthur knew that if we gave them a chance to dig in there, were would never turn this battle to our favor. Duke Cador didn't hesitate: he and his knights formed a wedge, their shields in front to protect them against the arrows raining down, and led a charge up that hill. But it was Mark who wound up leading the way. Knights were dropping to the left and right of him, including his father, who was downed by an arrow to the shoulder, but Mark was determined, and he was lucky. And once he reached the Irish lines, he was deadly. Slashing all about him with his sword, he downed at least two dozen bowmen single handed, then charged like a wild man against the wall of knights around King Rience. I've never seen a battle-frenzy turn any warrior as berserk as I saw Mark that day. He had cut down five knights single-handedly before some of Cador's other troops reached the Irish lines to help him. Then Arthur led a charge up the other side of the hill, and that threw them into confusion and their lines began to fall apart. In the chaos of the melee Mark killed nineteen knights and an untold number of archers, and, although it was Sir Balin and his brother Balan who ultimately captured the fleeing Rience, everybody knew it was Mark who'd won the day."

"So Mark wasn't just spinning tales when he bragged about his days as a soldier in the wars," Dinadan mused. "He was knighted after that, I suppose?"

"Arthur knighted him on the battlefield. And he had him at his right side when he held court in Dublin and accepted the surrender of Anguish, Rience's kinsman who was now thrust onto the throne of Ireland. It was there, in Anguish's train, that Mark first caught sight of Isolde. She was only eleven or twelve at the time, but Mark had never seen a girl so lovely. And he remembered her ten years later when he began to seek a wife. Of course, Duke Cador eventually died of his wounds. And Arthur named Mark his successor, but in gratitude for his good service, he elevated the Duchy of Cornwall to a petty kingdom and named Mark its first king. He even arranged it so that Ireland, which was forced to pay a tribute to Arthur's kingdom as war reparations, would pay the tribute directly to King Mark himself."

"That tribute is what made my homeland one of the richest in Arthur's realm," I put in.

"Of course," Merlin responded. After a pause, he added, "And we took the Giant's Ring and set it up on Salisbury Plain as a monument to that war."

I was busy working out all of the connections. So this was how King Mark came to the throne. This was how Arthur was conceived, this was how he was separated from his sisters, and therefore did not know who Margause was. This was why Tristram was sent to Ireland to ask for the hand of Isolde. There was no doubt that all Merlin had said went to prove the truth of my master Gareth's words: all the stories were the same story after all, it seemed.

When I glanced back at Merlin a change had come over his face. He looked much grayer, as if the strain of remembering had taken a toll on him. "My head," was all he said, raising his hand to his forehead and then reaching out before he slumped to the deck. He was breathing heavily and his eyes had become skewed—one bulged out like a frog's, while the other was squinted almost to closing.

Dinadan was shocked and moved to help the mage up, and I got down to the deck with him and shook him gently. "What is it, old man? One of your spells?"

"Listen," he spoke with a gravelly voice that came from somewhere beyond his consciousness. "The dog turns on its master. But there is another wolf with horns."

"Help me with him," I told Dinadan. "Help me get him back to the After Castle and lay him down. This will pass, I've seen it before. Sometimes it takes an hour, sometimes a day. But help me." Sir Dinadan hoisted Merlin under one shoulder, while I took the other side, and we carried the old man to a bed in the castle.

"What's he saying?" Dinadan asked. "What gibberish is this?"

I had recognized it at once. These spells came over Merlin on occasion, when the pain in his head became unbearable and he collapsed in exhaustion. As I explained to Sir Dinadan, Merlin always babbled something when it happened, something that was cryptic and indecipherable at first. This was how the necromancer had gained a reputation as a prophet—his words were ambiguous enough that they could be applied to situations that came up afterwards, and superstitious people would say, 'Yes, it's just as Merlin predicted, because when he was talking about the fish he meant the ship, you see, and when he said the fish was caught he meant the ship was going to sink, right?' "All bloody poppycock, for the most part," I told Dinadan. "But I have to admit that sometimes, when we've been working on a case, these spells do give us clues. It's his own mind, you see. He's been turning the case over in his head and he's put something together, but it comes out sounding confused because it hasn't, you know, sort of come to the front of his head yet."

It was the best I could explain it, and Dinadan seemed content, assuming a thoughtful look and responding with a "hmmph." Merlin moaned softly as we laid him down, then curled himself into a ball on the tiny mat we were given to sleep on in those very close quarters. Dinadan seemed a bit worried about the mage, the change had come upon him so suddenly, but I assured him I had seen this many times, and it always had to work its course.

***

Merlin lay unresponsive, curled up on his mat the entire night. I was restless, Dinadan bored, and there was not much to do aboard that ship if you weren't one of the crew. I rose early on our second day at sea and, leaving Merlin and Dinadan asleep in the Castle, I walked out on the deck to pace the ship nervously. I watched the sun come up on the left side of the ship—"port" the sailors corrected me—and saw its orange glow rolling toward us over the edge of the coastline of Normandy some distance off. Glancing over the other side of the boat, the "starboard" side I'm told, I could watch the long glistening carpet that formed the vast expanse of open sea. Turning toward the port side again, I watched the Norman coast, a shoreline we could follow all the way into the port at Saint-Malo, which I was told we should reach sometime after midday, perhaps around none. But coming up ahead, rising out of the sea like a green pavilion, was a small mountain that formed its own island off the Norman coast. Atop the mount was a human structure that looked to be a castle or monastery.

"Mont St.-Michel," said a voice behind me.

I whirled around to find Captain Jacques, commander of the duke's Breton guard, standing behind me, gazing intently at the island to our southwest. He'd not spoken to me prior to this, but I was glad for the company in the cool morning light. Captain Jacques had long dark hair, piercing brown eyes, and a bright red tunic that he belted with a sash that also held his sword in a long scabbard. He spoke with a decidedly Breton accent, but I felt a kind of kinship with him, knowing that the Bretons were close relatives of us Cornishmen.

"Mount Saint Michael's?" I countered. "That's a coincidence. We have an island off Cornwall with the same name."

"Of course," Captain Jacques answered. "Our people have a special reverence for the Archangel, I suppose, eh?"

"There are old stories about my Saint Michael's," I told him. "The legend goes that it was built out in the sea by a race of giants, and that the giant who lived there used to come to the mainland and steal children to devour at night on the island. The legend says that a young

Cornish fellow named Jack—ha, kind of like your name, no?—that this Jack was able to sneak into the island and kill the giant."

"Indeed?" Captain Jacques's eyes bulged with surprise. "This is an old story? How very strange. For we have a similar story about our own Mont St.-Michel!"

"What?" It was my turn to be surprised. "I wonder…maybe the story is so old that it goes back to the time when the Bretons and the Cornish were part of the same people, hundreds of years ago…for that," I explained, "is another of our legends."

"We are aware of our kinship," Jacques responded. "And if I were not, our language would bring it home to me. For we speak the same language, you and I, you Britons and we Bretons. Just a bit of an accent in your speech."

"I was thinking you were the one with the accent," I murmured.

"But that common history is not the origin of our story. No, our story is no legend but fact, and occurred within the living memory of many of our people."

"No!" I responded, fascinated. "Tell me!"

Captain Jacques put his hand on my shoulder and looked toward the island. But his eyes seemed to look much farther. "I was just a child, perhaps five or six. I lived in the port city, Saint-Malo, with my mother and father. He was a sailor in the service of the duke. I remember one day we heard that some great beast of an outlaw had moved onto the island. They said he was over seven feet tall and had legs like tree trunks. Some said he had come from Aragon or Castille, but nobody knew for sure. Before too long, daughters of the local community at Pontorson started disappearing. First the child of the town's blacksmith turned up missing one day. Next it was the teenage daughter of Pontorson's mayor. No one had seen him do it, but everybody was pretty well convinced that the giant on the mountain had stolen those girls. Then came the worst of it. The lady Helena, who was Duke Hoel's oldest daughter, disappeared one day from the rooms in her palace, and her nurse with her. The girl was fourteen years old, and the duke was mad to have her back."

Another daughter? My lady Rosemounde seemed to have sisters popping up like Hydra's heads. Why had no one ever mentioned this one? "And what happened to the young lady?" I asked Jacques, assuming she had perhaps entered a religious house—perhaps that same one I could see on the top of the mountain—and that that explained why Rosemounde had never mentioned her.

"I will come to that," Jacques answered. "I cannot tell my tale out of order. When it became clear that the giant had taken the duke's daughter to his lair on the mountain, the duke sent a fleet to surround the island and force the giant from his lair. But he had the strength of ten men, they say, and whenever any ship came close to the shores of the island, the giant would send huge stones raining down upon them. He sank two ships before the fleet backed off. No one was able to set foot on the island and no one could get near the giant to rescue the poor girl. That was when Arthur came."

That startled me. Was this another story that was connected to the rest? "Arthur? You mean the king?"

"The king himself," Jacques acknowledged. "He landed in Brittany with his whole army, bent on defending his realm from Lucius, the Roman. This was after the Irish wars, when, with his kingdom established, Arthur was focused on preserving it from outside threats. Anyway, after the fleet landed, Arthur learned what had happened. When he saw how distraught the duke was, Arthur took up the cause. His empire may have needed defending, but his good friend and adviser needed his help to save his own daughter, and Arthur put that first. Hearing how the giant had sunk the war ships when they came close in, he figured he'd sneak onto the island and take his chances. Under the cover of darkness, he took Sir Kay, his seneschal, and Sir Bedivere, his butler, in a tiny boat and rowed out to the island. They made their way as quietly as they could up the stony mountainside until they saw the light of a fire in a cave."

I have to say I was even more surprised at this, to learn that the obnoxiously obsequious Sir Kay had, at one time, been brave enough—and fit enough—to climb a mountain in pursuit of a giant. "So," I encouraged Jacques to continue the story. "They found the giant? They rescued the girl?"

Again Captain Jacques shook his head and cautioned me. "I'm not there yet," he answered. "From their hiding place amid the bushes, they could see a figure in a long black gown sitting despondently by the fire. Sir Bedivere volunteered to crawl closer to see who this might be. As it happened, it was the old woman, the girl's nurse, who was lamenting by the fire, sobbing uncontrollably. When she saw Bedivere peering at her from behind a boulder, she stopped and looked cautiously into the cave. Then she got up and walked toward him with a very light step. 'My lady, are you Lady Helena's nurse?' he says to her. She nods. "And where is the young lady herself? Is she all right?' he asks. She shakes her head, and points to the mouth of the cave. Bedivere squints and looks to the other side of the fire, and notices a body lying in gouts of blood on the cave floor. 'Oh God save us,' Sir Bedivere says. 'He's killed her then.' And the old woman nods. Finally she has her weeping under control enough to speak. 'The great beast unleashed his lust upon her, and was so violent that she died. In his anger and frustration he raped me as well, and my own pain is great, but I mourn more for my precious lady. But you need to go and go quickly. If he finds you here he will surely kill you—what with his great strength, only an army can defeat him. Come back with an army, and kill him. All I ask is that you let me deal the death blow once he is defeated. I would gladly rip out his pig's heart.'"

By now I was getting weak in the knees. I leaned against the ship's rail and took a deep breath of the sea air. This was why Rosemounde never spoke of her oldest sister. The girl had been brutally murdered by a cruel giant of a man. "What did Arthur do?"

Captain Jacques smiled. "Ah, now you are in the story. So Bedivere returns to Arthur and tells him what he's seen. Arthur is so enraged that the young girl's noble blood has been shed in this foul manner that he takes up Excalibur and charges in like a madman. Well by this time the giant has heard the commotion outside, and he shows up at the cave opening brandishing a club that's the size of a log, and he swings it at the king. Well Arthur had no armor—none of them were able to wear armor or shield while climbing that mountain—so he had no way to fend off that blow, and if it had caught him square it would have killed him for certain. But the king was able to duck and parry a bit with his sword, and the blow only glanced off his left side. So Arthur ducks in, toward the giant, where he can't swing the club, and stabs toward the giant's face. He gives him a wound in the forehead that starts bleeding so much it nearly blinds the giant, but the giant had pulled back in time to keep the wound from being fatal. So Arthur gets ready, expecting another swing of the club, but instead the giant uses Arthur's own trick, and rushes in close so Arthur can't swing his sword. Instead, the giant grabs him around the waist and lifts him from the ground. He's intent on crushing the life out of the king, you see? Arthur starts flailing away wildly with Excalibur, trying to get some angle to deal a deadly blow to the giant, but he can only get off some glancing strikes at his legs or his back. Finally, when he's about to pass out, Arthur realizes that instead of swinging the sword, he can use it to stab the one vulnerable spot on the giant—his neck, which is right there level with the king's eyes as the giant holds him. So up thrusts the sword, through the giant's unprotected neck and deep up into his brain. The creature falls like a great oak tree, dead as dust."

I realized that I had not been breathing for some time, and consciously took a breath at that point.

"Sir Bedivere and Sir Kay cheered at the sight, and insisted on removing the giant's head to show the people back in the village that they had nothing more to fear from the brute. Arthur allowed them the trophy but cautioned them not to celebrate the victory too excessively. After all, the girl was slain, and while the duke would be relieved to know that the giant could do no more harm, it was small consolation for the loss of his daughter. And although they had rescued the old nurse, the abuse and outrage she had suffered was unlikely ever to leave her. When the knights searched the cave, they found, to their sorrow, the bodies of the other two girls that the giant had stolen. More parents whose hopes would be crushed. The king said little when he brought the bodies, and the head, back to Duke Hoel's court. But it is said that he wept over the loss of those children, as if they had been his own."

Captain Jacques's story was at an end. I didn't say anything. I was trying to wrap my brain around the contrasting images of the king that were contending in my mind. Arthur, the King Herod figure who tried to kill a shipload of babies for fear of what one of them would do to him when he grew up. Arthur, the Saint Michael figure who overthrew the beast and wept at the children he was unable to save. Hero or Villain? Devil or Angel? Or was it Devil and Angel? The shades of gray were blurring my sharp black and white moral vision. Not that I hadn't known the complexity of moral character before. What, after all, was the queen but a conglomeration of virtues and vices? What was Sir Lancelot? Or Gawain, the most courteous of knights whose thirst for vengeance led him to ambush an unsuspecting Lamorak? Surely even Merlin, crusty blasphemous blustering carping big-hearted generous Merlin, was a study in contrasts. But the king. In him at least I had still believed in an ideal. If the ideal of chivalry was flawed, the glue that held Camelot together, then what hope was there in a dark world? It was almost as if my lady Rosemounde had shown herself imperfect. If that should happen, wouldn't all the stars fall from their spheres? But this good and courageous Arthur—that gave me some hope again. Not perfection but the striving for it was what was expected of the knights. And Arthur demonstrated that. The story had helped to restore me, or at least begin to restore me, to my faith.

All stories, it seems, are one.

CHAPTER SIX
SAINT-MALO

Saint-Malo was the main Breton port on the Narrow Sea. Some thirty miles south of the Breton Mont St.-Michel, it lay on an island at the mouth of the river Rance. As the *Rosemounde* neared the port, members of the crew struck the great square sail and lowered two small lifeboats into the estuary to tow the larger ship into the river's mouth, around the island through the strait between the city and a large fortified promontory to the south that Captain Jacques told me was called Aleth, on the side of the river called Saint-Servan. From the ship's deck I could see the tower of the cathedral rising over the walls of the city, and I knew that attached to it was a monastery around which the city had grown hundreds of years before, after its founding by its namesake, Saint Malo, a companion of the Irish Saint Brendan in the sixth century.

Merlin had finally roused himself and, a bit shaky, stood on the deck with Dinadan and me to watch as the ship was finally moored on the west coast of the island, the lee side between Saint-Malo and the mainland. We could see on the starboard side of the ship the rich farmlands and groves of hickory and fruit trees that were in bloom now in these gentle early summer days. Hard to believe that this pleasant looking land was the site of the tragic deaths of the famous lovers not many days earlier.

Captain Jacques had offered his services to us in obtaining an audience with Sir Kaherdin, who commanded the city. We disembarked with our luggage, a small sea-chest containing changes of clothes, a manuscript on heraldry I was trying to study, and our swords. The captain told one of the sea hands to take the chest to his own room in the palace. "You'll no doubt want to stay here in the palace while you are visiting Saint-Malo, and it will be convenient to pick it up in my own chambers when you obtain your own."

"You have a room in the palace?" I asked, surprised at this news.

Jacques shrugged. "It is a privilege of my military rank," he replied modestly. "Not of any special favor I may enjoy with Lord Kaherdin."

After the sailor went off with our chest, the captain walked us a short distance along the quay to a gate in the formidable brown stone wall that protected the city. There were well-armed guards at the gate, and a small watchtower over it where I knew two or three archers were stationed. The guards stepped aside at the sight of Captain Jacques, and he marched through without a sidelong glance. Merlin, Dinadan, and I followed in his wake, and I was suitably impressed by the captain's confidence and his apparent stature within the city. Dinadan, who had been living in Saint-Malo for many months, took it all in stride, and Merlin seemed distracted looking about at the people, hundreds of whom we saw gathered around street vendors just inside the gate.

"The lord's palace is just to the right as we enter the gate," Dinadan directed me as we turned to follow the captain toward an impressive stone structure at the northeast corner of the city. With the musical calls of the street vendors ringing in our ears ("Fresh apples! Apples here!" and "Onions and leeks, straight from the fields!" or "Meat pies here! Fresh meat pies!") all in their distinctive Breton accents, we strode toward the stark grey residence of Kaherdin, son of Duke Hoel and commander of the city. Before the building was a large town square, in which a small company of Breton cavalry were drilling, fully armed and on horseback, and I realized that the reason for all the activity around the square was that a good crowd of townsfolk had turned out to watch the drill.

Ten of Kaherdin's knights were mounted on great muscular destriers, armed in chain mail, helmets, shields, and lances, and wearing rowel spurs the better to control their horses. Their lances were the traditional battle lances, and thus were mounted with rounded metal heads coming to a sharp point, rather than the broader blunted, hollowed ends of the lances I used in jousting practice at the quintain, designed to break rather than run the opponent through. These lances were used with every intention of penetrating the enemy's flesh, even through their mail coats. The knights in the square queued up in a double line of five knights each, a formation called *en haie*, and cantered across the square at reduced speed, with lances couched under their arms and proffered toward what would have been the enemy lines if this had not been a drill. Essentially they were bent on training their horses to stay in formation, and an entire company of cavalry thus well trained could scatter any army's infantry. Except, of course, an infantry that had fortified its position with pikes, on which the charging horses would impale themselves. War was a gruesome business, I thought to myself as we circled around the square and worked our way to the front gate of the palace.

The fortress at the promontory across the estuary was the real defense of the city, and Kaherdin had that position well manned. So there wasn't a great need for the palace to have strong defenses, and indeed, it was only lightly fortified. There were two small round towers at the corners of the grey stone edifice. There were only perhaps sixty feet of wall between the towers, a fairly modest dwelling for a man who had no pretentions of being a great lord. He was his father's vassal and was not in line to inherit the duchy, and he knew it. His province was the port city of Saint-Malo. Duke Hoel ruled the duchy from his castle in the capital city of Rennes, some thirty-seven miles to the south.

Once again, at the palace gate, two guards stood, one on either side of the door. The captain asked us to wait a moment while he entered and announced us to the lord commander, and ducked into the chamber. To assuage the awkwardness, I thought to initiate an informal conversation with one of these grim looking guards. I looked at the one on the right, the one I was standing next to. He had a swarthy face that bore scars suggesting he was not inexperienced in his lord's wars. His eyes were dark and piercing, and his black hair hung over his forehead like that of an unruly pet. When he grinned at me menacingly, I was shocked to see that his two front teeth were actually made of gold. I had never seen such a thing before. Taken aback, I turned to the guard on the left. His unmarked face and pale blue eyes showed no expression, and his close-cropped blond hair gave him a stoic and uninviting look, but I was less put off by him than his companion, and so I addressed my remarks to him:

"Good morning!" I greeted him with a smile. Next to me I could feel Merlin's eyebrows rising to the heavens and his eyes boring holes in me. But I persisted. "I am Gildas of Cornwall, and this is the lord Merlin, and with him Sir Dinadan, Knight of the Round Table. We are visiting from King Arthur's court at Camelot. And you are?"

A bit to my surprise, the dour-looking guard picked up the gauntlet. "Sir William of Caen," he volunteered. "In the service of the city's commander. Lord Kaherdin, as you see," he shrugged slightly. "My companion," he nodded at the swarthy-faced soldier on his right, "is called Sir Neville of Acre." Sir Neville flashed a grin again, but remained silent.

"I know Sir William of old," Dinadan volunteered. "A good soldier. Not a lot of fun to go drinking and wenching with, I'm afraid, but somebody who could hold the fort while the rest of us caroused."

Sir William maintained his composure, though something in Dinadan's manner or banter seemed to have struck him. He turned his businesslike gaze on Sir Dinadan and shook his head slowly. "Ever the jester, Sir Dinadan. Perhaps someday you will find a cause to serve that is not a joke to you."

"And where would be the fun in that?" Dinadan responded, with his most winning smile—a smile that failed to melt the coolness of Sir William's reception.

"And do you enjoy your service here?" I asked William, curious, truly, as to what kind of master Kaherdin was.

"I serve the lord Kaherdin because I choose to," he answered simply. "He provides for me, I serve him. And will, so long as my arm can hold a sword."

"And just what is there about Kaherdin that inspires this kind of loyalty in his men?" I wondered aloud.

Sir William shook his head and finally smiled, though very faintly. "He is a strict disciplinarian and a courageous companion. But that is not enough. He has a quick temper and he often jumps to conclusions without having all the facts, but these things are not enough to make me question my loyalty. No, I remain loyal to Kaherdin because he is a champion of the right. He has never knowingly or willingly taken up arms in a wrongful quarrel, and I follow him because of that. And I do what he tells me to do."

"You do it without question?" I suggested.

"Without question. As I would a command from God himself."

"Well," Dinadan interjected. "Let's hope you don't ever actually confuse the two." At that point, Captain Jacques opened the door and beckoned us to enter, and the two guards stood aside to let us pass. We walked through a small courtyard, and I whispered to Dinadan, "Gold teeth? What was that about?"

Dinadan shook his head and shrugged. "Never met the lad before, though I've heard of some crusaders that came back with such teeth. It's a kind of status symbol among some of the infidels, I take it. This Neville seems a queer duck."

Through the courtyard we walked directly into what turned out to be the palace's throne room, where Lord Kaherdin received visitors.

The room was equally modest, being only about twenty feet wide and perhaps forty long, and at the end opposite the door we came through sat the lord himself on a slightly raised dais, flanked by two advisers. They were dressed simply but elegantly enough, the advisers in earth-colored tunics, dull hose and long leather boots, the lord himself in more supple-looking boots, dark red hose, a blue tunic covered with a fur-lined green cloak. I took a moment to take in the room: the only furnishings were the chair on which Lord Kaherdin sat, a small table to his right where a wine pitcher and a few bunches of grapes were placed for his refreshment. The adviser on his right sat at a small desk, and was shuffling papers like a clerk, and as we entered Kaherdin was saying to him "Get those orders off as soon as you can, Melias."

The floor of the chamber was wooden, and on the long walls of the hall were a series of high windows designed to let in both the morning and afternoon sun. Below the windows on each wall, and behind the lord on the north wall of the room, were a series of tapestries depicting, as far as I could tell, the story of Aeneas—from two great tapestries showing the wooden horse and the fall of Troy and then Aeneas and his crew's escape to Carthage on the west wall, to tapestries representing the death of Turnus and the subsequent marriage to Lavinia on the east. Behind the lord on the north wall was a huge tapestry depicting the Pious Aeneas turning his back on Dido's suicide pyre and the city of Carthage.

Before I was quite done looking around, Kaherdin said in a deep voice "Ah, Captain Jacques, welcome back. My father, I understand, has not made the return trip with you. Approach, approach, and tell me who you and Sir Dinadan have brought with you. But first what news of my father? Has he remained at Camelot?"

Kaherdin, stoic in his own way, had hair unusually close-cropped and was completely clean-shaven. He had large grey eyes that bulged in his head like a hare's, and though there was a strength about him he was quite slender, and though he was fairly tall he slumped somewhat in his chair, almost as if he was bored with his position. His thin face, with its high pronounced cheekbones, bent lower toward Jacques. I saw nothing in his lean face to remind me of his half-sister, my beloved Rosemounde, until he raised his left eyebrow quizzically while addressing the captain. That made me smile. But only with a slight twist of the mouth, since I did not want to appear disrespectful before the lord of the city.

"Lord Kaherdin," the captain said, with a slight bow. "Duke Hoel had urgent business with the king, and has remained at Camelot until it is concluded. He sent me home in the *Rosemounde* to bring these gentlemen, who are here on a mission specially commissioned by the queen and your own sister."

Kaherdin looked puzzled. "My sister? How on earth could Isolde have commissioned them in Camelot, unless she sent some message to the queen with you or father when you left?"

"No, my lord," Jacques corrected him. "I meant to say your half-sister, the queen's lady."

At that Kaherdin's face seemed to lose interest, and relaxed into indifference. "Oh," was all he said. "Well, what is your commission, gentlemen? We will do what we can to assist if it is not against the interests of Brittany. Who are you, first? Are you of Arthur's court? Is that why you have Dinadan accompanying you?"

While all this was going on I could feel Merlin next to me fidgeting with impatience. He had been slow moving, silent, and morose since getting up this morning, the aftermath of his spell the evening before. This was just the sort of thing he needed to set his blood moving again. "My lord," he began, stepping forward and taking charge. "Allow me to introduce myself. I am Merlin. I know your family well and was telling your father what to do when he was your age." An audible gasp issued from the young man on Kaherdin's right, and Kaherdin himself just stared, his eyes protruding even more than usual, and his jaw hanging slack for a moment, before, recovering himself, he rose and nodded toward the old necromancer in a way that suggested that Merlin and not he was the ranking noble in the room. There was an irony to it, of course, since Merlin was not only no aristocrat, but was known to have been born out of wedlock to a young nun. According to legend his father was an incubus—a demon of the air who visited his mother secretly at night and left her with child. Merlin loved to make the most out of that superstition. But he was certainly never mistaken for a nobleman by anyone in Camelot, though all of the knights feared his power and his influence. His reputation, however, seemed to have given him some sort of heroic stature in Brittany.

"My lord Merlin!" Kaherdin began. "I apologize for not recognizing you on sight, and for treating you with any discourtesy. For years my father has told me of your amazing feats of magic and prophecy. Know that I and all my household are at your service. This," he gestured toward the young gasper on his right, who now rose to greet us more courteously, "is my squire, Melias, son of the Count of Poitou. On my left is Sir Andred, my kinsman and close adviser."

Melias, the squire, was about my own age. His close-cropped hair and smooth face were barbered in emulation of his master. His was a broad, open face with brown fawning eyes that looked on the great mage and stammered "My lord." As for Andred, his flowing yellow locks and piercing blue eyes set him apart in this court, but his face had shown no expression—not when we walked in, not when Merlin announced himself, not now when he was being presented to us. He said nothing, but merely nodded almost imperceptibly in our direction.

"Sir Dinadan you know of course," Merlin followed Kaherdin's lead with his introductions, but he was clearly anxious to begin his investigations. "My young assistant is Gildas of Cornwall, squire to the king's nephew Sir Gareth of Orkney."

A short burst of laughter issued form Kaherdin. "Cornwall! One of your own countrymen, Andred!" The grim knight said nothing, merely glared at me. But Sir Kaherdin continued. "Sir Andred is from Restormel, aren't you Andred?" No response. "His father is the earl. And you, Gildas?"

"Launceston," I told him. I didn't add that my own father was no earl, count, baron or lord, but an artisan who made armor and who, through his profession, made various connections among the nobility and found a way to get his only son placed as a page in the household of the queen of Logres.

"Good," Merlin said. "Now that we're all bosom friends, let's move on to why we are here. We have been commissioned, as Captain Jacques told you, by Queen Guinevere and the lady Rosemounde to look into the unexpected and disturbing deaths of Sir Tristram and La Belle Isolde."

At this Kaherdin showed some surprise, sending his left eyebrow skyward again. Young Melias gave another gasp, and turned his fawning eyes toward his master. Sir Andred finally showed a slight crack in his demeanor with a miniscule pursing of the lips. "I tire of this reference to Isolde of Ireland as 'La Belle Isolde,'" Kaherdin griped. "As if my sister were not 'la belle.' But aside from that, I don't understand what on earth the queen expects you to find by 'looking into' this affair. Tristram died from a wound inflicted by Norsemen. Isolde of Ireland died of a broken heart. There. What more do you need to know?"

"Things are not always as they seem, my lord," Merlin answered. "What you say may be the case, but I would like to satisfy myself that the general interpretation of events is the accurate one. For instance, my lord, and I hope you will forgive me for saying this, but the general impression is that your sister is to blame in Sir Tristram's death." Kaherdin's face grew dark. "Not, of course, that she gave him the wound that killed him, but that her words—her lying to him about the color of the sail when your ship approached—took the hope from his heart and sapped his will to live."

Kaherdin's eyes shifted to Dinadan, standing next to me behind Merlin, and it was on him that Kaherdin's ire landed. "You told this story in Arthur's court? What need was there to air these things before the general world? These were private words between a husband and wife. Who are you to spread this…this slander?"

Sir Dinadan was not cowed. "My loyalty was to Sir Tristram first, and to the king. What I told King Arthur was the sole truth. I find it easier than lying. With lying, you have to remember which lie you told to whom, and my memory has never been that good."

Sir Andred finally spoke, and the sound was not pleasant. It was more of a growl than a voice. "Your truth may be your last testament, jester. What would you say if I told you I would wait for you with my sword in the courtyard this afternoon?"

"Why, I suppose I'd tell you to wait there as long as you liked, for I was unlikely to show up," Dinadan gave the knight an exaggerated bow.

"These japes are unseemly," Merlin broke in, trying to restore order. "My questions are neither affronts nor untruths. I say what is, and my purpose is to uncover what is not known, in part to preserve your own sister's reputation, Lord Kaherdin. God's ankle bones, can you not see this?"

There was a moment of silence while Lord Kaherdin considered this, Melias watched him with real concern in his eyes, and the rest of us hung fire. But finally the lord relented, sighed, and admitted, "You're right old necromancer." There was an audible easing of the tension in the room. "Let us help you look into these matters, then. What will you need first?"

"Free rein," the old man responded. "Nothing should hinder me in questioning any witness I deem important until I've gotten to the bottom of these events. For that I need your guarantee that people will cooperate with my questioning. Otherwise the investigation is simply sham."

"Of course, you shall have a letter from me to present to anyone you need to question which will make it clear that you conduct this investigation with my approval." Kaherdin nodded to Melias, who dutifully sat back down at the simple desk where a small candle burned, and pulled out a scrap of parchment and a bottle of ink. "Write it in Breton," Kaherdin insisted. "None of your Church Latin here. People whom they talk to are going to need to understand what they're reading."

"If they can read at all," Melias muttered as the clerk quickly scribbled something onto the scrap. "The only thing that really matters is that they recognize your seal." With a flourish Melias finished his task, looked to Kaherdin with an air of a dog who, having done a trick for his master, desires a treat, and then dripped a splotch of the candle's wax onto the bottom of the parchment. Kaherdin made a fist and punched his signet ring into the wax, making a sharp impression. Then he snatched the note from the desk and handed it to Merlin.

"There it is then, old man. You have what you've come for. And now if you will excuse us, we have pressing matters of state to discuss."

"No doubt, no doubt," Merlin said, carefully placing the sealed letter in an inner pocket of his long robe. "But I have a few questions first. As part of my investigation, I need to speak with the three of you, and of course your sister Isolde."

Three jaws dropped open at once, then the two flanking heads turned inward to see what Kaherdin's reaction would be. Andred's face looked dark and angry. Melias looked more concerned, as if he wanted to reach out and comfort his master. But as might have been expected, Kaherdin exploded. "You presume to question the royal family, you old fool? I should have you thrown into the river! Get out of here and be grateful I don't have your nose and ears cut off for your effrontery!"

That was enough for me. Patience is one of my great virtues, but Job himself would not have stood for this abuse. I stepped in front of Merlin as Sir Andred moved toward him. "Who does he think he is? He is the lord Merlin, most powerful wizard in all of Europe. He is the one whose magic brought King Uther to the Duchess Igraine and conjured the birth of Arthur. He is the one who made Arthur King of Logres through the device of the sword in the stone. He is the chief adviser to the king during the Orkney wars, the Irish wars, the Scandinavian Wars and the Gaulish Wars that gave Brittany its freedom. He is the necromancer that brought the great blocks of Stonehenge from the Irish wastes to the plains of Salisbury. You think you are dealing with some peasant here? Know when you deal with Merlin you deal with the right hand of King Arthur himself."

Captain Jacques, fortunately the only person in the room wearing an actual sword, tried with little success to assuage the prickly Kaherdin and the hackles his prickliness had raised among the rest of us. "My lords, my lords," he soothed, "let us have civil words. There is no need here for anger…"

Kaherdin sputtered in impotent rage, at which point Sir Dinadan stepped in to throw his own particular kind of oil on the waters. "And what was that exactly about 'royal family'? Uh…wouldn't it be 'ducal family'—unless you've got some kind of ambitions we don't know about? See, the actual 'royal family' are the ones that sent my lord Merlin here. So you're the one disobeying a direct command from the king. Now what do you suppose will be the reaction of King Arthur, slayer of the Giant of Saint Michael's Mount, when he learns how you've greeted his representative? I can see it now: 'Gosh, I wonder what's happened to my faithful and beloved Merlin in Brittany? Lancelot, old boy, why not take a hundred and fifty knights or so and take a look. Oh, and if you find one hair on that dear old man's head has been disturbed, raze the city of Saint-Malo to the ground and grind the bones of its leaders into the dust. Right then? All right, cheers.'"

Sir Kaherdin sputtered some more, finally proclaiming, "My liege Lord is Duke Hoel of Brittany!" to which Sir Dinadan added "And his is King Arthur of Logres. Do you really think the duke is likely to thank you for these shenanigans you've been engaging in today?"

My lord Merlin, who through all of this was unfazed, now bowed his head slightly to Kaherdin. "My lord," he began, "I regret that I am required by my charge to question you on these matters. I do so," he said as he reached into his robe, "on the authority of the commander of the city garrison at Saint-Malo, as this letter attests. If there is power in his seal, then you must give me audience."

"Conniving old cozener," Kaherdin muttered under his breath. His face was crimson with rage and with shame—the two seemed to battle to see which could redden him more. "In the name of the Protector of this city, ask your questions," he ended with some loud bravado.

"I shall not trouble you long, my lord," Merlin said, his mouth twitching up at the corner. "It's just that there are some details that only you can provide. First, for example, can you tell us briefly about the mission Sir Tristram sent you on to Cornwall?"

Kaherdin looked annoyed. "But you know all this, surely. He pleaded with me to take ship to Cornwall to bring back Mark's queen. He believed her healing powers could save him, as they had once before in Ireland. He told me to carry two sails, and to display the white sail if the queen was aboard, and the black one if she was not."

"This is all well known, my lord," Merlin nodded. "But some details are not. For instance: did you discuss any of these things with your sister before you left?"

"My…" Kaherdin's mood began to darken again. "And why would I do that? Isolde was already feeling the coldness of Sir Tristram's heart and of his bed. Why would I tell her that in his final days her husband was thinking only of seeing once more the adulterous queen who had brought about his exile from Cornwall?"

"Thank you my lord," Merlin nodded as if this was just what he had expected to hear. "Tell me, then, what happened upon your arrival in Cornwall? You went to the king's court?"

"I sought immediate audience with King Mark and his queen, and was soon granted it in the throne room. I addressed the king, and told him that his nephew Sir Tristram lay near death in Brittany, and had asked me to come there in the hope that his queen would return with me and save his life, as she had once before."

"And what was King Mark's response to this?" Merlin inquired.

"Far calmer than mine would have been, I can tell you," Kaherdin responded, with more truth than he may have realized. "His expression did not change a whit, until his queen suddenly knelt down beside him in a semblance of humility and begged him to return with me. He finally murmured his assent, and the queen leapt to her feet. 'I will go now,' she said. 'If the poison is so far along there is no time to lose. Please wait here for me, Sir Kaherdin, while I put together some traveling clothes and my medicinal kit. Of course I will want Brangwen to come along.' And the king accepted that as well. So within two hours, the queen and her lady-in-waiting, the loyal Brangwen, stood before me dressed for a journey and trailed by a large page carrying a small sea-trunk for the two of them. We left from there."

"Now, my lord, could you tell me how long it takes to sail from Saint-Malo to Cornwall?"

"Usually no more than a full day and night, in one of our new ships, assuming you have favorable winds..."

"So," Merlin mused. "Less time than it took us to sail here from Southampton."

"Indeed," Kaherdin conceded, now backing off a bit from his original comments. "King Mark abides at Restormel Castle, high above the River Formey near the Cornish capital of Lostwithiel. It's some miles from the coast, but is on the tidal estuary of the river and so it has a port. But it is not an easy thing maneuvering into that harbor from the coast."

I felt obliged here to assert my own Cornishness. "It is as he says, my lord Merlin. The new, larger ships draw more water than perhaps is safe traveling up that river."

"We lost a good twelve hours in that pursuit," Kaherdin agreed. "Still, I know what you are thinking. A day and a half to Restormel Castle, a mere few hours with the king, the entire trip should have taken perhaps three days—four at the most accounting for unforeseen weather delays and the like."

"And how long, in fact, did the journey take?" Merlin asked innocently.

Sir Kaherdin cast down his eyes, his lips pursing and unpursing with his tension. "Seven days," he admitted. "A full week."

"A full week," Merlin nodded. "What caused this unusual delay, my lord?"

Kaherdin was roused again. "Do you suggest I was less than zealous in pursuing my charge?"

"I suggest nothing! I merely want to know: why did it take you seven days to make the journey, while your friend was lying here dying of poison?"

"It was the winds!" Sir Kaherdin cried out in a kind of anguish. The shame and guilt that he felt at his inability to bring La Belle Isolde back to his friend in time to save his life was now manifest even to me. It explained some of his behavior. "There was a storm in the Narrow Sea the first two days, with winds blowing almost straight out of the south, and we holed up on the lee shore of the mouth of the estuary. But as it turned out, we may have been wiser to have braved the storm, because what followed were endless days of absolute calm. We could get no breeze at all. We sent the crew down each day to use two rowboats and try to row us into a wind, but it was futile, and after the first two days of exhausting labor, they balked at the idea of trying again. We were becalmed and there seemed no relief in sight. I despaired of achieving my purpose."

"He is right about those days," came support from the unexpected direction of Sir Dinadan. "From here we surveyed the sea hourly. Nothing moved on it. We could see nothing but the empty sea hour by hour, day by day."

"Of course he is right. Do you mean to suggest that my lord would ever tell a falsehood?" Melias rose to the defense of his master, but yielded the floor when Sir Kaherdin continued:

"Late on the fifth day, the weather finally broke. A breeze began from the northwest that caught our sail and brought us off the shore. We sped before it as quickly as we could, knowing that our delay may already have cost Sir Tristram his life. Finally, some seven days after our departure, we arrived back in Saint-Malo. I rushed the queen and her lady off the quay and through the gate and the city square, into the sick room which was in this palace complex. You know what we found."

"Indeed," said Merlin, with a slight raise of the eyebrows. "And… the queen? What was her demeanor all this time? How exactly did she react? When did you know she was…"

Surprisingly, it was the young Melias who took up the story here. "She was breathing heavily and seemed overheated as we hurried from the ship," he said, then cast his eyes down as we all looked with some wonder in his direction. "I…uh…I was the one assigned to escort her while Sir Kaherdin led the way."

"So you were along on this quest, young squire. And, I take it Sir Kaherdin, that your advisor Sir Andred made the trip as well?"

"Oui," the loquacious Andred grunted.

"So," Merlin continued, "to what did you attribute the queen's… fragility?"

"I assumed she was anxious about her lover. Wouldn't any of us be? Love is the most powerful of motives," the squire answered somewhat poetically. "And," he admitted in more mundane tones, "I knew that she had had some difficulties with *mal de mer* on the trip across. I knew her lady Brangwen had concocted some kind of herbal remedy for her that she had drunk a little earlier."

"The lady Brangwen is a healer as well as her mistress?" I asked.

"Of course," Sir Dinadan reminded me. "Have you forgotten the story? Where do you think the famous love potion came from?"

Merlin looked at him askance from under his great swath of eyebrow, and continued: "What had she been like on the ship itself? Did she speak to anyone?"

"Not to me," Kaherdin answered. "Just the occasional 'my lord' or some such greeting when we passed on the deck."

"She really did not speak with anyone," Melias agreed. "She and her maid remained together constantly. Sometimes she would pace the deck nervously as long as we were bound onshore. Most of the time she and the faithful Brangwen sat huddled together in the room in the After Castle we had given them as their quarters on the ship, Brangwen holding onto the queen and whispering comforting words in her ear."

"Did you ever hear what they were saying?" Merlin asked, curiously.

"Well, no…" Melias admitted.

"Hmmph," was Merlin's response. "I just wish I could find something about Isolde's…the queen's…state of mind before her own death. So Melias, you were saying that she was already feeling somewhat faint when you entered the sick room? And there you found…"

"That Sir Tristram had already died. She knelt down and took him in her arms, then saw that it was hopeless. Upon seeing that, she stood up straight, raising her face to the sky, then her eyes went back in her head and she fell like a stone to the floor. She was dead before she hit the ground."

"You have what you need then, old man," Kaherdin snapped with an air of finality. "You'll forgive us if we don't show you out, but I believe you know where the door is."

With that he turned and made as if to engage Melias and Sir Andred in other business, but, as Merlin had not moved, he had no choice but to come back to the interview. Rolling his eyes, he turned back to the old necromancer with an impatient gesture. "What is it?" He asked, not invitingly.

"There is one other matter, my lord," the mage began. "What can you, or either of your colleagues here, tell us about the skirmish that you had with the Norsemen on the day that Sir Tristram was wounded?"

"Well, your stooge the jester was there, can't he tell you about that?"

Sir Dinadan grinned at Kaherdin's characterization of him, but mentioned politely that he had already told what he could. "But as you may recall, I was near the fringe of the battle, and not in the thick of the fighting where Tristram was wounded. I did not see the wound, nor even know about it until the skirmish was over."

"Hmph," Kaherdin said. Then he thought for a moment. "Well, I took the garrison cavalry out that morning in pursuit of a band of Vikings who had been raiding country churches around the city during the night. They were on foot, so we were able to ride them down without a great deal of difficulty, up the coast toward Mont St.-Michel."

"How many in the garrison cavalry?"

"Twenty-four knights," Kaherdin answered. "There were perhaps thirty in the raiding party."

"And how were you armed?" Merlin asked.

"We all wore helmets and shields, and long chain mail shirts, belted with swords, and carried our war lances," Kaherdin responded.

"And the Norsemen? How were they armed?"

"They were a raiding party, and therefore needed to move stealthily and strike quickly," Kaherdin began. "They wore no armor, other than helmets. Each carried a sword or battle-axe, each to his taste. And of course each of them carried one of their Viking spears. It was one of those spears that did for Tristram."

"But how? Did Tristram fail to block a thrust with his shield? Did the spear puncture the chain mail?"

"The spear point apparently was thrust at Tristram from behind, while he sat on his horse, so that it wounded him in the thigh from beneath the mail shirt. A truly cowardly act," Sir Kaherdin answered, while Melias, and Sir Andred nodded their assent; apparently they had both been part of the skirmish as well.

"I see," Merlin said thoughtfully. "So without the poison, the wound would not have been life-threatening at all."

"True," Kaherdin agreed. "Making the act all the more onerous. Anything else, old man?"

"Just one thing," Merlin paused. "Did any one of you three actually see the wound occur that felled Sir Tristram?"

Kaherdin shook his head. "No, more's the pity. He was at my right hand as we rode down the Norsemen in a battering assault, lances proffered, horses galloping. We crushed most of them in that first charge, and most of the others in the melee that followed. Only those who ran away survived, and I assume got to their transport ship a bit farther up the strand. By then Tristram had got his wound, but I never saw how it happened."

"Nor did I," Melias concurred, looking toward Kaherdin as if for approval. Sir Andred simply grunted.

"Well, gentlemen," Merlin pronounced, in a voice that sounded like conclusion, "I have asked what I came here to ask. I appreciate your information, you have been most helpful. With your permission, we will be on our way now. Have a pleasant afternoon, and I assume that, should I have additional questions, I can call again?"

"With my permission and my intense pleasure, you may leave. I hope never to see you again, old man. However," he added with a dark look in Dinadan's direction, "if you find an additional audience necessary for your investigation, my door is open to you. Or at least, it is not locked. Good day to you." This time when Sir Kaherdin turned away, Merlin did as well, and the rest of us followed him silently through the back door and past the two guards, who seemed a bit unnerved, having heard some lively exchanges from within. Sir William was scowling after us, a thoughtful expression on his cautious face.

"Well!" I began as we started in the direction of the town square. "Old Kaherdin was certainly the paragon of hospitality, wasn't he?" Merlin gave me a meaningful look—the meaning of which was pretty clearly "shut your yammering trap, you fool of a Cornishman"—and then raised his eyebrows and shifted his eyes in the direction of Captain Jacques. Ah, I realized, I had been indiscrete. The captain, however friendly, was in the employ of the commander of the city, and it would not do to be too free and easy with my opinions while he was our guide.

It was, in fact, the captain who called to us before we went too far toward the main gate. "My lords! I'm not sure where you are walking to right now but it is my duty to inform you that if you do in fact want to speak with the lady Isolde next, you will find her here, within these palace grounds," and I thought, as he was speaking, that perhaps Merlin was on to something: the Breton seemed much more formal, much less affable, than he had before. Was he smarting a bit over our behavior toward his lord? "If you will follow me, I can show you."

With that he turned and headed to the left and then forward, toward a large, long, grey stone building that contained, as I surmised, the great hall of the palace. Upon entering the building, I realized it also contained a number of private chambers one of which must belong to the lady Isolde. Indeed, within a few steps of the circular south entrance to the building, Captain Jacques stopped to speak to a soldier standing guard before the door to one such private room. The guard nodded, and Captain Jacques beckoned us.

"This is the lady Isolde's private quarters," Jacques told us as the guard disappeared into the chamber. "The guard is preparing her to receive you, and will come to fetch you when she is ready. I must leave you now—I do have other things that call for my attention. My lords, when you have finished here, you will of course also want to question the doctor, Master Oswald. Him you will find attached to the cathedral, and you will have no trouble finding the cathedral from here. It is the building with the very tall westward towers that looks a great deal like a cathedral." The captain smiled at his little joke.

"Yes," Merlin smiled back. "I believe we saw it on the way into town. It should be easy enough to find."

"Good," the captain said. "Listen, though, I do not want to abandon you to your own devices completely. We will have quarters here in the palace to put you up in. Let us plan this: when you have finished with the priest, there is an inn just a street away from the cathedral called the Cock and Bull. I will hurry to meet you there as soon as I can, and there we can dine, and I can show you to your quarters. A pact?"

"Done!" said Merlin, and the two grasped hands. When the captain's steps were sounding their last on the floors of the great hall, I bent close to Merlin and whispered, "Something was going on there."

"Indeed!" whispered Merlin, as the door to Isolde's room opened. "We will need to talk about it later."

And at that point, the guard beckoned us into the room.

CHAPTER SEVEN
PEOPLE WEARING BLACK

The lady Isolde of the White Hands sat, cold and imperious as a marble stature, swathed in black samite on her bed on one side of the small room, directly across from a fireplace, which was dormant on this warm late spring morning. Next to her sat a young girl of perhaps fourteen, also dressed in black, with dark cow-like eyes and black hair uncovered. Isolde's own hair was concealed by a wimple. Her pale face showed ravages of grief and pain that had aged her far beyond her twenty-four years. I tried to find in her visage some semblance of her half-sister, my lady Rosemounde. But there was no sign of Rosemounde's twinkling blue eyes in Isolde's heavy, dark orbs, nor of Rosemounde's playful smirking mouth in Isolde's dour, cracked, frowning lips. Much more, I thought, Isolde's countenance resembled that of her haughty brother, and as we entered her chamber, she turned her nose up in such a way that she was actually able to look down it at us, even as we stood above her.

Merlin approached her with the caution of a diplomat. Bowing more deeply than I'd seen him bow to anyone, even the king, Merlin greeted her courteously. "My lady Isolde, I am the lord Merlin. I come as emissary from the court of King Arthur, who was your husband's liege lord as well as your own, and who sends you his condolences in this your season of grief. If there is anything the king can do to ease this time of sorrow for you, you are to name it to me and I will bring the request back to him."

The lady Isolde looked down at Merlin as if to say that such was her entitlement and expectation, and responded with equal courtesy: "I thank the king for his good wishes, and for his offer, though I cannot imagine what the king might do to ease my pain. My lord husband is gone, and nothing will bring him back. I simply need to adapt myself to the state of widowhood." I noticed that her eyes were completely dry as she spoke with us. The young lady in waiting at her side held Isolde's hand in a gesture of consolation, but in truth she seemed to need little comforting.

With a sudden inspiration, I was moved to address the lady Isolde myself. "My lady," I followed Merlin's example with my own deep genuflection, noticing as I bowed the old man's eyes glaring at me from beneath his thick brows. "I come as an emissary as well, but from a different source. I bring you the greetings and condolences of your sister, my lady Rosemounde, lady in waiting to Queen Guinevere."

I was *not* prepared for the response I got to *that* comment—nor, judging by the look on his face, was Merlin.

"That little bitch!" Isolde spat. "Daddy's favorite. The family's one Messiah. By what arrogance does she presume to send me greeting. Let alone condolences, as if I would wish any from that wench. Take her condolences back to her and spit them in her face for me."

"My lady," Merlin responded, as I stood by open-mouthed. "We were unaware of this animosity between you or would have refrained from delivering this message. But will you deign to share with us the cause of your bitterness so that we may understand it the better?"

"Why should you care to understand it?" she asked. Rhetorically, it turned out, since she really had no intention of giving away the floor to anyone. "The lady Rosemounde, as you call her, is my father's sole heir. Did you know that?" she challenged us. "My brother has received all he will from the estate: lordship of this town in fealty to the duke. As for me, I received a dowry when I married Sir Tristram. Upon his death it has reverted to me."

"A generous dowry?" Merlin asked.

"Harumph," was her answer. "What do you think? Look at this sparse room! A nun's cell, I call it." The room itself was not ostentatious. It was probably a bit larger than a nun's cell, but was sparsely decorated. There were no tapestries hanging on the walls, only the semi-ornate fireplace and wall slots for candelabra. Although it did seem to me that the lack of decoration was a product of her own choice, not of her poverty.

"The lady Rosemounde," Isolde ranted on in bitter irony. "The *legitimate* Lady Rosemounde. What has Daddy not planned for his little treasure? *She* must inherit the entire duchy, mustn't she? *She* must be fostered in the queen's own chamber! *She* must have negotiated for her a marriage into the royal family itself, mustn't she? Oh *she* is your dear one, dearest Daddy! And I? It seemed if I wanted a husband I must fend for myself. I thank God I had a brother who still cares somewhat for his family, and who had a friend in need of a wife—a knight of Arthur's table, no less. One without money or property—or even, as it turned out, a homeland—but one of the highest reputation that I would not be shamed to marry. Thus I became the wife of the famous Sir Tristram."

I began to grow increasingly uncomfortable with this. There was a twinge in the back of my neck, and I was beginning to feel drops of sweat trickle down my spine. It was not simply that I was beginning to realize that the lady Isolde had rather serious father issues. But it was also that, by her description, Isolde was bringing home to me the utter hopelessness of my love for Rosemounde. How could I ever hope to satisfy Duke Hoel as a suitor to his daughter, when I could bring no title to the marriage? How could I ever hope to see myself as de facto Duke of Brittany? Me, an armor-maker's son from Cornwall?

I glanced over toward Dinadan, who crossed his eyes at me as if to say, "What we have here is a major loon." But I could see that Merlin was endeavoring somehow to bring the interview back to the questions he wanted to pose. It was going to take some doing.

"My lady," he began, with another exaggerated bow. "We are here to discuss your own affairs, not those of your sister. One of the king's chief concerns in this case is your own reputation, Lady Isolde. There is gossip, perhaps unfounded, that your own words to Sir Tristram as he lay dying had the effect of stopping his heart. The king, of course, puts no credence in such rumors, but I have been asked to clear up that matter, if you can tell us in your own words what happened."

"What happened? You know what happened. Everyone knows what happened. He lay there, day after day wasting away from that poisoned wound. More and more listless as the days went on. Nothing I could do would ease his pain. Not that he cared if I did anything. I may as well have been invisible. Everyone knew the rumor: it was common knowledge that my husband was awaiting the coming of his former lover on a ship sailed by my own brother. Somehow everyone's expectations rested on the girl. A white sail and she was coming. A black sail and she was not. White was life, black was death. Yet every day, day after suspenseful day, we heard the same words from the watchman on the tower: bleak and empty the sea. Even though my husband—like my father before him—never saw me as a person, I felt in those days at least that I was a part of the drama. Then came the report. A sail! And the sail was… white. The girl was coming to displace me physically as she already had emotionally. When my husband finally turned to me, seeing me as the one to provide him his answer, I did not hesitate. Black. The sail was black, I told him."

"And he died?"

"Almost immediately. And when the little twit came in and found his corpse, she fainted dead away and fell to the floor right on top of him. It was the best day of my life."

Merlin seemed somewhat shocked by this, but certainly not surprised, given her state of mind. "And do you believe, my lady, that you caused either of their deaths, either directly or indirectly?"

"Oh my God, I hope so," she declared. We each took a small step back. "What?" she continued. "You think I should feel remorse? Why? Being married to Tristram was hell. It was like being my father's bastard daughter all over again, with his favorite little Isolde of Ireland playing the part of my baby sister, the perfect Rosemounde. Three years we were married. The first few nights he made excuses to me about some old war wound. After that he had a cough. After that I gave up. I never asked again, and he never approached me."

One thought flashed through my head. All stories are the same story.

"And your brother Kaherdin?" Merlin asked quietly and cautiously. "Was he aware of the situation?"

She gave a bitter laugh. "After the first year or so, I suppose he must have been wondering why I was not popping out little Tristrams here and there. One day we were out riding together, and we came upon a shallow pool of water. 'Just ride through it,' my brother told me. And so I did. But there was a deep point in the pool where the horse had to struggle to stay on his feet. The water splashed against my thighs, which made me cry out in shock, and then I couldn't help bursting out in laughter. My brother was concerned, and asked why I laughed. I told him I was laughing at the irony: the cold water splashing my thighs had taken liberties with me that my husband Tristram had never dreamed of. Hmph. My brother was enraged. He confronted Tristram and my loving husband revealed to my loving brother precisely how things stood between him and the wife of the King of Cornwall. And what do you suppose my loving brother did? Did he compel my husband to fulfill with me the marriage debt? Did he insist on a true marriage or threaten to annul ours so that I might take another? Oh no. He understood Sir Tristram's plight, he told him. He sympathized, he told him. My sister is in fact beneath your contempt, he may as well have told him. So that, Lord Merlin, is that. That is my story, or as much as I am willing to share with you. You have our permission to leave now."

The girl, who had spent the entire time holding Lady Isolde's hands and looking into her face, now got up and went to open the door for us to leave the room. Sir Dinadan and I began backing away, both of us nodding and mumbling "my lady" as we exited. Merlin himself gave her a curt nod, his face showing a bit of irritation—I thought perhaps because of Isolde's slipping in the use of the "royal we." As he turned to leave the room, Isolde called after him: "As for your king, tell him I appreciate his concerns, and that I look forward to paying him my respects some time. Good-bye, my lord Merlin." And with that the door closed on us.

***

By now I really felt like I had to get out of the stifling atmosphere of that palace, and headed purposefully toward the exit to the town square. Merlin and Dinadan seemed equally happy to be done here, and all through the walk to the gate I could hear Sir Dinadan muttering, "Pure balmy, that's what she is. Completely crackers, I can tell you." Which were my sentiments precisely, though I had a little more trepidation about expressing them while still within the walls of the palace.

When we burst out into the light and air of the town square I drank in deep breaths like a drowning man gulping fresh water. It felt such a relief to be away from that family of smothering arrogance and mendacity. "Well, Gildas my lad," Sir Dinadan ventured. "How do you like your potential in-laws, eh?"

I stared back at him and at Merlin, who was looking down at me curiously. "I can't help wondering how Sir Tristram was able to stand it, day after day, with those two his main companions."

"I was with him much of the time," Dinadan offered. "I suppose the soothing balm of my presence enabled him to carry on. Though the fact is, he was so miserable away from La Belle Isolde, that exile in hell could not have made things worse."

"Well, one thing is certain," Merlin mused. "Anyone in that palace is capable of having murdered Sir Tristram. But did one of them? That is the question. Perhaps the monk will have the answer for us. Let us find the cathedral."

"Found it!" Dinadan said, pointing south where the tower rose over the rooftops.

Before we could cross the square, however, we needed to wait for another group of Kaherdin's soldiers to move on from the part of their drill they were exercising directly before us. It was a completely new group from this morning's and, I noticed, included Kaherdin's squire, Melias, and his advisor Sir Andred, both of whom sat atop their destriers with a kind of arrogance caught, like a contagion, from their master. Like the morning's group, they were armed in chain mail and helmets, carrying their fighting lances, and displaying their shields. Melias's coat of arms displayed a simple vert (green) chevron on an azure background, symbols of protectiveness and loyalty. Sir

Andred displayed a rampant bull in gules (or red), on a dark sable background: the one connoting strength or valor, the other grief. Each of them bowed to us in turn as they trotted in formation across to the other side of the square. Then I noticed Sir William of Caen as well, similarly armed with lance and shield, his arms displaying a gold unicorn rampant, on a field azure. I thought it an odd emblem, so fanciful, so idealistic, for a man who struck me as so practical and businesslike. Across the bottom of his coat of arms was emblazoned the motto *Veritas*, "truth"—a motto, too, that suggested a significant portion of idealism, particularly considering what I'd seen of *this* town. Sir William too gave me a nod as he cantered past. And then Sir Neville trotted into view, carrying a shield with a blazon as strange as himself: a figure that looked like nothing so much as rat couchant argent, on a field sable. Sir Neville rode by, flashing us a golden smile as he passed. After him there was a break in the line of horses, and we all hustled across the space, having no desire to be trapped on the other side for the duration of the military exercise.

It was not difficult to find the wide thoroughfare called "Rue St. Vincent" that cut southwest from the square, from the side nearest the quay. From there it appeared to be only perhaps a quarter mile to the cathedral. We started walking at a leisurely pace among the crowds of the city, for that street was lined on both sides with various shops and businesses. On the right was a bakery, then a butcher, then a candle maker, while on the other side was a glover, and behind his shop a tannery, as our noses told us, next to a goldsmith, next to an armor-maker's shop. I often felt a sense of pride when I saw one of those, and this was especially so today, as I remembered the honest and humble roots from which I had sprung. Admittedly, at times it was a disadvantage to me to come from such stock, but after the past few hours it seemed pure blessing.

It had passed sext and was well on its way to none when we started toward the cathedral, and so Merlin decided we should stop at one of the local food sellers' carts. Each of us walked away with some bread and cheese for lunch, and a small cup of ale. Thus we walked the street, chomping and drinking, toward the church.

Merlin, though, was lively, and seemed to want to talk more about what we'd seen and heard earlier that day. "Gildas, my lad, what did we learn this morning?"

"We learned," I mouthed through my bread and cheese, "that Duke Hoel's bastard children are a pair of uncompromisingly arrogant hypocrites."

"I beg to differ," Sir Dinadan chimed in. "I did not learn that at all. Having resided here with Sir Tristram for the past three years. I have known this truth for some time."

"Well," Merlin munched thoughtfully. "Arrogant yes, that's clear. But why do you say hypocritical?"

"Well, all this dressing in black and the show of mourning they put on, when in fact it appears that either of them could have run Tristram through with ease and not missed breakfast."

"Definitely a possibility, I'll admit, in terms of motive. For all Kaherdin's show of friendship to Tristram, he was surely under his sister's constant nagging regarding Tristram's failure to consummate the marriage. But why go to the trouble of bringing La Belle Isolde back here from Cornwall?"

"Perhaps they wanted to kill them both," I suggested. "They might have been working together to plan it, and wanted to destroy both family enemies at once."

Sir Dinadan shook his head. "Much as my gorge rises at this family's overinflated pride, and much as I wish I had a pin to prick it with, I have difficulty believing they would have plotted together in such a way. Isolde's attitude toward her brother doesn't suggest it."

Merlin nodded, murmuring "Granted" in a thoughtful way.

"Kaherdin maintains that he saw nothing, no foul play regarding La Belle Isolde either on the boat or in the city, and he is supported by both Melias and Andred," I contributed. "And it's not clear how either of them could have gotten to Isolde while at sea if what they say is true. But it seems to me clear that both Melias and Andred would lie in whatever way necessary to protect their master."

"I'm not sure I agree," Merlin answered, sipping thoughtfully on what was left of his ale as we passed a side street which seemed to be lined with blacksmith shops. "Sir Andred perhaps—he is one bitter man who seems to trust no one. The squire Melias, however, I thought much more amenable, and as far as I could tell seemed to be concealing nothing."

"I have to admit, that is my view as well," Sir Dinadan answered. "And…" with this he grimaced and rolled his eyes upward, "to give the Devil his due, I have no personal knowledge of Kaherdin showing any ill will at all toward Tristram. He admired him and, if it can ever be said that he loved anyone, he loved Tristram as his closest friend. At his death…he wept as if it had been his own brother who died. I can't believe Kaherdin had ought to do with Sir Tristram's death. Kaherdin was truly close to Tristram, despite his other shortcomings. And they are legion, believe me."

"So," Merlin moved on. "The case is not so obvious anymore, eh? But Gildas, your bringing up the lady Rosemounde certainly roused the grieving widow, did it not? I admit I did not anticipate that."

"Nor did I, my lord," I answered. "The lady Rosemounde certainly harbors only the most familial of feelings toward her sister."

"Or at least wants the world to think so," Merlin mused, though I did not like him speaking so of my lady. "In any case, if Isolde of the White Hands did lift her hand in violence at any time, it is difficult to consider whether she believed it was her father or her husband she was killing. Or whether it even mattered to her which one."

"Yes, and realistically, she clearly couldn't have stabbed Tristram, unless she had an ally who was part of the cavalry. Nor, for that matter, could she have poisoned Isolde, if that's what happened, since she was never near her before she died," I reasoned. Then, thinking back to Merlin's earlier comments, I changed the subject. "But what was your concern about Captain Jacques?"

"We must speak with some care in this city," Merlin cautioned me. "Everyone who deals with us is not necessarily our ally. I don't know how far to trust Captain Jacques, but one thing I know for certain is that he is under the command of Sir Kaherdin as part of the city's garrison. That does not necessarily make him our friend."

"I did notice a kind of change in his demeanor after we had visited Kaherdin," Dinadan agreed. "Do you think it may have been because he had seen how unwelcome we were to his commander?"

"I can't say why," Merlin mused. "Maybe we'll be able to feel him out when we meet him later at the Cock and Bull."

"It would almost certainly be to our advantage," Dinadan proposed, "to have a conversation with Sir William of Caen. He is dull as pondwater, it's true, but as intelligent a knight as there is in this city. And one of Kaherdin's inner circle. He has a reputation for honesty, and may know things or have seen things that he'd be willing to tell us about."

"And we can trust him?" I asked. "If he's as close to the ruling family as you say, and as devoted to Kaherdin as he says himself, how can we believe him?"

Merlin shrugged. "If he lies, I think we will see through it. But Dinadan has a point. He may be a good witness, and the parchment I have from Kaherdin should convince him to talk to us. We'll have to find a time to question him."

"What about his companion, that Sir Neville?" I asked.

"Too strange for my blood," Dinadan muttered.

And Merlin seemed to agree, but changed the subject: "But look, we seem to be here!"

The Cathedral of Saint Vincent of Saragossa was named for a fourth-century martyr who, like most fourth-century martyrs, had died by the hand of the Roman Emperor Diocletian. I observed now at closer range that the single tower we had seen from a distance was an old Roman tower that rose above the transept of the church. Most of the rest of the structure was fairly new, built of white and red sandstone in thick Romanesque walls. There was no elaborate west work, but only a fairly simply portal into the nave. The west portal, like the tower, seemed of a much greater age than the rest of the church.

Ancient or no, the western portals of churches always hold a fascination for me. That was always where you found the Last Judgment tympanum. And there it was. The old sculptor, hundreds of years earlier, was no genius with stone but had rendered a passable semblance of Christ sitting in judgment, of a large group of souls on his right being led by an angel into eternal bliss, and a large group of sinners on his left, goaded by a hideous demon into a great fiery hellmouth. And there, at Christ's upper right, my favorite image of all: father Abraham sitting in paradise, lifting his robe so that he revealed the tiny, innocent souls spending eternity in Abraham's bosom. That's where I wanted to wind up, I always thought. There, in the bosom of the patriarch—if I could somehow remain innocent, uncorrupted by the world of the Tristrams and the Isoldes. And the Kaherdins and the Marks. And the Hoels. And the Arthurs, I thought, remembering the birth of Mordred.

Merlin and Dinadan stepped into the darkness of the cathedral, and I followed. Inside, the nave was dark, lit only by a pair of high windows on the side walls. There were two aisles supported by six rectangular stone columns. The apse in the chancel was flat. There had been some small attempt to decorate the church with frescoes over the years, and I could make out on one wall along the side aisle what appeared to be a procession of martyrs, led, apparently, by Saint Vincent himself, carrying his palm. The other martyrs all seemed similarly Roman in their provenance. I understood from Captain Jacques, who had discussed the cathedral with me on our crossing from Southampton, that the abbey attached to the cathedral was allied with the Marmoutier order—monks from an abbey founded by that other most Roman of saints, Martin of Tours. No mention anywhere in the cathedral of the city's founder, Saint-Malo, who as a companion of Saint Brendan would have brought a Celtic form of Christianity among the Celtic people of Brittany, and whose monastery would have followed the ancient Celtic rule, rather than that of the Roman Benedict. Were there any adherents of the old ways still active in Saint-Malo any more, I wondered, even after some centuries? Such things were not unheard of, this clinging to the old ways, especially in places like Saint-Malo, where anyone who was *not* of Celtic heritage was a recent import.

"Hello!" Merlin called to the empty church. "You'd think there'd be a sacristan at least around somewhere, wouldn't you?" He asked us, looking about with his hands on his hips. He called out again: "Is there anyone here?"

I caught a sudden movement out of the corner of my eye, and looked to see a face, peeking as it were from behind the rood screen in the front of the cathedral. I pointed, and called out, "Are you the Sacristan?"

The head shook and spoke, "Oh no, I'm not. Saw you approaching though. Have a pretty good idea who you are."

Squinting into the darkness, Sir Dinadan announced. "That, gentlemen, is Master Oswald. We've found our man."

"Looking for me I guess?" Master Oswald came from behind the rood screen and bustled his way up the left side aisle to meet us. "Sir Dinadan, such a delight to see you again."

"And you, master." Dinadan smiled down at the diminutive monk. "Master Oswald, this is the lord Merlin, famed counselor from the court of King Arthur himself."

"Ooo," Master Oswald cooed, his brown eyes growing round with enthusiasm.

"And this," Dinadan continued, "is his assistant, the squire, Gildas of Cornwall." I nodded to the monk. He was quite short, a good two inches shorter than me, and I was the shortest of our group. But what Oswald lacked in height he made up for in girth, for his body was nearly as round as his tonsured head, and the black Benedictine robe that swathed it must have taken the wool of a significant number of Breton sheep to construct. Master Oswald wore no belt; I suspected he could find none large enough to encircle his perimeter.

"Cornwall, hey?" Master Oswald reflected. "Some personal interest in this business here that's gone on in the past weeks? That's why you're here with Dinadan?"

"Not exactly personal," I replied. "But certainly an interest. That's why Merlin and I are here…" I said, looking up at the mage.

"The king has asked us to inquire into the rather unquiet deaths of Tristram and Isolde," Merlin began, as diplomatically as possible. Pulling out the parchment that the squire Melias had prepared for him, he also showed that to Master Oswald. "As you see, the lord Kaherdin has given us leave to question people in the city as we look into the case. Our understanding is that you were there when they died—indeed, other than the lady Isolde of the White Hands, the only one who was present for the deaths themselves. In addition, of course, you tended Sir Tristram during his debilitating illness following on the wound that poisoned him. How much do you know about poisons, Master Oswald?"

"Ah," the rotund monk cried. "So that's the way of it, eh? We'd better be seated then. I suppose this may take some time. Come, please," and he motioned us to sit on the small benches available for congregants who chose to sit through mass. We gathered four of the seats into a circle, Master Oswald's looking as though it may collapse at any moment. And then he began, as if we were all old friends exchanging stories.

"How much do I know about poisons, you ask, my lord Merlin? Well, certainly more than any man in Saint-Malo. And I would venture to say as much as anyone in all of Brittany. This is not boasting. I am herbalist to this monastery, and have spent every day of my life growing and gathering plants and herbs of remarkable variety, to keep my cupboards stocked. Been doing it now for twenty years. I know what every one of those herbs and plants does because I've used them, tending the sick in the abbey and the town when called upon, as I was in the case of Sir Tristram. Don't just rely on trial and error though, no, no. I have manuscripts of Pliny, Dioscorides, an Anglo-Saxon herbal, a Latin manuscript of Avicenna, and a new treatise by a German nun, Hildegard, called *A Book of Simple Medicine*. All of this is me. But does Tristram trust me to cure him? No. He calls for his old girlfriend. Isolde of Ireland, whose reputation is she's the greatest healer in the world. And on she comes, to save the day."

"Well, she *had* cured him of a similar wound before, hadn't she?" I ventured.

Master Oswald scoffed. "In Ireland, not? Sure, he was wounded by a poisoned blade. In Ireland. A blade borne by *her own brother*. She knew exactly what the poison was that her brother used, and so she knew precisely what the antidote was. It doesn't take a great herbalist to do that. It just takes somebody's sister."

"But isn't it likely to be the same kind of poison, if it's used on a weapon?" I asked. "I mean, how many different poisons are there that somebody would envenom a blade with?"

"Dozens," Oswald answered. "That is, unless that was a rhetorical question. Look, it's really a pretty unusual thing for someone to be poisoning their weapons anyway. Why do it? It takes a particular streak of cruelty. You want to make sure that you maximize the kill, that if you just slightly wound the enemy, he's going to die. A person like Marholt might do it: his job was to defend Ireland single-handedly, so even if he lost, there was a chance he'd prevent the enemy from entering his country. But why should a Norse raiding party do it? They care about plunder and then about getting away. What do they care if one of the defenders dies long after they've left? He wasn't their target. But I guess I'm off on a tangent here. The point is, you make your poison from what's available. In this case they used snake venom. The toxic venom of the asp viper."

"You're sure of this?" Merlin asked. "How can you be certain?"

"By the symptoms," Oswald shrugged matter-of-factly. "Acute pain. Swelling due to edema. Discoloration. Heavy internal bleeding. Some loss of vision, difficulty breathing and swallowing. And by the end he'd lost all feeling in his right leg, the leg with the wound. It was snake venom. No doubt. Now, answer me this. There are no snakes in Ireland, is that not so? Saint Patrick cast them all out, like demons, isn't that what they say? So if there are no snakes in Ireland, how was Isolde of Ireland going to know what to do to save Tristram? Huh? How?"

Merlin pursed his lips, then frowned and raised his eyebrows, as if to say, well, she couldn't.

"Of course she couldn't. If I were a betting man, I'd say he stood a better chance with me than with her. Of course, I'm not a betting man," Oswald laughed. "Gambling is probably a sin. In fact the odds are three-to-one that it is, I'd say. If I were a betting man. But then, look, it gave him some hope to think she was coming. That might have bought him a few days. But trust me, he was a dead man from the time he got that wound. All we did was stave off the inevitable."

The loquacious monk had a tendency to talk all around a topic before finally putting it out of its misery, but Merlin did seem not only to be amused, but to be getting something out of Master Oswald's ramblings. "Tell me, Master Oswald. In your opinion, did Isolde's lie about the black sail play a part in Sir Tristram's death?"

"A part? Oh dear me, I suppose it might be said to. Not a major part, certainly, but if his hope had allowed him to hold on that long, taking the hope away from him did send him into his death throes. But I'd say it may have hastened his death by only a few minutes. Once he had actually seen his Isolde of Ireland, the hope would have been achieved, and it couldn't have sustained his life any more. No, white sail or black, the man was dead, I can tell you for a certainty."

"Well answer me this then," Merlin continued. "In your professional opinion, what do you think killed La Belle Isolde?"

The monk smiled wanly. "A broken heart, what else? She comes in after the long journey, after being separated from the love of her life for three years, and thinking it would be forever, and what does she find? Only that he has died, but scant minutes before. How else could the story end? She *must* die. The story calls for it."

Merlin smiled back sadly. "An oddly romantic notion for a consummate professional like yourself, wouldn't you admit?"

"Well, as to that," Master Oswald looked down. "Sometimes there is no reason to disturb the common belief. Let the people have their story as they want it. Besides," he went on in a conspiratorial tone, "I had no time or opportunity to examine the body. The thing was done, the stage must be cleared and struck before the next farce began."

Merlin folded his arms and leaned back to study the little round monk's face. "If you were a betting man," Merlin challenged him. "What would be your best guess as to what killed La Belle Isolde?"

Oswald licked his lips, looked around, and whispered rather loudly to Merlin "She was poisoned as well. Five will get you ten it was with Belladonna. It's the most toxic plant found in Europe. Now when she came in, she was shielding her eyes against the light. Dilated pupils and a sensitivity to light are symptoms of Belladonna poisoning. She was also flushed, staggering, seemed unbalanced, seemed to have blurred vision because she didn't look like she was seeing clearly, had slurred speech, and then fell in a great convulsion to the floor."

"All symptoms that would seem consistent with broken-heartedness," I ventured.

"But more clinically, all symptoms consistent with Belladonnna poisoning. Twenty years of experience, young Gildas, and you know what I've never seen? I've never seen anyone die of a broken heart. The odds are…well, they're not even worth considering."

"So she was poisoned," Merlin concluded.

"She was absolutely poisoned," Master Oswald affirmed. "And it was done not long before her disembarking from the ship."

"But how is that even possible," Sir Dinadan wondered, "when the faithful Brangwen was with her every step of the way from Cornwall to Saint-Malo?"

"Or so Kaherdin and his friends told us. But here again, we have only their testimony. How much can we believe what they say?" Merlin reasoned. "Is it really possible for the two of them never to have parted company that entire week? I mean, we would say 'she never left her mistress's side,' and be sincere about it, even though we know that at some point she must have gone off to use the necessarium, or to stretch her legs while perhaps her mistress was sleeping, or any one of a number of excuses that would cause her to leave her mistress unattended for a few seconds, even a few minutes at a time. That is all that would have been necessary for a poisoner to do his work."

"Well," Master Oswald said thoughtfully as he scratched the side of his close-shaven face. "I think maybe if I was you boys, I'd want to talk to the lady Brangwen then."

"Well of course we'd like to…" Merlin began to snap at the monk, and then realized: "Wait, Master Oswald, are you saying that the lady Brangwen is here? Now? In Saint-Malo?"

The monk shrugged. "Where else would she be? I mean, she was left pretty much alone and friendless when her mistress collapsed, and no one had taken much thought as to what to do with Brangwen when it was all over. She is trying to find passage on a ship that will take her back to Cornwall, although it may turn out to be much faster for her to go back on the ship that takes the three of you to Southampton, since she can probably get overland escort to Cornwall from Camelot. Likely granted to her by the king himself, known the world over for his generosity."

"But, where is she?" Merlin wanted to know. "Where can we find the lady Brangwen?"

"Here, here," the monk answered. "There is a small room outside of the monks' living quarters, within the cathedral itself in fact. I arranged to have the lady Brangwen housed there temporarily, as long as she is abandoned and friendless here. One of our young monks is seeing to her needs as best he can while we try to help her figure out what to do next. Look, I will speak to the abbot on your behalf, and get you an interview with the lady tomorrow morning, if you think that will suffice."

"Perfect," Merlin agreed and rose to go. "We'll return in the morning at about terce, then, will that be agreeable?"

"Good then," Master Oswald also rose and began showing us to the door. "We shall meet again in the morning. I do hope my thoughts on these matters were of some help to you."

"Invaluable, invaluable," Merlin told him. Then suddenly Merlin turned toward him with some agitation, as if he had just thought of something new. "Oh, one more thing, Master Oswald! I wonder if you can tell me something about the shape of the wound on Sir Tristram's leg. Was it a deep cut or slash, or was it more of a hole? Please, you were the only one who looked at the wound closely, can you describe it?"

"Strange you should mention it, and word it exactly that way. Yes, I did notice that there was a rounded shape to the wound. Why? Is that significant?"

"It may well be," Merlin answered "Until tomorrow morning, then," and with that, we exited into the street.

CHAPTER EIGHT
A COCK AND BULL STORY

It had not been difficult to find the Cock and Bull Inn. The colorful sign hung outside a shop on a corner just down the street from the cathedral: an angry looking red bull with a colorful rooster perched on its left horn. We soon discovered the reason for the name: Everything on the bill of fare was either some dish made of chicken or some kind of beef preparation. We sat now near a glowing fire in the dark inn, heads close together at a dark wood table.

I was eating a beef meat pie, with gravy and some local vegetables mixed inside the crust. Sir Dinadan was eating a creamy blancmange with shredded chicken breasts. And Merlin was enjoying an omelet made with local oranges and lemons, cooked in olive oil. We had a pitcher of Bordeaux wine on the table, and were eating better than we had since leaving Camelot. And we were going over what we had heard that day from the witnesses we had interviewed.

"How believable is the monk?" Dinadan was asking.

"He's the only one I'm absolutely certain is not lying," Merlin said. "And I do believe he is quite right about Isolde's death. Poisoning very satisfactorily explains what happened to her—far more satisfactorily than any broken-hearted nonsense. As for Tristram, his fate seems to have been sealed when the poison from the weapon entered his body. Nothing is likely to have saved him."

"But it's like Master Oswald says," I asserted. "There wasn't any reason for the Norsemen to poison their weapons. What would it matter to them if Tristram died a lingering death? They just wanted him out of the way so they could escape."

"I have heard," Dinadan mused, "that the Norsemen's favorite god, Balder, was killed unexpectedly by a sharp missile that did not at first seem to pose any danger to him. It may be that Norse warriors regularly poison their weapons for that reason. I have little experience fighting against them myself."

"Well I have," Merlin announced. "In Arthur's Scandinavian wars. And what you say about the god Balder is true, but we did not run into any poisoning of the kind you suggest. The point is moot anyway, though. Sir Tristram was not wounded by a Viking blade. He was wounded by the lance of one of the city's guard. One of Sir Kaherdin's men."

That pronouncement, made so confidently and matter-of-factly by the old mage, left Dinadan and me staring at one another's gaping jaws. After a moment or two of stunned silence, I babbled, "But... but how can you know that, for sure?"

"God's nostrils, boy, didn't you hear what Master Oswald said about the wound?"

"About it being round you mean? Why is that important?"

"Dunce of a Cornishman!" Merlin cried, exasperated. "It's of primary importance! What kind of a spear does a Viking use as a weapon?"

"Viking spears have iron heads that are thin and sharp, like knives," Dinadan volunteered. "I remember that much. They'll use them to thrust, as was done to Sir Tristram, or to throw, or sometimes, when they have long heads, as a cutting weapon."

"Precisely," said Merlin. "No Viking weapon made that rounded wound. Sir Dinadan, perhaps you can enlighten young Gildas as to what weapon would have made that wound."

Speaking through a mouth full of blancmange, the now-enlightened Dinadan said with some confidence, "It was made by a fighting lance, of the sort borne by Kaherdin's troops. Tristram was wounded from behind by one of his own men."

The news came as a shock to me, but not a complete surprise. The poisoned wound was too personal, the bitterness in this city too virulent, for Tristram's death to have been an accident.

"The question, of course, is who was behind the attack," Merlin continued.

"Well my money's on the wife," Sir Dinadan said. "I was here with Tristram for a long time. And I was never shy about telling him how he treated his wife worse than a serf or villain on his land. If he had had any land. But she was about as cold and vengeful as any woman I've known. That performance about the black sail was about as cold-hearted as it could be."

I felt a pang in my stomach, as if instinctively I needed to rise to the defense of my lady's sibling. Even though Isolde seemed to despise Rosemounde, Rosemounde had charged me specifically in this case to find a defense for her sister against the charge that her words had caused Sir Tristram's demise. "Well, look, to be fair, how could she not be bitter? She was in an impossible situation, wasn't she? What was she supposed to do? So she struck out with some hurtful words. That doesn't make her a murderer, does it?"

"Well, obviously, she didn't stab him herself. She would have had to hire or convince somebody in the guard to do it for her," Dinadan said. "But I think she hated him enough to do that."

"What about her brother?" I asked. "He could easily be behind this. He knew all about his sister's marriage. His family pride—and there's an awful lot of it there—couldn't possibly allow him to just let that insult to his family go."

"I can't see it," Dinadan said. "Remember, I've been here with Tristram for a long time. Kaherdin was his closest friend, except maybe for me. And to be completely honest, I can't stand him. He's got that quick temper, he's arrogant, he's unpleasant. But he's always been loyal to Tristram, I'll say that for him. I would have a really difficult time believing he could have wounded his friend from behind with a poisoned lance."

"He was on the ship for days with Isolde," I reminded him. "Somebody poisoned her on that boat. Maybe he couldn't bring himself to kill Tristram because Tristram was the love of his life, or whatever you're saying, but he needn't have any compunction about killing La Belle Isolde, right? Somebody on that ship was a murderer."

Dinadan was turning red, and Merlin, having calmly finished his omelet while Dinadan and I had been speculating, broke in with an obvious point: "We don't really know anything. The two of them have motives, but there are other things to consider. What about King Mark himself? He seemed quite reconciled when we spoke with him. But wouldn't the murderer want to seem innocent? And if Isolde or Kaherdin were guilty, why would they have shown us their worst traits when we interviewed them?"

"I can answer that," Dinadan said. "They think they are beyond reproach, beyond the law, because of their status. It wouldn't even occur to either of them to cover up a crime, because if they did it, they'd think it wasn't a crime."

Merlin gave a little half smile, recognizing that there was indeed some truth in what Dinadan had to say. But he had one other caveat. "There is another fact to consider. Captain Jacques had such a sudden change of mood earlier, after we had interviewed Kaherdin and his men, that it seemed that he might be hiding something. Or know something that he wasn't telling us."

"Captain Jacques? You really think he may be a part of this?" I asked.

"I think he knows something. Perhaps even just realized that he knows something. But he's not sure what it means."

"Well, I know for one thing that he couldn't have been responsible for Tristram's wounding, or even witnessed it, because he was left behind to guard the city when the bulk of the garrison went after the Norsemen," Dinadan volunteered.

"Well, we'll just have to see if we can get him to tell us what was affecting him. But enough of that for now. I want to know one thing: on the ship, when I had my spell, what did I say? You haven't told me yet."

"You haven't asked," I reminded him.

"What is this about?" Dinadan wanted to know. "You mumbled something that made no sense. This is an infirmity, is it not? What can your crazy ramblings have to do with anything?"

Merlin shrugged. "Those spells are times when I am touched by God," he said simply and with surprising calm. The silence at the table was palpable. "They call me a prophet. But it's a kind of a trance. The things I say during those moments, before I black out, always prove to be true. But since they are always cryptic, I usually can't understand them until the time is past."

"Well," Dinadan said, "God touches you in a funny way, then. Little cosmic joke of his, sending you messages you can't interpret?"

"*The dog turns on its master. But there is another wolf with horns*," I said. "That was what you said when you went down."

"Well, that's crystal clear isn't it?" Dinadan scoffed. "So all we need to do is find a dog, right?"

A long snout poked in front of me just then, looking for a mouthful of my beef pie, which, fortunately, I had already finished. "Down girl," said a voice, and the long head was pulled back. I followed it and looked up to see Captain Jacques, holding a large dog on a leash. "So," he said, you found the place and you're already eating. I'm glad to have found you. Please allow me to join you," and he pulled up a chair, telling the dog to "Sit, girl!"

The dog was tall and built like a deer, with long delicate legs and a sleek body. She reminded me a great deal of the queen's greyhounds, Dido and Aeneas, but was a good deal taller and was covered with a long wavy coat of russet and white fur. She had an intelligent, curious face, and her brown almond shaped eyes stared at me with an almost calculating expression.

"What is she?" I asked, fascinated by the dog's face and generally aloof demeanor.

"Ah, she's what they call a Borzoi," Captain Jacques answered, absent-mindedly petting her deer-like head, which the dog tolerated while looking about inquisitively. "You don't see them around here much," he continued. "I won her off a seaman from Ragusa a year or so ago, when she was still a pup. She's a great hunting dog—fast as a greyhound. The seaman told me that in Russia they train them to chase down wolves. Anyway, I usually keep her with the other dogs of the garrison in the kennel, but sometimes when I'm out and about in the evenings, I like to bring her along. She senses things that I might miss."

One of the bar wenches sauntered up to the captain and flirted a bit before taking his order for a meat pie and ale. She was ruddy and round-faced, with sparkling blue eyes that fixed solely on Jacques. "You know Captain," she said, batting her dark eyelashes at him. "You probably ought to get a new girlfriend. That one's too skinny, if you ask me."

"Hello Meg," Captain Jacques replied. His eyes wandered over her own ample hips and bosom, which were noticeable even in the shapeless grey dress she wore, with its sleeveless brown tunic and leather girdle around the waist. Her blonde curls protruded from her wimple. "I notice that's not a fault of your own, now, is it?"

"No sir," she murmured over her shoulder as she walked off to take care of the captain's order, wiggling her backside at him as she stepped away.

The captain laughed and waved her off, and then looked at Merlin with some seriousness, asking, "So, old man, have you found out anything useful in your questioning of people today?"

"Well, you saw my limited success with Kaherdin and his men. I must say that Master Oswald was especially helpful with his learned observations. As for the lady Isolde, she was most forthcoming about her feelings. Feelings of bitterness and vindictiveness seem to run deep here in Saint-Malo."

Captain Jacques nodded as he drank from his glass of ale that had just arrived. "It is true," he said, putting down his glass. "It is even part of our reputation, I'm afraid. Ah, the things I could tell you…" and he trailed off, though Merlin was leaning forward expectantly. "Listen," the captain suddenly said, putting up his finger for quiet. I listened. A bird's song was floating in with the night, a loud song full of whistles and trills.

"Beautiful," I murmured.

"The nightingale," Captain Jacques continued. "There are a few orange and hickory trees even here in the city, and the birds will nest in them, and entertain us with their songs at night. My friends," the captain stretched out, taking a bite from his meat pie. "You know that Brittany is famous for its storytellers. Well, let me share with you a story of our city that has become widespread throughout Brittany. People call the story 'The Nightingale.' It may tell you something about the character of the people of Saint-Malo."

"Well, let's hear it then!" Sir Dinadan asked. "It'll help pass the night, and maybe teach us a thing or two."

"With your permission," the captain nodded to Merlin, and the mage nodded back his assent. "All right then," he began. "So, it seems that once upon a time in a village near Saint-Malo there were two great knights, who lived in palaces that were right close up near one another. Now one of these knights, let's call him, I don't know, 'the husband' or something. Well this husband has just married himself a very courteous, noble lady. Now the other knight, we'll call him 'the lover' or just 'the knight,' is a bachelor and a chivalrous one, spending his time in tournaments and such, giving his riches away to other knights and his own retainers. But all this time, you see, the knight was pining away with love for the wife of his neighbor.

"Well, he pleaded with her for her love, and did noble deeds, and all of those things that knights are supposed to do who love courtly ladies. And so after certain years, he finally won her over, and she granted him her love. But though they lived so conveniently right next door to each other, the two of them found no way to meet for a tryst anywhere on the grounds of either estate, for the husband watched over his wife more closely than a hawk. The lovers needed to find some way to meet, if only to talk to one another as an outlet for their unconsummated love.

"Now there was a tall stone wall between the two houses, right outside her closet window, separating her casement from the lover's on the other side. The lady would often talk to her lover on the far side of the wall, and the two of them would sometimes toss love tokens over the wall to one another. So they passed a number of months, pretty much as happy as they could be under the circumstances of their separation, and the husband none the wiser.

"Well, it got to be the early summer—this very time of year we're in now. The meadows were green, the trees were in bloom, and the nightingales were singing. The wife and her lover listened to one particularly vocal nightingale who sang in the trees near their houses, and they thought only about their love. When the old husband had gone to sleep in his own room, the lady would come in the evening to her window and stand, under the pale moonlight, and call to her lover over the wall, while they listened to the nightingale. He was always waiting for her, and always answered.

"Eventually the husband came to realize that his wife was waking every night and standing at her open window, and became suspicious. He demanded to know what in the world she was doing there. She told him it was only to listen to the nightingale, whose song was the most beautiful in all the world, and that no one could know true joy who had not listened to the song of that beautiful bird. Well, her husband listened to her, but he didn't believe a word of what she said. He gave an angry laugh, and stalked off.

"His plan was to trap the nightingale. He set every one of his household servants to set snares all around the house and the orchard. They put traps in the trees, coated the branches with sticky lime, until, of course, the nightingale was finally caught. The servants immediately brought the ensnared bird to their master, the angry husband.

"Her lord brought the little bird in his bare hands to his wife's chamber, and told her with a cruel smile that he had caught the nightingale. He showed it to her, saying, 'Here, my lady, is the bird that kept you awake and kept you from sleeping in my bed night after night—disturbing your peace. Well, that will never happen again. Watch how I take care of this.'

"The lady was aghast. She pleaded with him to let her have the bird and to do it no harm, but in a fit of brutish cruelty the husband took the bird between his hands and broke its neck. Then he threw the dead bird at the lady, splattering the front of her dress with blood. In the end he stalked from the room, leaving her to weep over the dead bird.

"When the cruel husband was gone, the lady picked the tiny body up in her hands and, weeping sorely, cursed the entire household that had helped her husband trap the bird. And within herself she mourned the fact that she could no longer spend the evenings speaking with her lover over the wall—and she knew, too, that if she did not come to the window, her lover would think she had forgotten him and was no longer true.

"She thought it through for several hours, standing there in her closet clutching the lifeless body of the nightingale. Finally she determined to send the nightingale's tiny body to her lover next door. She took the murdered bird and wrapped it in a piece of black samite that she had in her room, embroidered in gold. She called her personal page to her chamber, and gave him the bird to deliver to her lover. The page greeted the lover from his lady, and placed the samite-swathed bird into his hand. Then he told him everything that had transpired in his neighbor's house.

"The knight was so saddened by these events that he wept openly. Then, thanking the page, he took the bird, and called to him the best goldsmith in Saint-Malo. When the goldsmith had come to his palace, the knight bade him make a golden reliquary, studded with precious stones, to house the body of the blessed bird that had been the symbol of his ill-fated love. From that day until this, the knight has carried that small reliquary with him everywhere. He never lets it out of his sight. The lady is still married to the cruel husband, and he holds her like a small bird in a cage. She hates her husband, and he knows it, but is satisfied with the power he has over her. Misery seems fine with these people, so long as one is properly avenged."

It was the kind of story that left its audience sobered and silent, and that was the mood of the table when Captain Jacques had finished his tale. A low whine could be heard from Jacques's side, and I suddenly realized it was the dog, whining as if she understood the story. Of course, as Jacques realized, what she was doing was begging for food, and he gave her a piece of his beef pie to eat directly out of his hand while the rest of us were recovering from his narrative.

"So what are you saying with this," Dinadan wanted to know. "You're implying that people like Kaherdin, like Isolde of the White Hands, like their servants and countrymen and retainers, are like the husband in the story? That they will gladly harm anyone around them, including themselves, to make sure that no one impugns their honor in any way?"

"That is, perhaps, one thing that the story suggests," Jacques admitted. "But don't forget that the lady and her lover are also of

Saint-Malo. So the story tells of those who love strongly, against all odds, and remain true even when love is hopeless."

"A land of complex and utterly human motives," Merlin nodded. "But you forget, my good captain. Tristram was Cornish. La Belle Isolde was Irish. Mark is Cornish. The story is universal, Captain Jacques. It reflects values and deep emotions that are as strong among others as among those of this land."

Captain Jacques smiled grimly. "But of course. That is the strength of stories. But this particular story—the story of Tristram and his two Isoldes, and Kaherdin and Mark, played out its final scenes right here, where the nightingales still sing."

"Indeed. Well, on that note, I think my friends and I should be finding our way to our evening rest about now."

"There I can help you," the captain responded. "My lord Kaherdin has instructed me to extend to you the hospitality of the palace while you are in Saint-Malo. I can show you a room where you are welcome to stay, and have your sea chest brought to you before you settle in for the evening. It is still in my room, you'll recall."

"Ah!" Merlin said. "Well, this is generosity we had not looked for. I expect we will be quite grateful for the offer," and he rose from the table, as Dinadan and I followed suit.

The captain did not move. He held on to his dog's lead and looked over his shoulder, searching for someone. I realized that he was looking for Meg, the kitchen wench he had spoken to earlier. "I have a small bit of personal business to attend to before I can go with you," he said rather awkwardly and, seeing his dilemma, I made the best of it and said, "We'll stretch our legs for a moment, then, and meet you out in the street when you are ready."

Captain Jacques looked relieved, and nodded at me gratefully, and as Merlin, Dinadan and I made our way to the door, the Borzoi turned her nose up and looked around as if to say that she was done with us as well.

We were no sooner out the door when Dinadan exploded. "Stay in the palace? What kind of offer is that from someone who virtually threw us out on our ears when we interviewed him? And in the same complex as that vengeful wife of Tristram's? I don't know about you, but I don't feel safe there, especially as Tristram's closest friend. If they wanted to get him, what would keep them from doing away with me too?"

"I have to say I'm not happy about the idea of staying there either," I concurred. "Don't we put ourselves right in the power of those we don't really trust at all?"

"Now, let's just think about this for a moment," Merlin cautioned us. "If we want to find out all we can about those that live there, where better to be than right under their noses? It's perfect for our investigation."

"Perfect for *your* investigation, perfectly awful for *my* safety," Sir Dinadan countered, but suddenly Merlin put up his hand and glanced to his side. I knew what he was doing, because I had seen the same thing: A movement in the shadows. The sun had set some time ago, and the streets were becoming quite dark. We could see each other reasonably well as we stood in the light coming through the window of the Cock and Bull, but across the street, or to either side of us, there were only shadows. And I now realized that a number of those shadows were moving.

I still had no sword, nor did Sir Dinadan—they were in that chest in the captain's quarters. Merlin had the staff he usually walked with, but if these thieves were armed, we had little defense. Dinadan reached into his belt and pulled out a knife. I looked around on the street for anything—a large stone, a brick, something that I could use to fight back.

Merlin, however, was way ahead of us. He was rolling something around in his hands, and I knew what he was about to do. He raised his right hand and boomed out in a powerful, stentorian voice, "*O Fiat, Domine, hun ignem terrent stolidis mentibus abstulit*!" with that he hurled a shining ball into the darkness where the shadows seemed to have gathered the deepest and there, across the narrow street the ball exploded in a bright incendiary flash. In its brightness we caught sight, for a brief moment, of six skulking figures, dressed like simple artisans, armed with knives and clubs, except for one who had a crossbow pointed in our direction. Before the flash faded away, I caught the slightest glimpse of something on that crossbow-wielding villain's shrouded face that glinted in the flash. The tiniest spark of light, too quick to register, or even to remember afterwards.

"Away with ye, foolish peasants, or my next explosion will take you all up in flames!" Merlin called out, bluffing, as I knew, since he never carried any more of that incendiary powder than could make a single flash. It did seem as if a few of the shadows slunk off but there was a cry from one of the others, and at that moment it seemed that some three or four of the thugs came rushing toward us. I steeled myself for the attack, preparing to defend myself with my bare hands, when suddenly two forms shot past me, coming from within the inn. One was calling "For Saint-Malo!" and waving a glittering sword. The other was a streak of blonde fur and a snarl.

Captain Jacques may have wounded two or three of the bandits before they turned tail and ran away into the darkness, The dog had run down one of the fleeing culprits and had torn half of his hose off and was shaking them about, as if trying to break the neck of the shard of clothing.

"What was that about?" I blurted out. "Is this common behavior on the streets of Saint-Malo at night?"

"It is not," Captain Jacques insisted. "This is not some wandering band. There are no such criminals in this city. The city guard patrols the streets regularly; I have been on such assignment myself. The lord Kaherdin would never hear of such a thing in his town."

"Then you are saying that this group was hired deliberately to attack us?" Merlin asked.

"Well I…no, I did not mean to imply…"

"If there are not groups of brigands who wander the streets at night, as you insist, then this is a special group, and one that could have only one purpose—the purpose they were employed for at this inn at this time: someone in this city wanted to stop us, to kill us if need be, to stop our investigation. This is what follows from your comment."

The captain had no answer to that. But suddenly his eyes grew very round as he looked past Merlin and into the street. "Sir Dinadan!" he cried out.

When I turned to see where his eyes had traveled, I saw what he had seen, and froze for an instant. Sir Dinadan was lying face down in the street. Merlin quickly bent down to look at him and turned him over onto his back, revealing a cross-bow dart buried in the upper right part of his chest. But his eyes were open, and his chest rose and fell unevenly with his breathing.

After an instant of shocked silence, Merlin took charge. "God's earlobes, you lunkheads, don't just stand there. Gildas! Captain Jacques! Lift him up and bear him back to the monastery. Master Oswald will need to be called in to help him right now. Follow me to the abbey—I know it is this way down the street. Follow me now," and he led on, his staff pointing before him and the dog at his side as he started on his way, looking over his shoulder to make sure we were keeping up. I had Sir Dinadan's legs and was scampering after the old man as quickly as I could, as Captain Jacques held Dinadan up by the shoulders and kept pace with me, trying not to jostle the wounded knight any more than absolutely necessary.

We were at the gate to the abbey in a matter of moments, and Merlin was pounding away at the door and calling "Ho there, in the abbey! We have a visiting knight who may die without medical attention." I glanced back to see Dinadan's face and saw him wince as he mumbled, "Don't sugar coat it, old man. I wouldn't want you to give me any false hope." Captain Jacques was rolling his eyes and the dog began whining and pawing at the door once she realized we were trying to get in.

After what seemed an eternity, a grizzled monk opened the door to us and glared unwelcomingly. Captain Jacques took over at this point. "My good brother, perhaps you know me; I am Jacques, a captain of the city guard."

"And what's that to do with me?" The old monk responded in a surly voice. "What are you doing mucking about and disturbing people in their homes at night? Come back in the morning if you've any business with this house."

"Wait, brother," Merlin intervened as the ancient monk began to close the door. "We come on urgent business. This man has been attacked in the street. He has a crossbow dart in his chest. We seek Master Oswald for his medical expertise. Can you not bring us to him and save this man's life?"

The monk opened his eyes wide and shook his gray, tonsured pate. "God protect us!" he exclaimed. "You would bring the violence of street gangs into this house of peace? Begone, brigands, or I'll call the watch!" And again, he moved to close the door.

"I *am* the watch, you blithering idiot!" Captain Jacques exclaimed. But the ancient fellow continued to push the door closed.

By now Merlin had had enough. He had been deferential to those of rank in the city, but after being attacked in the street he was not about to let himself be insulted and pushed aside by the doorkeeper of this Breton monastery. Now he rose to his full height and glared down at the fellow, shoving his staff in the door to keep it from closing. In his most booming of voices, he cowed the monk into submission.

"I am Merlin, you clownish lout! Right hand of your sovereign, Arthur of Logres. Maker of kings, adviser of emperors. You will cease your pointless drivel, open this door, and show us to Master Oswald this minute, or the king will reduce this abbey to ashes at my command. *Do* it. *Now*."

The monk began to babble incoherently, or perhaps I should say even more incoherently, but he did open the door and managed to choke out an audible "Follow me, then," followed by a softly grumbled, "They're just getting out of compline." Captain Jacques and I carried Dinadan—mumbling "Good for old Merlin. For a second there I thought I might be in trouble"—along one of the cloister walks and up a steep staircase to a cell on the upper floor, where Master Oswald was sitting on his bed. He looked up at us in astonishment, saw the wounded Dinadan, and understood at once what the situation was. "Brother Thaddeus," he said with some authority. "Show these men down the hall to the sickroom. I'll be right behind you." And with that we carried Dinadan a bit farther, to the end of a long hall, and into a larger room with several cots in it. We placed Dinadan carefully into one of these beds as Master Oswald bustled in, tsking away and chattering about the safety of the streets and the danger of thieves after dark. He sat on a short stool at the side of the cot and looked Dinadan in the eye, saying, "I need to draw out the dart. Hurt a great deal, but it must be done. Can you brace yourself for it?"

Dinadan nodded and gritted his teeth. "All right then," Oswald said. "On the count of three…One!" And with that he yanked out the arrow. Dinadan gasped in surprise, then fainted with the pain. Master Oswald saw my mouth agape and winked at me, saying "Always better to take the arrow out when they don't expect it. Saves them anticipating the pain, and odds are that anticipation is worse than the real thing. Also, they're not all tensed up, so the arrow comes out easier."

"But…look," I said. "He's fainted with the pain."

"Well, yes," Oswald replied. "He was just shot in the chest with an arrow. What do you *think* he's going to do?"

At that point the dog's long nose darted in to sniff at the wound, and Master Oswald, taken aback, fell backwards off the stool onto his substantial bottom. Captain Jacques reached in and grabbed his dog's lead, saying, "No girl, stay with me," but Oswald, sitting on the floor, was not amused. "The dog must leave. Can't get in the way here. This is a delicate matter."

"She won't interfere again," Jacques promised. "I've got her now."

"No, it must leave," Master Oswald insisted.

"Well," the captain said. "We were about to start on the way back to the palace anyway. What about you?" He looked at Merlin. "Are you content to sleep at the palace and leave your friend in Master Oswald's capable hands?"

"Sir Dinadan needs a friendly face," I interjected.

Merlin seemed to agree. "I must concur with my young colleague," he said, and then of Oswald he asked, "Would we break some rule of the abbey if we were to stay with Sir Dinadan, perhaps sleep in this room with him?"

Master Oswald shook his head and shrugged as he examined Dinadan's wound carefully. "You may stay here if you want," he said. "It will be a long watch with him. Your friend is in some difficulty I think. If I were a betting man, I'd say he will probably pull through, but I'd want odds. No, only the dog needs to leave."

"Well then, I'll be off," the captain declared, though he seemed hesitant to leave. Finally, in low tones, Merlin asked him "Was there something else, Captain?"

Jacques answered him in a whisper. "There is something I believe I should tell you, Master Merlin. Now is probably not the time, what with Sir Dinadan's wounding. But you are, I believe, still planning to speak with the lady Brangwen in the morning?"

"Indeed, we hope to," Merlin answered.

"Then I shall return to the monastery tomorrow at around sext. That should give you enough time to speak with her, but trust me: I don't think I should wait much longer to talk with you about this."

"Good," Merlin nodded. "Then sext it shall be." The captain nodded in his turn, then left the room with his dog at his side.

"What do you think that's all about?" I asked softly when Jacques had left.

"The good captain has a clue. I knew there was something, and I thought perhaps he had some sort of information that he didn't quite know what to do with earlier today."

"Yes, but why didn't he tell us at dinner? Why did we get that story of the nightingale instead of the story of his evidence?"

"I can't say," Merlin mused. "It may have had something to do with his conversation at the inn afterwards, when we were outside."

"I have to admit," I told him. "When he didn't come out with us, and we were attacked by those bandits, I couldn't help thinking that he had set us up."

"I must confess, the thought crossed my mind as well," Merlin told me. "Until he and his dog came out and chased them away. Unless the intent was simply to scare us, and he was a part of that. Or unless the plan was always to destroy Sir Dinadan. But why? Does Dinadan know something that he may not be aware he knows? It doesn't really make sense that Captain Jacques was a part of the attack. Particularly since he now wants to share some kind of evidence with us. No, I think we have to assume that those brigands were hired by someone from the palace. Someone who does not want our investigation to continue."

"It seems to all come back to Kaherdin, doesn't it? I mean, if King Mark were behind the murders, how would he have been able to send that group after us?"

"He could have an agent here in Saint-Malo—the same agent, in fact, who murdered Tristram, and is now feeling the pressure to get rid of us before we stumble on the truth."

By now Master Oswald had concocted a poultice that he was applying to the wound in Dinadan's chest. "A mixture of garlic and myrrh, which should keep the wound from mortifying, and comfrey, which should help the healing process. When he is conscious, I will have him drink a tonic containing wormwood, which Dame Hildegard recommends as a kind of cure-all. If the bleeding proves difficult to stop, I have sutures made of calves' intestines that I can use to sew up the wound, but I don't think that will be necessary. The dart has not come close to his heart, which of course is the most important thing. But if it has punctured his lung, there may be no way to save him. We will need to watch his breathing tonight. If it remains strong and healthy, I think that your friend will weather this attack. But who, do you know, could have done this, and why? You were attacked by random vandals in the street?"

"They were not random, Master, not random at all," Merlin answered. "This was a very deliberate attack. Someone wants us silenced. That is one reason we wish to stay here tonight. First, I expect there is some safety here in the abbey. But even if that safety is breached, I want to make sure we remain together. I want nothing to happen to any of us that I do not know about."

The monk shivered with a kind of aversion. "To think that it has come to this. Someone among us here in Saint-Malo has killed, and has no shame in continuing to kill to keep his crime hidden. Sometimes I understand why Saint Benedict bade us stay within the cloister. The world outside is no place for human beings."

"Master," Merlin asked. "Will you be retiring to your cell, or do you intend to watch with us tonight?"

"Think I will stay here," Oswald said. "Least until I believe he is out of danger, though that may indeed take all night. We can put out the candles if their brightness hinders your sleep."

"No, no," Merlin answered. "Everything is quite fine. If he does seem to be out of immediate danger by morning, young Gildas and I will still want to interview the lady Brangwen, who you told us was staying here."

"Yes," Oswald murmured. "I remember. She is in a room in the cathedral itself, as I think I told you earlier. The abbot, by the way, has given permission for you to interview her. So I can have one of our brothers show you the way in the morning, once we've determined Sir Dinadan's progress."

"Good," Merlin agreed. "Then Gildas, I see no reason for you to watch at the moment. I am not really sleepy, and you young whelps need your beauty rest. So I will sit up a while, but I suggest you stretch out and get some sleep. It has been a long day."

It had indeed been long, and I was very grateful to stretch out on one of the empty cots in the room, keenly aware of the sound of Dinadan's breathing as I did so. He had come so close to dying on the spot—in fact, all three of us had—that only now did I realize how shaken I was. There was evil here in Saint-Malo. An obsessive evil that was linked with revenge and unrequited love, like the characters in Captain Jacques's story. Where was it coming from? The palace itself? Cornwall? Even Ireland? I couldn't help but remember the hatred felt for Tristram among La Belle Isolde's own family, after he had killed her brother in a duel. Perhaps the faithful Brangwen would be able to tell us something about that. I thought again about my beloved Lady Rosemounde. She would be happy to learn that despite what rumors claimed, her sister's vengeful remarks did not cause Sir Tristram's death. But how could she thank me if we discovered, after all, that her sister or her brother was, in fact, behind the cold-blooded murder of Arthur's great knight?

Drifting off to sleep, I thought again about Merlin's prophesy regarding this case. A dog. A dog what? Turns on its master. It seemed too clear—was Captain Jacques' dog going to turn on him somehow? What did that have to do with the murder? And what was the other part? *There is another wolf with horns.* That made no sense at all. Something symbolic, I suppose. A wolf in sheep's clothing? A fierce, wolf-like murderer? With horns? As I finally dropped into sleep, a coat of arms passed before my eyes, and on it was a creature. A creature with horns.

CHAPTER NINE

THE FAITHFUL BRANGWEN

In watching his patient, Master Oswald had been spared singing matins and lauds, but one of the younger monks had come up and called him to prime, and with that I awoke to find Merlin still sitting up—I never knew whether he had dozed off during the night or not—and Dinadan himself sleeping peacefully and breathing normally. He had made it through the night and, I was now convinced in my heart, he was likely to survive this attack.

Master Oswald rose and stretched, and then confirmed my optimism. "Your friend seems to be out of immediate danger," he told us. "Must go to sing prime now. Perhaps you would still like to watch with him for awhile. When I come back, I'll change his dressing, and we'll see how that wound looks. Odds are it will be looking better. When the service has ended, I will have young Brother Aaron here show you the way to the lady Brangwen's cell in the cathedral," and with that he nodded at the youthful tonsured lad who had come to fetch him, a boy younger than me. "She may even be at the service. She often attends prime and vespers," Oswald added. "If she is there this morning, I'll warn her that you're coming."

"Thank you, Master, that would be good of you," Merlin said as the two monks left the sickroom. Then he plopped down on the other bed and told me, "It's good you're finally awake. You ought to know better than to practice your filthy sin of sloth here in a house of God. You watch Dinadan for a while, boy, I need some rest." And with that he curled up in a ball and seemed to go to sleep instantly.

And so I sat for some time, listening to the two of them breathe and thinking vaguely about my lady Rosemounde and the queen, when Sir Dinadan gave a brief cough and suddenly opened up his eyes. He looked confused, and tried to get up, but I laid a hand across him and gently pressured him to stay prone. "Gildas!" he exclaimed, though in a weak voice that made him look confused, as if he did not recognize it as his own. "Where am I? What's happening?"

"You're in the monastery of Saint Vincent," I told him. "We brought you here last night after you were shot by a crossbow dart, remember? You're in the care of Master Oswald."

"Oh great," Dinadan replied. "Well, I sure hope he'll have better luck with me than he did with Tristram. Isn't there another doctor in this town?"

"He seems to know what he's doing. At least it doesn't look like the arrow that pierced your chest was poisoned."

"Well, I'll tell you one thing, Gildas my lad. I'm not going anywhere else in this town without my sword. Where's that captain fellow? Send him round to fetch it from our luggage, and you won't soon see another one of these wounds in me, I'll tell you that much."

"Right," I agreed. "But you're not going anywhere for a while. You've got a serious injury that needs to heal."

"You're telling me!" Dinadan responded. "I'm the one who can feel it. And trust me, it really, really hurts."

"Well, maybe when Master Oswald gets back, he can give you some juice of the poppy. That might salve the pain."

"Ach, the pain I can stand. I don't want to be stupid from the drug." By now Sir Dinadan was panting.

"Don't exert yourself, my lord. Your wound is too fresh, and still too dangerous."

"Perhaps you're right," Dinadan replied, settling back into the bed. "Truth is, I really feel like sleeping some more right now. Maybe a good deal more."

"That's fine," I said absently, leaning forward on my stool with my face cradled in my hands in order to rest until Master Oswald returned, or until Merlin woke up. But Dinadan's voice broke in on my reverie, well after I thought he had gone to sleep. In soft, dreamy sounding tones, I heard him murmur, "You waste your time suspecting Kaherdin. Kaherdin would not have harmed Sir Tristram. He loved Tristram. Truly. Loved him."

***

I started when Oswald came back in through the door. I must have dozed off again. Merlin started as well—he had been pretty soundly asleep until that moment. Dinadan merely grunted and rolled over to his side, and I felt obliged to mention to Oswald that Sir Dinadan had awakened, seemed lucid and healthy, but still tired. The monk was happy to hear that, and said, "I'll stay here with him through the day to see whether he needs anything else and to monitor how well he responds to the medicines. I do want to change his dressings as well. But I haven't forgotten your goal, my lord Merlin. This is Brother Aaron. He will guide you to see the lady Brangwen, as you wish. In fact I did see her attending the service for prime this morning, and informed her you would be visiting her, so she is actually expecting you. Don't worry about your friend; he seems to be making good progress and I will watch him closely."

Merlin rose, and I was already standing. Brother Aaron was waiting at the door of the infirmary. We thanked Master Oswald and turned to follow the young monk out the door, Merlin tossing back the promise, "We'll be right back after we've finished with the lady Brangwen," and Brother Aaron led us out of the infirmary and down to the ground floor to the cloisters once more.

I was fairly certain that there had to be a direct way into the cathedral from the abbey; it seemed absurd for all of the monks to have to exit onto the street and then come around the corner to enter the church from the west door. And yet that was the way the young monk was taking us. But I realized after a moment that the part of the cathedral that the lady Brangwen must be staying in had to be separated from the monastery itself, so that the monks could not have direct access to her—or she to the monks—because of their strict rule of chastity.

And so we entered the west door of the cathedral of Saint Vincent. Brother Aaron, his brown curls bobbing over his tonsure, was chattering as we walked. "The lady is staying temporarily in a room here in the cathedral," he informed us, concerned with giving us a firm grasp of the obvious. "She waits only until she can find passage back to Cornwall. Or Logres—she can get back to Cornwall overland from there, if that is her quickest option." The youth's large, brown, innocent eyes looked up at Merlin and blinked. "She was quite devastated, you know, when her queen died. She would not be consoled."

"So…she wept uncontrollably? Wailed perhaps without ceasing? What did she do?"

"Oh, nothing," Brother Aaron answered, without a trace of irony. "I mean, she was like a stone. She would not speak, or respond, or react in any way. Like a marble statue. A beautiful marble statue."

"Brother Aaron," I asked, recalling my own infatuation with Guinevere when I served as her page, "are you the monk assigned to serve the lady Brangwen while she stays here?"

"Oh yes," he said proudly and somewhat protectively. "That is my duty. And a very welcome duty. The lady is quite kind and truly in need of someone like me to help her. I mean, she is in a somewhat vulnerable position here, surely you can see that."

"Indeed," Merlin said. "We wish only to help the lady, and to console her in her grief." By now we had climbed to the second floor of the church, where in a corner on the clerestory level, behind one of the small pillars that separated this area from the nave, a small closet was built. This had to be the space belonging temporarily to the stranded lady Brangwen.

Brother Aaron knocked on the door and, upon hearing a soft "Yes?" from inside the room, he opened the door and, bowing with palpable deference, announced, "My lady, the ambassadors from Camelot are here to see you…"

I smiled at the promotion he had given us. "Ah, thank you, Brother Aaron. Please show them in," came a soft, sensuous voice from within. The young monk stepped back out and, swinging the door open wide, motioned us into the closet. I noticed he waited outside, for the room was quite small, and three of us visiting with the lady within may have been uncomfortably crowded.

Everyone always raved about the unparalleled beauty of La Belle Isolde, princess of Ireland and queen of Cornwall, wife of King Mark and lover of Sir Tristram. A woman whose beauty was legendary. Nowhere had I ever heard anyone praise her chief lady-in-waiting, the faithful Brangwen. But I could see, as I entered that small room, that this was a mistake.

She wore an olive green gown, fastened in front by a row of ivory buttons, with a frill around the collar that folded onto her upper chest in two points. Over the gown was a tight jacket that reached to slightly below her waist. The jacket was light brown, embroidered with colorful flowers, and trimmed with a dark brown fur. She wore her red hair plaited as it hung down over her left shoulder, and her head was uncovered since she was, though certainly at least thirty years of age, as yet unmarried.

But it was her large green eyes that captivated one on first sight. She sat on the only small chair in the room, her hands holding a nosegay and placed primly in her lap. Her wide, honest-looking face lay open and sincere as those substantial emerald eyes stared out at me from her fair, freckled skin like those of a loving puppy. I found myself smiling shyly as Merlin cleared his throat and addressed the lady.

"My lady Brangwen," Merlin began, bowing his head slightly. "My name is Merlin, chief advisor to his majesty, King Arthur of Logres. My companion is my assistant, Master Gildas. We understand that you have no transportation back to the kingdom of Cornwall, where you wish to return now that your queen has died. We can offer you passage on the boat that takes us back to Southampton, a sturdy ship that brought us here and is at our disposal thanks to the generosity of Duke Hoel. While this is not a direct path to Cornwall, it will get you to Logres, and allow you to find transport by land back to Mark's kingdom, if that is where you wish to return. Or I believe I can offer you King Arthur's protection, if you choose not to return to Cornwall, and would like to resettle in Arthur's kingdom. I think I can even promise that, should it be your wish, King Arthur would see to it that you could be returned to your original home in Ireland itself. Tell us your wishes, my lady, for we are at your service."

I had not expected this from Merlin. Knowing that the faithful Brangwen was perhaps our only reliable witness to La Belle Isolde's journey on the ship that brought her here, and the events that led directly up to her death, it surprised me that Merlin was taking this circuitous route to get to that subject. Perhaps, like me, he was somewhat smitten by the unanticipated beauty of the lady herself.

"Your courtesy is most welcome, Lord Merlin," the lady Brangwen answered, her sweet intoxicating voice wrapping itself around each syllable of her response. "I have no wish to return to Ireland, I'm afraid. My lady Isolde worked quite hard to make herself unwelcome with her own family and all the other nobles of that island. My association with her would most certainly make me *persona non grata* as well. As for the offer to stay in Camelot, I thank you and your gracious king for that kindly proposed hospitality, but I would be alone in that court—I have no friends or kinsmen there, and although I am certain the members of Arthur's magnificent court would be welcoming and courteous, like yourselves, I would not be at home there. I have lived in Cornwall for some years now. That is where I feel most at home, and that is where I want to return to live out my days."

"Forgive my asking, my lady," Merlin began. "But I had heard at one time that you were residing at the Convent of Saint Mary Magdalene in Caerleon, in Arthur's realm. Were you not placed there by Sir Tristram?"

Lady Brangwen's eyes widened with surprise. "I was not aware, Lord Merlin, that my whereabouts were the common gossip of the court. I had not thought that anyone in Camelot would have even heard of me."

"I was close enough to Sir Tristram that he occasionally confided in me. I assure you that this was not common knowledge. But I was given to understand that after King Mark discovered the ruse that you and La Belle Isolde had concocted, by which you would take her place at night and sleep with the king—begging your pardon, my lady—that there was some worry about your safety, and that Tristram brought you to the convent to keep you safe."

At that the lady Brangwen's smile grew strained and cold as her eyes narrowed at Merlin. I wondered myself what he was trying to do with such a bald statement about her sexual life.

"I see my estimate of your courtesy may have been somewhat hasty," she began. "Sir Tristram seems to have felt completely at ease discussing even the most personal details of my private life with his comrades in the inns and drinking establishments of Caerleon. What are you seeking from me, old man? You seem to know everything. What is there left for me to tell you?"

Merlin once more assumed his deferential pose, and spoke quietly, his eyes lowered. "My lady, I mean no disrespect. As I stated earlier, we will be happy to help you and to give you passage back to Logres, and we mean you no harm. But I admit to needing your help and cooperation, indeed, I implore you for it. The truth is, we are here chiefly to investigate the unsettling deaths of Sir Tristram and Queen Isolde. King Arthur has sent us to look into the matter, and I have, as well, a letter from the lord Kaherdin giving us license to question the folk of this town."

Brangwen scoffed. "Put your parchment away, I care nothing for Kaherdin and his self-aggrandizing poses. He's a nobody who thinks he should be somebody, and that's always a dangerous combination. But I do respect the king. Ask your questions, old man."

Merlin inclined his head toward her in a polite acknowledgment of her permission. "Much has been said about the events surrounding Tristram and Isolde's deaths, and of the story of their affair that led up to that point. If your own story is known, as you say, it is known because of the circumstances surrounding it, and your involvement with the chief players in the story: your own queen, the prince Tristram, and King Mark. If you can help us by either verifying or correcting those stories as they have circulated, it will be of significant help to our investigation. And so, my lady, as I understand it, you were a guest at the convent of Saint Mary Magdalene. But I understand you returned to Cornwall?"

Brangwen let out a sigh, as if to say "all right, let's get on with it, if you're going to insist." She even went so far as to roll her eyes, a gesture that did not go unnoticed by Merlin, whose mouth curled up in the corner for just a moment in amusement. "All right, yes, of course I returned to Cornwall. How else could I have come here with the queen? After Tristram left for Brittany, I had a letter from my mistress, begging me to return and saying that now, with Tristram out of the country, King Mark was far less angry, and not at all inclined to revenge as he had been at the time Tristram spirited me from the court. Well, I was grateful to the sisters for providing me that protection, but I had no desire to stay in the convent—taking the veil was the farthest thing from my mind—and so I hired a wandering minstrel who was traveling in that direction to escort me to Cornwall, and received a fine welcome, from both my lady and King Mark, when I appeared again in court. The minstrel did not fare as well—he sang a song at supper about a pair of lovers cuckolding a lord and was thrown from the palace for his pains. But I was home, and happy to be there."

"Sorry," I interrupted. "I'm a little bit confused. Why was it that Sir Tristram had taken you to the convent in the first place? What danger were you in?"

She looked at me as if seeing me for the first time. She lowered her eyelids and then raised them again, and continued. "It was for fear of King Mark. You see, he had just discovered the uncomfortable fact that he had been sleeping with me every time he thought he had taken Isolde to bed. He asked for her company perhaps once a week, and it was always the same. I would escort her to the royal bedchamber, and we would both be veiled. The lights were put out, and it was I rather than Isolde who slipped behind the bed curtains and paid her conjugal debt for her, while she waited outside until we were finished, and then escorted me out of the room. In the dark we were difficult to tell apart physically, and since he had never actually slept with her, he had nothing to compare me to, and it was relatively easy to keep him fooled. But rumors around the court raised his suspicions after some time, and one cursed evening two knights came into the chamber with torches, revealing our ruse."

"That must have been dangerous for both of you. What did you do?" I asked.

"My lady was always quick witted. She told the king that physicians had discovered that she was barren, and that she had arranged for him to sleep with me in the hope of providing him with an heir, which she could pretend was her own babe after it was born. King Mark actually believed that story, though of course it was a bald-faced lie. In fact, the truth is, I am the one that doctors have pronounced barren." She looked uncomfortable, then closed her eyes and shook her head as if shaking off a pesky insect. "Why else do you suppose I am still unmarried at my age? But although Mark was appeased temporarily, Tristram and Isolde worried that he would eventually see her excuse for the lie it was. They also feared the gossipmongers of the court, who were busy filling Mark's ears with stories of Isolde's infidelity with his own nephew. Tristram finally concluded he must leave the court, and he took me away for fear Mark's wrath would fall upon me. And that, young man, is why I was at Saint Mary Magdalene. And why I left."

"Forgive me, my lady," Merlin asked, his lips pursed and a look of curiosity on his face. "But this is a very strange ruse for you to have been involved in, or shall we say for you to have consented to. Can you tell us how it came about?"

Another sigh escaped those lips red as roses as she turned her catlike green eyes back to Merlin and seemed almost to sag in her seat at the thought of what she now must confess. "It began with the first night in Cornwall. Naturally, King Mark was eager to have his new bride in bed with him. The problem, of course, was that she had been advertised as a virgin, and by that time she definitely was not. She and Tristram had coupled like rabbits on the boat over from Ireland. So what were we to do? If he found her to be damaged goods, who knows what the king's wrath may have urged him toward? It may have been her very life at stake—and for all I knew my own as well, just for being a bad chaperone. In any case, that night we pulled the ruse for the first time, and, once that had worked, we kept it up. Once he thought I was Isolde, I needed to remain Isolde, or he would know that he had been tricked from the beginning."

"Gossip claims that the entire ruse was your idea, a way to save your mistress from harm. It is why you are so often called 'the faithful Brangwen' when people speak of you: to make such a sacrifice for your mistress is something only the most faithful of companions would take on."

"Yes," Brangwen said, her mouth tightening. "So it is said. Consider it, my lord Merlin. Is it likely that the first thing that would spring to my mind would be permitting my body to be used in such a way in order to save my lady from the consequences of her adultery? I agreed, after my initial shock, that the plan may in fact be the most prudent course of action, the one that was most likely to get us all out of a very difficult situation and keep us safe. But no, it wasn't my idea."

"In some way, though, didn't you bear some blame for the situation? I mean, as the story goes, it was you who accidentally gave the two of them the love potion that first drew them to one another on the crossing from Ireland."

The lady looked at me now as if I had grown a second head. "That is how the story goes, is it? Yes, yes, I have heard similar rumors, begun I suppose by Tristram and perhaps my lady herself. Isolde's mother, the Irish queen—isn't that how it goes? Like her daughter a great expert in herb lore, concocted a potion for her daughter and her husband King Mark to drink upon their wedding night. A potion that would make them fall instantly and permanently in love with one another. Well let me tell you my young friend, nothing of the kind exists, or ever existed. Oh, surely there are certain herbs and medicines—the mandrake root, for example—that are purported to increase the desire for fornication, but the advantages of such potions are mainly in the mind. Let me tell you, I have been a practitioner of the healing arts for some fifteen years—everything my lady and her mother knew I learned as well, and assisted them in all of their cures. But I have never known an aphrodisiac to last longer than a single bedding, and as for a potion that would actually make two people truly love one another, and do so forever, that is pure fantasy, and has never been anything but."

"So…there was never a love potion?" I asked for clarification.

"Not unless you count the wine they drank on the Irish Sea on our trip to Cornwall. That I will claim credit for supplying. But it didn't take much of that to get them going."

"My lady," Merlin struggled to maintain control of the interview. "What we are in fact most interested in is the journey from Cornwall here to Saint-Malo. The last journey that you took with your queen. The one that ended with her sudden death in Sir Tristram's sickroom."

"What of it, then? We spent a week in a boat, on a trip that should have taken a day and a half. It was cramped and unpleasant. The food was bad and the company was worse."

"The company?" Merlin followed up. "Who exactly was on board the ship? Aside from the lord Kaherdin himself, I mean."

"Well, he had three of his men with him—that Sir William of Caen fellow, his cousin Sir Andred, and his squire Melias. And then there were the crew and their skipper, and Captain Jacques of the guard. I think that was everyone."

"Captain Jacques was on that ship?" I blurted out, surprised. "Why wouldn't he have told us that?"

Merlin seemed less moved by this information. "Perhaps he didn't feel it was important," he said, glaring at me with eyes that said, "Not now, dolt of a Cornishman, we'll discuss it after the interview."

"We have reason to believe that La Belle Isolde's death was connected to something that happened aboard that ship," Merlin continued. "Can you tell us whether you noticed anything unusual while you were at sea—anything that might have affected your lady's health..."

Brangwen scoffed through her nose and mentioned, "Well, she was sick with the *mal de mere* for nearly the entire voyage, if that's any help to you. The wind was blowing for days, keeping us from leaving the shelter of the shoreline, but the ship was tossing about like an untamed horse the whole time. I was kept busy fixing potions for her of anise, and then chervil, trying to settle her stomach down. I tried feeding her quinces and pomegranates. Nothing helped."

"Excuse me," Merlin interrupted. "You say that you gave her potions every day. Did anyone else on the ship attempt to give her anything?"

"No, no," Brangwen shook her head. "My lady stayed in our quarters in the ship's castle the entire time. I don't know that anybody else on the ship even saw her during all that voyage. Or if they did, it was not without me at her side. I was with her even up until her entry into Sir Tristram's sickroom. And there, if she seemed weak and dizzy when she got off the ship, I would imagine it was because of the seasickness, wouldn't you?"

"So you attribute her fainting to her sickness?" Merlin pressed.

"Of course. That and her shock at seeing Sir Tristram in that state, so close to death."

"But seasickness isn't a mortal condition," I put in.

"Of course it isn't," the faithful Brangwen agreed. "Her weakness was caused by the sickness. But she died of a broken heart. Anyone there could have seen that."

"My lady," Merlin began again. "You are yourself an expert in the mixing of potions and the use of herbs and medicines. You have been a healer for many years. You are seriously telling us that you believe Isolde died of a broken heart?"

"Of course," Brangwen shrugged. "It is what everybody thinks. It certainly seems more likely to me than poison, don't you think?" And with that she lowered her eyes.

"Just one more question, my lady," Merlin said. "In your opinion, who would have reason to desire the deaths of Tristram and Isolde?"

I did not expect the response that this question elicited from the faithful Brangwen. She laughed aloud for several seconds. Finally she responded, "Ask me rather who *didn't* want them dead. I could give you a shorter list."

"Perhaps you could be a little more specific," Merlin calmly prodded.

"Well, the entire royal family of Ireland, and anyone who supports them, to begin with," Brangwen enumerated. "Tristram killed their son Marholt, forced them to pay tribute to Cornwall, and then stole their daughter away from her rightful husband, in their view. Why wouldn't they want him dead? And Isolde as well, for that matter, whom they could only see as having betrayed them. So that's one nation that wanted them dead. What about Cornwall? King Mark saw them as traitors, and anyone who adhered to Mark had to see them as criminals as well. And some of the court would have been jealous, especially of Tristram, the king's nephew, who received all kinds of benefits that they didn't get, and then betrayed his uncle anyway. So you can add anybody Cornish to your list of suspects."

"Well, not anybody," I inserted, but she was just getting started and didn't hear me.

"Then you have the folks right here in Brittany," she continued. "Isolde of the White Hands, the loving wife that Tristram wouldn't love? Lord Kaherdin, the loving friend whose sister Tristram spurned? How many knights, how many ladies-in-waiting, owe their allegiance to those two, who rule Saint-Malo? Anyone in this town had a motive. Even Duke Hoel himself—it was his daughter, after all, that Tristram insulted. How many allies does he have? Of course, we're forgetting anyone in King Arthur's court, but should we? What about Sir Palomides? He was the most ardent suitor for Isolde's hand, until he was defeated by Sir Tristram on the jousting field. But that doesn't mean he ever gave up his love for my lady. Or that he ever gave up his hatred of Tristram. Why wouldn't he want Tristram dead? Is that enough suspects for you, or should I go on?"

"Can you?" Merlin challenged her.

She gave him a wan half-smile. "Perhaps if I think about it for a while," she answered. "But I am pretty sure I am finished with this interview now. Good luck with your quest. I assume that the sooner you make your determination, the sooner you will be leaving Brittany and will take me with you back to Logres. I hold you to your word."

"And I have given it," Merlin answered. "With your permission, my lady, we will take our leave now, and we thank you for your help in this matter."

Brangwen waved us away and turned her face. "Begone, if you please. Leave me alone with my thoughts." And with that, we backed out of the room, and found Brother Aaron waiting for us on the other side of the door.

***

The presence of the young monk made it difficult for Merlin and me to share our thoughts about that remarkable encounter with the one person who could tell us the most about the private affairs of Tristram and Isolde. As Brother Aaron led us back out of the cathedral and, as Merlin requested of him, back toward the sickroom in the abbey, where we could check on the progress of Sir Dinadan, I only gave Merlin the very noncommittal comment, "Well, quite an interesting woman, the faithful Brangwen, wouldn't you say?"

"Oh yes," Brother Aaron began, waxing eloquent upon his favorite subject and precluding any answer from Merlin, whose face told me he had not been likely to give me one anyway. "She is like an angel come to earth, isn't she? Those green eyes against her fair skin—like emeralds set in a silver reliquary, didn't you think?"

"Brother Aaron," I began, a little taken aback by his attitude. "You are committed to your monastic vows, are you not?"

The little brother flushed crimson, even to the bald spot of his tonsure, which I could look straight down upon. "Of course," he whispered hoarsely. "I am only admiring her because she seems to me an image of the angels of heaven. She puts me in mind of paradise."

Yes, I thought to myself, I've been to that kind of paradise too: with the lady Rosemounde, in my dreams.

By now we were coming to the corner where we would turn toward the small gate into the abbey, and I suddenly became aware of a wailing that sounded from that direction. At first I thought it was the completely unrestrained mourning of a woman who had lost that which she'd loved most ardently. But as we walked further I realized it was not a human voice at all. It was a howl of raw animal pain that could not be consoled by any human comfort. As we walked toward the gate, I saw clearly what it was: Captain Jacques's borzoi, lying upon a bundle of rags near the convent gate, her head flung back as in wild grief, her throat heaving great shrieks of sorrow, her eyes closed against the harsh reality she must be dealing with. About a dozen people had come out of their shops and houses in the neighborhood, and stood in the street, surrounding the dog but at a safe distance. As we drew closer, the bundle of rags on which the dog lay resolved itself into the shape of a man whose garments had been rumpled in some sort of struggle. A sticky red pool under the man's face was still spreading out, suggesting that the throat had been slit quite recently. Merlin quickly knelt next to the body and felt for a pulse, then looked on me grimly and shook his head when he found none. Even if he had still been alive, there would have been no way to save him, with his throat slit that way and with so much blood lost. Captain Jacques was quite dead.

Shaken to the core and feeling helpless, I sat gingerly on the cobblestones next to the dog and stroked her deerlike head. Once I was able to get my breath again, I told her in low tones, "That's all right, girl. I know you're sad. Let it all out now, and later we will find the villain who did this, you and I."

The dog, grateful for my presence, my attention, and my gentle strokes, stopped her wailing. She laid her head in my lap whimpering quietly, and panting in the exhaustion of her grief.

CHAPTER TEN

ON THE SCENT

"The captain was on his way to see us, because he had some sort of information he wanted to pass on. Someone followed him here, waylaid him, and killed him to prevent our receiving that information. That means it was important. Whoever killed him must have been behind the attack on us last night, and so behind the near slaughter of you, Dinadan. And he is almost certainly also the one who killed Sir Tristram. And that means that unless we find the killer, Captain Jacques will have died in vain. God's cheekbones, Gildas, I will not let that happen!"

We sat in the abbey's infirmary, on a bed across from Sir Dinadan, who was conscious and seemed well on the way to recovery, though far from able to get out of bed yet. The dog lay on the bed next to me (Master Oswald hadn't been in to catch her in the sickroom this time), her head resting on her paws and her intelligent eyes looking up at me with what looked like concern.

"What could he have known?" Dinadan wanted to know. "And why on earth didn't he give us the bloody evidence last night?"

"He wanted to," I recalled. "Your wounding last night postponed it, but he wanted to come to us right away this morning."

"By thunder, he did at that," Merlin remembered. "And do you recall when he told us about this evidence—when he said he wanted to talk with us?"

"It was after he came out and helped us fight off those brigands," I recollected. "After he had talked in private with that tavern wench—

what was her name?"

"Meg," Sir Dinadan answered confidently. When both Merlin and I turned to look at him, he added, "What? I'm wounded, not dead. Meg was not someone I'd easily forget."

Merlin nodded and continued, "Meg it is. Whatever Jacques planned to tell us, Meg must be the key. It was only after speaking with her that he decided to confide in us."

"So that means…that something took place in the inn that Meg witnessed…" I proposed.

"Or that she was the captain's confidante and whatever he knew, he wanted to discuss with her before deciding to tell us," Dinadan countered.

"And if that's the case, then my guess is that the captain witnessed something on the ship that brought La Belle Isolde and the faithful Brangwen here," I guessed.

"Your instincts may prove right, Gildas," Merlin mused. "We didn't know until this afternoon that he had been on that ship. Which means he kept it from us on purpose. And he may have done so because he suspected there was something not quite right with that journey. We need to find out what he knew. And the only way to do that, it seems, is to question this Meg herself."

"You need to go see her. You need to go now," Dinadan said. "Don't worry about me—Master Oswald will look after me. The only thing I regret is I won't be with you to question that tavern wench. My, she was a sweet looking girl, wasn't she?"

"We'll give her your regards," I told him as Merlin and I got up to leave. We exited the room to the sound of his laughter. It was good to see him feeling that well—last night we weren't so sure Sir Dinadan would still be in this world by this time today. I couldn't help but admire Master Oswald's healing powers, and was more than ever convinced that nothing could have saved Sir Tristram from the poison in his body, if Master Oswald had failed.

As Merlin and I made our way out of the monastery, we passed the chapel in which Captain Jacques's body had been laid out. Two of the brothers were with him now, preparing the corpse for burial. Brother Aaron had been sent to Lord Kaherdin to let him know of the murder of his officer. Looking at the body through the door, though, sent a cold shiver down my spine. It was pale and naked, drained of much of its blood, and drained too of the unique personality that had given it life. I felt in some ways like the dog who walked by my side: Even she was not especially interested in what was left of Captain Jacques—by now the body no longer smelled like the living Jacques, and she recognized that all that was valuable in that shell had deserted it. The light was out. I put my head down and took the dog by the leash, feeling the urge to get out of that place as soon as I possibly could.

Merlin had been silent since we left Dinadan's room, but now spoke softly to me as we exited the convent, walking by the place where we had found the body. A pool of blood still stained the street. "He was a good man," the old mage said simply. "We'll get to the bottom of this."

That wasn't what I was thinking about right now. "The prophecy," I said. "Those things you said in your…your vision or whatever it was. 'The dog,' you said. 'the dog turns on its master.' I don't see how that fits. The dog didn't turn on Captain Jacques. She was with him until the end—until after the end. She never turned on him. She loved him."

"She's faithful as a dog can be," Merlin said. "Which is saying a lot. I've never met a human that could rival a dog in faithfulness. But can we be sure that the prophecy refers to this particular dog?"

"Oh…I…I was so sure that this dog has something to do with the answer…"

"Oh, I'm not saying she doesn't," Merlin assured me. "This is a dog that actually witnessed the murder of Captain Jacques. She will have a lot to do with the answer to our problem. But these 'visions' of mine are never literal. So the 'dog' referring to an actual dog would be pretty unusual. And remember the other part of the prophecy: a horned wolf? Obviously that's not literal, because there is no such thing as a wolf with horns. Both the wolf and the dog are metaphorical, young Gildas. Surely you realize that, being the love poet that you are."

I pulled a sarcastic face upon him and shook my head, but suddenly an idea struck me. "Merlin, the horns. Do you think it's an allusion to cuckolding? You know, the husband whose wife is cheating on him grows invisible horns on his forehead? Is the horned wolf King Mark himself, maybe? I mean, I know he hasn't been here in person to have a hand in killing either Tristram or Isolde, but isn't it perfectly logical that he might have sent an envoy to do his bidding? That he ordered the murders and sent his minions here to carry them out?"

Merlin shrugged. "Possible, yes. Likely? I'm not so sure. It would have to be someone in the court who has not been here long, someone who arrived only after Tristram did. I don't know that we've met anyone that newly arrived."

"True, but there are a lot of members of the guard that we haven't met. It could be any of that faceless multitude that do their drills in the town square." But I noticed at this point that we were approaching the cobbled street directly outside the Cock and Bull Inn, and so I quickly changed the subject. "Have you thought at all about how we are going to break the news of the captain's murder to Meg? It appeared to me that she had some special interest in him that went a little deeper than what he wanted for dinner last night."

"Hmmph. Really? I must have been preoccupied," the old man said absent-mindedly. Despite his deference to nobility, a tact he had learned from decades of servile flattery of royalty in order to advance his own purposes, I knew that his bluntness could sometimes be too sharp for someone in a vulnerable state. And Meg could very well be quite fragile upon learning of Jacques' murder.

We entered through the heavy wooden door, leaving the bright sun of midday for the close, dark atmosphere of the tavern. Beams of light poured through the inn's small windows, but we sat down at a table in the corner of the room. There was no fire this early in the morning, but the smell of the ash from last evening was still in the air, along with some of the cooking smells that were already wafting out to us from down the hall: simmering beef and chicken and the tender brown crusts of pies. The dog, sitting quietly at my left side, twisted her head and caught the scent, and began to whine quietly and lick her chops.

Quite abruptly, the substantial flesh of buxom Meg came bustling by us, still wearing her gray dress and brown tunic but now unwimpled, her blonde curls trailing behind her as she moved with rapid efficiency around the tavern room, slapping a white rag over each table to clean it. "Sorry lads," she told us. "We're closed till after none. Oh!" she cried when she caught sight of the dog. "Hello girl!"

The borzoi padded over to Meg as if she were greeting an old friend, and while Meg held her face in her hands, the dog pressed her nose forward and stroked her head against Meg's cheek. "Oh, my Sweetie," Meg cooed. "Where's your daddy this morning? What are you doing with this lot?" She smiled and winked as she glanced over at us. Merlin cleared his throat. I looked down at the floor. Perhaps it was time to break the ice. And I judged that I may be able to do this with an iota more tact than Merlin was likely to do.

"Meg…if I may call you Meg?"

"That's my name, so what else would you be calling me?" she said, looking at me quizzically. I was feeling more and more trepidation about breaking this news to her.

"Meg, Captain Jacques will not be joining us today," I began.

"Oh?" she said, feigning indifference. "And what's he doing this time that's so important?"

"Well," I tried to explain. "It's not that he's doing anything, *per se*. It has more to do with the…condition he's in." When I looked over at Merlin, the old necromancer's eyebrows had reached the top of his forehead, and his eyes appeared to be looking up at them.

"Oh, I see," Meg said, giving a hearty laugh. "So he's drunk, is he? Or hung over? That's not like him, but I'm always telling him he needs to unwind and live a little. So was it you two naughty boys who led him astray…"

"No, no," I interrupted. "He's not drunk. It's more serious than that, I'm afraid…"

"You mean he's sick?" Now she seemed concerned, and turned to the dog saying "Is your daddy sick? Does he need me to bring him some nice chicken soup?"

"He's dead." Merlin said, decisively and with finality. Meg immediately turned completely white and her jaw dropped open as she stared at him with eyes the size of carriage wheels. I looked over at Merlin and shrugged, as if to ask what on earth he was thinking to blurt it out in that way, but he shrugged back at me and said, "Your way is like torment, Gildas. It's as if she had an arrow in her arm and you were trying to pull it out by small increments over a long period of time. Yank it out immediately, man. It will be painful, but the pain will be quicker."

The initial shock having passed over her like a great wave, Meg was now wilting in sorrow. Her eyes filled with tears and she let out an anguished, inarticulate cry. She reminded me of nothing so much as the dog herself when we found her hovering over Captain Jacques's body. Perhaps out of some fellow feeling, the dog put her paws on Meg's shoulders and leaned her body into her, licking at Meg's face with her tongue. And Meg, of course, put her arms around the dog, holding her close. She was the last part of Captain Jacques that Meg could touch or feel.

"We found the captain this morning," Merlin continued, his voice informative and objective. "He had been murdered perhaps a little after prime at the gate to the abbey. His dog was with him"

"Murdered! Now Meg's face changed again, this time slowly reddening with anger. "Who would do such a thing? Why? What could *mon capitan* possibly have that anyone would think was worth killing him over?"

"Information, we think." Merlin explained. "The captain was on his way to see us when he was killed. He told us last night that he wanted to tell us something, and he made it clear that it had to do with the case we are investigating."

"Case?" Meg echoed, but was paying little attention. Now she broke down completely, melting in tears. "He promised, you know to take me out of this place. He..." she blurted out between sobs, "He said he loved me. Told me he was saving his money and one day I would leave this place and go to live with him, once he had his own house in the town instead of quarters in the guards' fort. It's why he volunteered for all those extra tasks, like going on the ship that brought you two here He would always get some extra something from Lord Kaherdin, that he could put toward his own little fortune that he thought would make me comfortable once we were married. I didn't care about all of that. And now he's gone…and we were never able to marry as he wanted…" Once more she broke down, wailing now with such intensity that I feared we would get no more out of her this day. I raised my eyes questioningly to Merlin, but he was determined to move on.

"Young lady," he began again. "Can you tell us…"

"Murdered, you say?" She was back to being angry. "Why does his dog have no signs of a fight on her? Surely she would have tried to defend him if he was accosted in the street…"

"Captain Jacques's throat was cut," Merlin declared indelicately. "The killer must have followed him, or lain in wait, then come up behind him with rapid stealth and slit his throat in one quick motion, slinking away before the dog even knew what had happened."

"A professional killer then," I mused out loud. "A soldier."

"My lady," Merlin pleaded, giving her a bump in social status while he was at it. "If you are as angry about this as we are, you must help us find this monster. The same person who killed Jacques is almost certainly also the one who killed Sir Tristram and La Belle Isolde as well, and tried to kill us last night, nearly succeeding with our friend Sir Dinadan. We need to stop him before he kills somebody else. Perhaps even makes an attempt on your own life, if he thinks you know something!"

"I take it you two think I know something, or you wouldn't be here. Maybe talking to you is what got my Jacques killed. Maybe if they see me talking to you, they'll come after me too!"

"They, or he, will come after you in any case," Merlin asserted. "Was your affair with Captain Jacques a secret? If anyone else was aware of your relationship, then this killer will soon know about it, if he doesn't already."

"Well let him come, then!" she called out defiantly, standing up and striking the table with her fist so vehemently that the dog retreated back to my side and sat quietly again. "We've got half a dozen strong lads working here, and a few wenches that can hold their own as well. And a kitchen full of knives. I hope he does come looking for me. It'll be the last thing the bastard ever does."

Merlin nodded. "God's whiskers, I believe you'd do it, too. But remember, others may be the target before you are. But if you help us, it may be that we can catch this murderer first, before anyone else is harmed."

"And what would be the use of that?" She was back to her despondent mood once more. Tears poured from her eyes as she choked out, "It will not bring him back. Nothing will bring back my beautiful captain," and with that her sobs overcame her again.

Before Merlin could open his mouth again, I thought I would try a different tack. "Are you sure that the captain was serious when he told you he would marry you? I mean, some of these men say these things to all kinds of women, but are only toying with their emotions…"

"He loved me!" Meg exploded, her voice cracking between sobs. "He had no other women! It was I that he came to when he needed to confide in someone."

"Like last night?" I prompted.

"Yes! Exactly like last night." And with that she narrowed her eyes at me, as if I'd tricked her into something.

"You need to tell us what Captain Jacques talked to you about last night," Merlin stated definitively. "You know that the final outcome of that meeting was his decision to talk to us about what he knew of the murder suspects. He couldn't tell us last night because we were attacked—attacked, I say again, by the same people who killed him. You owe it to his memory to tell us what you know."

"Ha!" Meg spat, clearly veering toward the angry once more. "He wouldn't be a memory if it weren't for you people! Him deciding he was going to talk to you is the thing that got him killed! Don't you know that? Why in the world should I help you?"

Merlin, unflappable, challenged her with his reply. "Because by not helping us, you're helping whoever killed Captain Jacques. You let them get away with his murder. And with other murders. Can you live with that?"

"No." she said quietly. "But I don't like you."

"You don't have to," Merlin conceded. "You just have to tell us."

Meg blinked and wiped some of the persistent tears from her red eyes. But she seemed determined to get through this testimony before she allowed the heaviness of grief to overwhelm her at last. "He was concerned about something he had overheard," she began. "While he was on that long voyage that took him to Cornwall and left him becalmed there for days. Something he overheard on the boat."

"Overheard?" Merlin repeated. "Who was he listening to? Was it La Belle Isolde herself? Her lady perhaps, or the lord Kaherdin?"

"Are you telling this or am I?" Meg said with some vehemence. When Merlin silently conceded to her, she went on: "This was on the voyage back from Cornwall, during the evening, so it was dark. Captain Jacques had come up out of the hold onto the deck. He said there were only a few of the crew on deck, and two of Kaherdin's close advisors, who were leaning over the ship's rail with their backs to him, and he perhaps ten or twelve feet behind them, but obscured by the mast in the middle of the ship. He heard them talking about Sir Tristram and the lady Isolde—the Irish Lady Isolde is the one I mean. And he came to me last night and he wanted to talk about it with me, saying that he'd heard this but he didn't know what it meant and he didn't know who it was who said it, so he was unsure whether he ought to tell you two or not. Because, you know, it wasn't at all certain, but it was really bothering him."

"Yes, of course, I understand," Merlin said. "But God's knuckles, woman, tell me what it was he overheard!"

"Well, all right then, one of the fellows leaning over the railing says, 'Well, this is the funniest trip I've ever been a part of. I wonder if we'll get this Queen Isolde back to Saint-Malo in time to save Sir Tristram from the poison in his wound,' and then the other one snaps back with a 'Sir Tristram is done for, take my word for it. That poison in his system has got no antidote. He's food for the worms.'"

"But who was talking? Which one of them said this?" I wanted to know. But Meg narrowed her eyes at me and chided me back.

"I told you, didn't I, that Jacques couldn't see them except from behind, and that in the dark he couldn't tell which one was talking. Do I have to keep repeating myself here?"

"No," Merlin said, looking down at me and lowering his own eyebrows menacingly. "Please, go on and tell us the upshot of this."

"Right," Meg continued. "Well the first fellow doesn't like what he's hearing, and he says 'What do you mean, the poison's got no antidote? How do you know what the poison is?' And the second fellow gets a little nervous then, you see, and he hems and haws a bit and says, 'Well, from what I hear, anyway. They say that when those Norsemen poison their weapons, it's with a really powerful poison that has no known antidote.' And I guess the first fellow lets it go, then, and they don't talk about it anymore. But that's the whole story. That's what Captain Jacques told me about, and that's what he said he was going to tell you this morning. And so that's what got him killed. And now you've got what you came for, so I'd appreciate it if you would leave. I'm going to need some time to be alone and cry as much as I can."

Merlin gave a slight bow of his head and said, "My dear, we share some small part of your grief. Captain Jacques was friendly and helpful to us, was an excellent ambassador for the city and for Brittany, seemed kind and competent. His loss is felt, even by those of us who had met him only very recently."

Meg nodded, holding her hand to her mouth and momentarily holding back her tears. But Merlin continued, "Is it possible, however, for us to talk with the manager of this establishment? I understand you will want to find a private place, but if we could speak to someone in charge—no, this doesn't concern you or Captain Jacques—we would be most grateful."

I knit my brows inquisitively at him, and Meg seemed slightly put out, but bellowed loudly "Claude!" at which a burly man with scraggly black hair and beard and a food-stained apron darted out of the kitchen holding a large meat-clever. "You are all right?" he asked Meg. "These men, they are causing problems?"

"No, no," she answered him. "They just want to talk to you. Listen, I've got to go lie down. The captain is dead." And with that she covered her face and rushed from the room, out the rear door of the tavern into, I assumed, private quarters in the back. At the same time, a side door to the outside opened, and another tavern wench entered, dressed similarly to Meg, but in a brown dress and gray tunic. She had dark brown hair under her white wimple, and carried a bowl full of butter that she had just been outside churning. She seemed somewhat spent from the effort. "Here, Claude, is butter for the ale for tonight and…hello, what's this? Sorry gents, but we're not open until after none."

"It's all right, it's all right," Claude said, waving his meat cleaver around like a baton. "It's almost none; Let them stay." The girl shrugged and walked into the kitchen. At that point my stomach started growling as I thought about buttered ale, and realized that neither Merlin nor I had broken our fast all day, so much had been happening. I was craving some tavern food.

"Now what's this all about?" Claude wanted to know, turning toward us with his meat cleaver. The dog tilted her head curiously and looked Claude in the eye. It was a kind of a standoff. Either that or the dog was hoping that the cleaver meant there was some unclaimed meat somewhere.

"Sir, what Meg says is true, I'm afraid. Captain Jacques has been murdered. We are fairly certain that he was murdered by the same person or persons responsible for the murders of Sir Tristram and La Belle Isolde."

Claude scoffed. "Tristram was killed by Norsemen. You're telling me that there are Norsemen wandering the streets killing our citizens, and nobody has seen them?"

"Tristram was stabbed from behind by one of Lord Kaherdin's own guard, a murderer who planned his crime out well ahead of time, anointing his lance with poison to await his chance to kill the knight secretly. And Captain Jacques had evidence damaging to this person that he was about to pass along to us."

"You? Why you? Who in the devil's name are you, anyway?"

"Merlin and Gildas," the old mage replied, "at your service. We were sent here from Logres at the command of King Arthur to investigate the death of one of his most valued knights."

"Well, Merlas or whatever your name is, I don't care who sent you here and I never cared much for your Tristram nor any of his Isoldes. But Captain Jacques, he was a man worthwhile. He was a man to be missed."

"They cut his throat. Right on the street," I put in.

"And the ones who killed him are safe and secure. They feel like they can kill anyone who might get in their way. And the next ones in their way are us," Merlin added. I hadn't expected him to say that. It hadn't been on my mind at all, but when he said it I realized it was true. Why else would Dinadan be lying in the abbey infirmary if we weren't targets of the same assassin who had murdered the captain?

"We are almost certainly their next targets," Merlin said. "And the killer, or killers, seem to be working quickly. That means we will be fortunate to make it through the night." At this I sat down at a table and let out some breath. I felt a cold sweat chilling my forehead and the back of my neck. Of course he was right. How I hadn't seen it before I had no idea, but I certainly could see it now.

Merlin continued: "We have reason to believe, based on Captain Jacques's own evidence, that the murderer or murderers are in Kaherdin's court, living in the palace. And that palace is where they've given us rooms to stay while we are here. Our belongings are there. Including our swords. But if we go there to sleep tonight, we make ourselves targets."

I put my head in my hands, elbows on the table, and added, "Last night we slept in the abbey, because we wanted to watch over our friend Sir Dinadan, wounded by these same killers. But they know now that we have slept there. So…if we go back there, we may be targets as well."

"So what you're saying to me is that you want to spend the night here in the inn?"

"You understand us perfectly, sir," Merlin answered. "This is an inn, correct? You do have rooms to let?"

"Well…" Claude considered, laying his meat cleaver down on the table. "You would think so, wouldn't you? We make most of our money from the meals. We have only a few rooms, and they tend to fill up pretty quickly, what with the sailors who move in and out of the city. It's a busy port, you see. We don't have a room we can let you have tonight."

"We don't really need a room of our own!" I asserted. "Maybe we could spend the night right here in the tavern? As long as we stay in the building until daylight, I think we can be safe tonight."

"Well," Claude rubbed his hand across his scraggly chin. "We might be able to do better than that. There is room in the attic, if you don't mind the dark and the cramped quarters. We could set up two pallets and you could sleep there. We're glad to do anything to keep you safe from those bastards. How's that? Will it work?"

"Absolutely!" Merlin said, sounding relieved.

At that point, the bells of the cathedral could be heard, tolling none. An instant later, the door opened and a few local patrons walked in, looking for a late midday meal. Claude called into the kitchen after the young woman who had brought in the butter. "Nancy, customers!"

Nancy pulled a face on Claude, saying "Really? Thanks for helping out a poor blind girl," and then shouted out the back door with more than a hint of irony in her voice, "Meg! They're pouring in from every direction!"

But Claude stopped her. "Nah, leave Meg alone for a while. She's had a bit of a shock. I'll get the old lady out of the kitchen to help."

"What, Helen? Oh Lord, spare me that kind of help," Nancy responded, and then sauntered over to a table that had filled with four burly lads of middle age, cooing, "Now then, gents, what's your fancy today, eh?"

"We're square, then?" Claude asked us. "You'll stay in the attic tonight? I've got to get back to the kitchen and start cooking…"

"Right," Merlin said. "And we thank you so much for the shelter. We'll pay for it, of course."

Claude shook his head. "Wouldn't be right to charge you like you was staying in one of the guest rooms. No, you go ahead and stay there—anything to thwart those bastards what killed the captain."

At that Merlin sat down at the table where I was already seated, declaring "I dare say my young friend here is famished. We'd love a couple of your meat pies and some buttered ale while we're here!" Claude winked and left for the kitchen, saying "I'll send Helen out to wait on you," over his shoulder as he walked away. I and my empty stomach said a prayer of thanks. The dog licked her chops.

***

The attic was indeed small, cramped, and uncomfortable. Claude and Nancy had done what they could to make it as homey as possible with fairly soft pallets, warm blankets and several long candles, although there was still a small draft coming from somewhere where one of the rafters sagged or the roof tiles were missing. I was glad that the candles were large enough to burn all night, for I could see tiny eyes shining out at me from the shadows in some of the dustier corners of the attic, and I hoped that the light of the candles would keep the vermin at bay until morning.

In that hope I had the assistance of the dog, who lay next to me on my pallet and pushed her back into my side in a full-body snuggle, but whose ears were alert all the time, belying her relaxed pose. And there was a low but continuous growl coming from her throat as she sensed the presence of the rats we shared the attic with. I was relieved to think that they were not likely to take a chance on showing themselves with our large carnivorous borzoi as a guard. I was becoming more and more attached to the dog every hour, and began to think that perhaps it would be good to give her a name.

But I didn't have time to think about dog names right now. Merlin was sitting up, his arms folded, thinking about the case. It was now much clearer where the murderer, or murderers, must be lodged: in the palace itself.

"We know that the murderer is one of Kaherdin's men, one of his closest advisors, don't we?" I said, trying to spur Merlin on to talk about the case. "That narrows it down to Andred or Melias, doesn't it? I mean, isn't that what Captain Jacques's story tells us?"

Merlin shrugged. "Perhaps. But why rule out advisors or retainers of Kaherdin who are not quite as close as Melias and Andred—Sir William of Caen, for instance. But I suppose it's more likely that the captain had those two in mind in particular. They are the ones who seem to be Kaherdin's constant companions. But what Jacques overheard was not a confession of guilt. It was only an indication that one of those two—and we do not know which one—knew something about the poison that was killing Tristram that most people were not privy to. It could mean he was the murderer, yes, but it could also mean that he knew who the murderer was and had spoken with him."

"I guess you're right," I began.

"You guess I'm right? You dolt of a Cornishman, if I'm ever wrong I'll let you know. Meanwhile, you can assume that I am the oracle of truth and wisdom."

"But I was just going to say," I continued as if I hadn't been interrupted at all, "that either way, it's likely one of those advisors is in on the murder plot. Obviously there are more people involved here than a single villain. Look who attacked us in the street! There were four or five of them at least, wouldn't you say?"

"Six," Merlin corrected, but went on to add, "But I doubt very much whether any of them were in on the murder of Tristram. They were probably not members of the city guard, or Captain Jacques would have recognized some of them. No, no, I am fairly certain that they were a small group of local thugs hired by the real assassin for the sole purpose of doing away with us if they possibly could, and throwing a scare into us at the very least, and so encourage us to give up the investigation and return to Logres."

"Well, they did a pretty good job of throwing a scare into me, I can tell you that. But I have no intention of quitting. I want to find this killer and bring him to justice. And how do you know the captain would have recognized them? It was dark. At least one of them might have been a guardsman." I didn't indicate that what I was really thinking about was how the true danger I was in would make me look in the lady Rosemounde's eyes: I would have gone on this quest for her, and the quest proved to be dangerous and therefore, dare I say it, heroic. How could she help but be impressed by me? I stroked the dog's head as I daydreamed of Rosemounde, thinking about how soft the borzoi's satiny fur felt, and how that softness might compare with the softness of Rosemounde's alabaster cheek—which in fact I had never touched and could only imagine.

"Good lad," Merlin responded. "The danger should make us even more determined. Anyone who would do these things to us must be brought to justice before he can practice his evil arts on others."

"So," I continued. "It's certainly one of the city guard who went into the skirmish with the Norsemen with Tristram, because he stabbed him from behind. It must have been either Melias or

Andred, or someone they were working with, like Sir William or that spooky Sir Neville. Could it have been masterminded by someone else? I mean, what about Kaherdin himself? Either one of those two would have done it on Kaherdin's orders in a heartbeat, it seems to me."

"As would Sir William, for that matter. He told us so himself," Merlin reminded me. "As for Kaherdin as the mastermind, I have my doubts. Sir Dinadan knows him well, and thinks it highly unlikely."

"What about Isolde—I mean the Breton one? She's about crazy enough to have enticed one of Kaherdin's men to kill her husband for her. Might something like that have been going on?"

"Anything could have been going on. So which of Kaherdin's followers is she likely to have seduced?"

"Well, I'll tell you what I think. Sir Andred is a pretty surly brute. He seems suspicious to me."

"What, because he wouldn't chat with you about your home town in Cornwall? Not being friendly doesn't make him a murderer."

"Well it doesn't make him a saint, that's for sure," I countered. "And if it's Melias, what would his motive be? He's also probably too young to have been seduced by Isolde."

"Oh, I don't know," Merlin pointed out. "I mean, look at the young Brother Aaron and his infatuation with the faithful Brangwen. She's a good deal older, but he admires her maturity and sophistication. Why not Melias and Isolde?"

"Well, maybe. But you know that's just a wild guess. It's probably more important that Andred is from Cornwall, right? So isn't he the only one with a clear motive?"

"And that would be?"

"He was from Cornwall himself. He could easily have been sent here by King Mark to avenge the king on Tristram."

"I thought you were looking to clear Mark's name?" Merlin goaded me.

"Well…somebody killed Tristram and whoever it was had to have some motive. Maybe it's like King Mark himself said—and the faithful Brangwen too, for that matter—that anyone who had been a member of his court in Cornwall would have developed a jealousy and hatred of Tristram, and could have brought that hatred here to let it fester until he killed him."

"Perhaps," Merlin conceded. "But all we know is that Andred is from Cornwall. We don't know if he was ever a member of the court there."

"Then maybe we should talk to Sir Andred!"

"Or Sir Dinadan," Merlin suggested. "Remember, Sir Dinadan was at Mark's court the entire time that Tristram stayed there. He'd have recognized Andred if the knight had been one of Mark's retainers."

"We'll ask him tomorrow, then," I decided.

"Yes," Merlin agreed. "But we have to make some sort of decision tomorrow. Ideally, we need to name the murderer. If we don't, and we don't see him in custody, we remain in danger from a ruthless villain dedicated to killing anyone that might put him in danger of discovery. I don't want him loose for another night, because I'm not sure we can be protected if we have to spend another night in Saint-Malo with the killer on the loose."

"That reminds me," I ventured. "We believe that Captain Jacques was killed because he was about to give us the information about what he overheard on the ship. If that's true, how would the killers have found out that he had overheard? Meg said that he was hidden and they didn't see him. So how would they know? And how would they know he hadn't already told us about it?

Merlin looked at me with his mouth agape. "God's thumbnails, Gildas, you're absolutely right. But if it wasn't for that information, why kill the captain at all?"

"Unless, of course, he only *thought* they hadn't seen him," I reasoned, thinking out loud, "but they actually knew that he had been eavesdropping."

"But even if that were the case," Merlin answered, "why, as you said, should they assume he hadn't told us yet?"

"Could it be," I ventured cautiously, "that Meg is not what she seems? That in fact she passed the story along to some member of the guard? One of those brigands could have come back to the Cock and Bull after the captain had chased them off, and cajoled or coerced the story out of her."

Merlin wrinkled his nose and then shook his head. "No one is that good an actress. The girl was genuinely aggrieved, and genuinely shocked, when we gave her the news this morning. If some brigand had forced her to tell her story last night, then this morning she would have been expecting news of the sort we brought, and instead she was blindsided by it completely. Besides, the killer must needs have been following Captain Jacques closely for some time to know all of his habits and to know that he might confide his secrets to a particular tavern wench at a particular inn. They'd have no reason to keep Captain Jacques in their sights until the past two days, since he began to help us. They would not know to question Meg. The answer must be somewhere else."

"Well, it's beyond me right now," I yawned.

"I'll give it some thought," Merlin said, lowering his eyes and folding his arms. "The answer is probably staring us in the face. I'll sleep on it. Things may be clearer in the morning." And, effectively calling a halt to the discussion, he settled in for the night.

The dog rubbed her back against me all the way down to her tail, and let out a long contented yawn as she stretched and settled down to sleep. Merlin, rolling onto his side and away from me, advised, "Let's get some sleep. You'll need it for tomorrow. It's going to be a long day."

He was right about that, I was pretty sure. Glancing over into the shadows of the attic, I could still see the glowing red eyes of the rats, and I lit another candle from one that was beginning to burn down to the leavings. When I put my head down on the pallet and cuddled into the back of the dog, I began to drift off almost immediately. But before I fell asleep completely, I remembered something that I felt I needed to point out to Merlin. "Merlin," I called to him. My only answer was an inarticulate grunt. "I just remembered. When the guard was drilling in the town square, remember Sir Andred's shield? His coat of arms was a horned bull. And what does your prophesy say? Beware the wolf with horns, isn't it? So who's most likely to be that wolf? The horned bull, right? It's Andred."

Whether or not Merlin agreed with me I couldn't tell. The only thing coming from his side of the room was a loud snore. In that, I joined him in a couple of minutes.

CHAPTER ELEVEN
SIR WILLIAM PAYS A VISIT

It was well past prime when we awoke the next morning. No light penetrated into the attic, so we weren't awakened by the morning sun. It was the whining of the dog, begging to go outside, that finally roused us from our exhausted sleep. I shook off the last dregs of slumber and rolled off my pallet, figuring it would be to my advantage to let the dog out before she got desperate. Merlin sat up suddenly, crying "God's kneebones, what time is it? We can't sleep the day away. We need to see Dinadan and we need to find Kaherdin, and we need to do it quickly."

"Right," I agreed. "But our dog here needs to do something else and needs to do it even more quickly. Let me get her out."

"When did she become *our* dog?" Merlin wanted to know as I stood up, stoop shouldered under the attic eaves, and followed the dog down the narrow steps that led downstairs into the back room of the inn. I took her out behind the inn and glanced around the neighborhood as she went through her morning rituals. The sun was already well up in the eastern sky, and I gauged it must be nearly terce already, a beautiful early summer morning that promised a pleasant afternoon and evening. There were a few folk walking here and there, mostly toward the town square where the peddlers had by now set up their carts, and I wondered whether the hooligan gang of the previous evening had been active last night, and if they had been looking for us. When I went back into the inn, dog in tow, Merlin was up and sitting at a table, while Claude stood next to him, the perpetual meat cleaver in hand. He turned toward me when he heard me enter, and said, "Ah! Here is your young friend. I have set Nancy to fetch you some small beer and bread and cheese from the kitchen to break your fast," the last part addressed directly to me.

"You are too kind, monsieur," Merlin told him.

"Not at all," Claude said, waving his cleaver around deferentially. "Any enemy of Captain Jacques' murderers is a friend of ours. Only promise me you will bring the beast who killed him to justice, and my hospitality will be well-rewarded."

"You have my thanks as well," I told Claude. "But I wonder if you might have some table scraps or bones from yesterday's dinners that the dog could have?"

"Ah, but of course!" Claude cried. "This is the captain's borzoi. She has been in here many times, and we all love her. Any dog of the captain's will never go hungry at the Cock and Bull. I'll go and fill a bowl for her."

As Nancy came in with a tray of breakfast for us, Claude went out to bring something for the dog. I sat next to Merlin at the table and looked into his face. His jaw was set and his eyes burned with a fierce glow, and I knew that he expected this day to make or break the case—perhaps even to make or break the two of us. It was getting serious now.

***

The street in front of the abbey gate was littered with debris this morning—broken furniture, for the most part, and large stones, strewn about with no rhyme nor reason. The gate itself that barred the way into the monastery was scarred and scratched, as if having withstood a siege. The dog looked around cautiously, sensing that things were not as they had been before and wondering if this new state was a good thing or a bad. It was Brother Aaron who opened the gate for us into the abbey when we knocked. His eyes were red and he seemed on the verge of collapsing. "Brother Aaron!" I cried on seeing him. What's happened? Are you ill?"

"Worn out from watching and from fear," he answered hoarsely.

"You will want to see Sir Dinadan, I suppose. I'll take you to him. But then I must take you to the Abbot. He has demanded to speak you, to better understand what has happened here."

"What *has* happened here?" Merlin wanted to know.

"The abbey was assailed during the night by some six or seven brigands, who shouted for us to give up the foreigners, by which they must have meant you—and, I suppose, Sir Dinadan. We must deliver you up to them, they demanded, or suffer whatever consequences they would mete out."

"Good Lord, what did you do?" I asked, as we stepped around more debris inside the abbey wall: burnt out torches and more large stones, and, on the stones of the walls and the cloister, blackened marks, presumably scorched into the stones by those same burnt-out torches. We walked tentatively, as the dog sniffed and whined, her eyes and her head darting about and gingerly sniffing the remains of the burning brands.

"The abbot shouted down to them from the high window in the dorter, telling them that this abbey and church were sacred ground and anyone behind our walls was accorded sanctuary. He also told them they had no legal right to make such demands, and that even if they had, the Peace of God superseded any earthly authority. According to the law of the Church, if they set foot in, or even laid violent hands upon, the walls of the abbey, they were excommunicate and imperiled their mortal souls."

"I don't imagine that stopped them," Merlin commented wryly.

"It did not, sir." We had reached the stairs now that led up to the infirmary, and Brother Aaron now recited the litany of horrors from the previous night. The bandits had hacked at the doors of the abbey, trying to get in with swords and even with an axe. The monks tossed chairs, furnishings, anything they could find that seemed heavy enough, down from the dorter windows and onto the bandits, and drove them off for a moment. "When they came back, they were carrying torches. They tossed them over the wall, tried to set fire to the doors, anything to try to burn us out. They could not harm the stone of the abbey walls, but they continued to shout and harass us for the better part of the night, hurling large stones into the cloisters and cursing without regard for God or man."

"Why was there no city guard patrolling the streets? Why were they not alerted to this?" I demanded.

"Why indeed," was all Brother Aaron could say. "Finally a group of folk from the neighboring houses, realizing what the commotion was, came out to see what was happening. The brigands, born cowards that they were, ran off. But the abbey has been in turmoil, and the abbot as angry as I have ever seen him. With the first light he sent Brother Michael and Brother Gabriel to the palace to protest to the lord Kaherdin and to demand he find and punish those responsible. Much of the morning Sir Andred has been leading a troop of about ten knights around the neighborhood, searching for the culprits, but it was too little too late, and he has returned to the palace, I assume to report to Kaherdin."

"Setting the fox to guard the henhouse," I mumbled under my breath. But by now we were mounting the steps that led to the infirmary, and were quite taken off guard when we came face-to-face with Sir William of Caen, coming down the steps on his way to exit the premises. He seemed less surprised to see us, and nodded cautiously as he squeezed by us down the stairs, murmuring, "Gentlemen, a good day to you," and leaving us to stare open-mouthed at his retreating back as it descended the stairs and headed for the abbey gate. "So, what do you suppose he was doing here?" I whispered to Merlin. "Maybe checking out the damage to report it to Lord Kaherdin? That would be a legitimate reason to be here…"

"Perhaps," Merlin said, sounding unconvinced. "Or perhaps to determine what damage his men caused when they ransacked this place—if he's the one behind the attacks."

"Well, yes," I conceded. "But is there any reason to suspect him in particular?"

"Is there any reason not to?" Merlin countered. "Everyone in Saint-Malo is suspicious to me at this point. I don't know that we've met an honest chap since we arrived. Nor an honest woman, neither."

I could have argued that I'd found the folk at the Cock and Bull sympathetic and friendly enough, but I refrained, not eager to get Merlin's dander up so early in the morning. At last we reached the infirmary and found Sir Dinadan sitting up in bed waiting to see us. There were, however, three monks lying on beds as well, each with some injury—lacerations, bruises bloody heads—sustained, no doubt, in the assault the previous evening. The dog looked around here, too, and then sat at my side, subdued and letting out an occasional soft whine.

On the bed closest to Sir Dinadan lay the ancient Brother Thaddeus, looking at us with a mixture of accusation and pleading. On his head was a bandage with a great stain of blood on the left side, and his left arm was splinted and in a sling. His body seemed listless but his eyes were alert, and when he saw my gaze move to his arm he spoke: "Broken bone, Brother Oswald tells me. Never heal at my age. This all started when you three came to the abbey." With that he turned away and faced the wall.

"We thank you for your help and courtesy, Brother Aaron," Merlin said, glossing over the old monk's comments, "and will come to speak with the abbot as soon as we have conferred with our colleague. Please convey to him our deepest regret for what has happened to this holy place, and our determination to see that it shall never happen again."

"I'm sure he'll be glad to hear it," Brother Aaron replied. "But he's already making his own plans to prevent any such thing from happening again." With that he gave us a quick nod and headed off to find the abbot.

When he had left, Dinadan broke into a smile. "Well, you should have seen these monks under pressure. They were more than anxious to strike a few blows for the right, let me tell you. I think if the abbot had turned them loose, those craven villains would have been scattered quicker than a portly abbot downs a fat swan, if you know what I mean."

"God's shinbones, man, you're in a jolly mood for somebody who was nearly killed two nights ago," Merlin remarked.

"*Almost* killed, that's the key. I was saved two nights ago and, truth be told, the monks saved me last night. I could have been dead twice, but I'm not, so why shouldn't I be celebrating? Looks like you two made it through the night unscathed as well."

"So we have," Merlin nodded. "And what have you been up to this morning? Watching the monks clean up the mess those outlaws made of their abbey?"

"No, no," Dinadan murmured, his eyes looking toward us with a mischievous twinkle. "I've actually been spending the morning chatting with Sir William of Caen."

"Sir William was here to see you?" I asked, somewhat taken aback. "But I thought he was strictly Kaherdin's man, as resentful of our being here as his master."

"True to a point," Sir Dinadan answered, adjusting his body on the bed, trying to get comfortable. "He's loyal, as I told you, but that's because he values chivalry, so he puts loyalty to his liege lord above most other considerations."

"Most?" I pressed.

"But not all," Dinadan threw me a close-mouthed smile. "Honor and truth are higher on his list."

"All of these things are abstractions," Merlin grumbled, shaking his head. "Suppose you tell us what Sir William's visit to you was about, here on this physical plane." And with that he sat on one of the empty beds in the infirmary, facing Dinadan's.

"Sir William is a member of the city watch," Dinadan explained. "He heard this morning about the brigands that threatened us and put me in this infernal infirmary, and he heard, too, about the rough treatment the abbey received last night at the hands of those same villains. Word reached our friend, the city's Lord Protector, this morning, and he sent his lieutenant Sir Andred with a gaggle of guardsmen to make a show of looking around the neighborhood. But William didn't go with them, he came straight here."

"Why?" I wondered.

"First to apologize. I think he was kind of appalled that such events could happen in a city he was guarding. Or at least that he was supposed to be. He said that the watch had specific orders the last two nights to patrol an area of the city across the river near the garrison. Said there were warnings of suspected criminal activity in those parts, but he got to thinking pretty quickly that the whole assignment was bogus. William says they wasted their time there, that everything was completely quiet. Except, of course, for the nightingales." Dinadan flashed another of his grim smiles, and I answered it with one of my own, remembering Captain Jacques' tale of jealousy and violence.

"And did he happen to mention where those orders came from?" Merlin wanted to know.

Dinadan shrugged. "He didn't say. I suppose the captain of the guard, who, as far as I know, is Sir Andred. But that means little—he takes his orders from above."

"From Kaherdin," Merlin agreed, thoughtfully. Then he continued, "So that was all he wanted? To, as you say, express his regrets?" Merlin raised the great tangled hedge of his eyebrows as he voiced the question.

"No, no. He wanted to know, too, if I saw any of those hooligans clearly enough to identify them."

"And did you?" I wondered. "Because I couldn't see a thing in the dark. Something I'm pretty sure that gang was counting on."

"Like rats lurking in the shadows, waiting their chance to strike a cowardly blow at the unsuspecting or the vulnerable," Merlin mused, and I shuddered, thinking of the night we'd just spent.

"Well I hadn't really recognized anyone, or seen any distinguishing features—they all kept their faces pretty well hidden. But I remembered when he asked that something struck me when Merlin played his little game with the fiery flash. You know, it lit up their faces for a moment, and even though they were keeping them covered, I did notice a kind of *glint*, just for one brief instant, as if one of the thugs had something on his face that reflected the light."

I had forgotten that until now, but cried out "Yes! I noticed that too but didn't think anything of it at the time. Did it mean anything to Sir William?"

"Well he wasn't giving anything away, but he did seem to perk up a bit when I said that," Dinadan conceded.

"God's molars!" Merlin exclaimed. "Are we all thinking the same thing?"

"Gold teeth!" Dinadan and I shouted in unison, and the dog barked with excitement, too. She didn't know what we were so animated about, but she knew it was something sensational.

Merlin slapped himself on the forehead and went on, "This answers our quandary of last night, Gildas! Captain Jacques was not killed because it was feared he had overheard the exchange on board Kaherdin's ship. He was killed because of the fear that he had recognized the mysterious Sir Neville among the villains who attacked us before the Cock and Bull!"

"So what's Sir William going to do about it? Did he say? Can he arrest that freak Sir Neville? Or turn him in at least?"

"But to whom, Gildas?" Merlin stopped me for a moment. "How does he know he won't be turning Sir Neville in to the very person who ordered him to do what he did? Whether it was Kaherdin, Melias, Andred, Isolde, or someone as yet undetermined. I do wish this Sir William were working with us, rather than on his own. There is something uncomfortable about his asking questions of us, when it is we who are supposed to be conducting the investigation."

"I suppose he thinks about the two situations as separate matters. His concern is with the misdirection of the guard and with the misbehavior of the brigands the past two nights. He sees ours as finding the facts behind the death of Tristram and Isolde…"

"Behind the murders of Tristram and Isolde, you mean," Merlin corrected him. "That becomes more and more clear the deeper we search. But both stories are clearly the same story, even a blockhead of a Norman like Sir William of Caen should be able to see that. No, no, Dinadan, I'm finding it hard to trust this Sir William of yours. How can we be certain he did not visit you in the hopes of finding your wounds much worse than they were? How do we know he was not simply spying for his superiors—Kaherdin or Andred, say? Was he testing you to see whether you recognized Sir Neville in the dark, and if so did he fear you may then be able to trace the murderers straight back to him or to his masters in the court? One thing we know about him for certain is his absolute, one may say his blind, loyalty to Kaherdin. God's earlobes, Dinadan, how can we know there is any truth in him? We can't, and until we are certain, I will hold Sir William, like everyone else in this devious and dangerous town, highly suspect."

"Old mage, you don't have to tell me. I've been a cynic about human nature for most of my adult life, and poked fun at the posers and the hypocrites in at least three courts—here in Saint-Malo, in King Mark's court in Cornwall, and in Camelot itself. So don't think you need to lecture me about being cautious with my trust. After all, I followed Sir Tristram, didn't I? I know full well how far the weak flesh falls short of the willing spirit, how the ideal beloved becomes Isolde after all." I shifted uncomfortably, remembering Gareth's story of the king—which, as far as I was aware, even Dinadan did not know.

"But I'll tell you a story, Merlin," Sir Dinadan continued, as a sardonic smile began once more to play around his lips. "A story of love and honor. This is a story of what I know about Sir William of Caen, and why I believe we can trust him in this case."

Merlin leaned further back on the bed and breathed a loud sigh out through his not inconsequential nose. "Proceed then," he directed Sir Dinadan, but without a great deal of encouragement in his tone. "Just don't be all day about it. Gildas and I must see the abbot and will have other stops to make as well. You, I realize, have nowhere else to go and can spin tales from your comfortable bed all the livelong day if you set your mind to it."

"These saucy magicians nowadays!" Dinadan groused, rolling his eyes. "But to my story. Gildas, at least, is probably interested. At least it keeps him from hearing your endless lectures for a little while." Merlin snorted in response.

"It was a few years ago now, just after I'd followed Sir Tristram to this bloody port, and after he'd married the delicate and blushing lady Isolde of the White Hands. In those days I used to spend my evenings supping—and drinking—at an inn nearer the harbor called the Mermaid's Anchor. There was a serving wench there had a roving eye and I used to go there hoping it would rove in my direction."

Merlin rolled his eyes. "And you a knight of the Round Table. Not really seemly, is it?"

Dinadan scoffed. "Please. You'd question my purity when Tristram was in the room? Anyway, I don't recall any part of that Pentecost Oath containing a vow of chastity. We're knights, not monks, whatever else they say about us. But that's not the issue here anyway, so let it go. As I was saying, I'd visit the Mermaid's Anchor several nights a week, sometimes by myself, sometimes with Sir Tristram when he needed to get away from the smothering atmosphere of that court. But that wasn't often, since Tristram generally eschewed strong drink and only occasionally let himself have more than one glass of wine. But there were a few occasions when Sir Sagramore came over to visit us and bring news of the courts, both Camelot and Cornwall. It was on one of those nights that I first saw Sir William of Caen."

"In the inn?" I asked. "But I thought when we first met him you said something about his not being one to go out carousing with the rest of the guard?"

"Yes," Dinadan closed his eyes. "A comment that I admit was in somewhat bad taste, for I was thinking about this night in particular when I said that. Sir William had come in, yes, but with no intention of drinking. I remember seeing him come in the door wearing his sword and armor and looking around with his eyes squinting, and I was thinking 'This boy's not here for the ale.' Nor was he. He was there looking for his wife.

"A good number of guardsmen were there drinking, and some had women accompanying them, and a few of them were getting a bit rowdy too. One of those women was a young raven-haired beauty who was laughing louder than the rest, her hair long and flying free like a young virgin's, sitting with a tankard of ale on the lap of one of the roughest looking of those guardsmen. I watched Sir William's eyes narrow on her, and his face looked…well, it had an expression of deep sorrow, but not so much anger. And she—well, she turned pale and stopped laughing pretty quick. She stood up and William says to her 'My lady Evelyn, this is not seemly. Would it please you to return home?'

"And she's ready to start for home, but the bloody bounder she's with grabs hold of her arm and says something like 'Hey, wench, you can't tease me like that and walk off. Come back here and pay what you owe!' But William, now, he strides over to them and stands between the guard and the woman, draws his sword and holds it to the man's neck. And he says "I'll assume the lady's debt, sir. And I will meet you in the parade field before the castle at terce tomorrow, where I shall undertake to pay you what you deserve. If you desire payment, meet me there at that time. If I do not see you then, I will consider the debt canceled.' Well, the big drunken lout blustered a bit, and William and his wife walked out of the inn."

"And did this brute of a guardsman meet him the next day?" I asked. "Was there a duel in the center of Saint-Malo?"

A half-smile twisted Dinadan's face. "Sir William stood in full armor in that public square from terce until sext the next morning, but that scoundrel of a guardsman never appeared. Some said he was afraid of William's prowess. Some said he had given up the woman as not worth the trouble. But within days, he had left town and good riddance. I cannot recollect his name, but that's probably a good thing. A man like that doesn't need a memorial."

"Well Sir Dinadan," my tongue dripped with sarcasm, "*that* was indeed an exciting story. A little thin on plot, though, I thought. Not much of an ending…"

Dinadan puckered his face up in exasperation and then spat out, "I'm not telling you the story to entertain you, you dolt of a Cornishman…"

"Hey, only Merlin can call me that…"

"I'm telling you the story to make you understand who you are dealing with when you deal with Sir William of Caen. When the burly guardsman failed to appear to fight him, Sir William returned to his home and took his wife by the hand, and, though she had been conducting an affair with that blighter for months, William knelt before her—or so the story circulated—and proposed that she remain with him and be his loving wife. And she did."

"And there was no animosity between them? No bitterness and reproach to sully their reunion?" Merlin wanted to know.

"None that we know of, or that was ever spoken of," Dinadan answered. I pursed my lips and mused. Dinadan's story was so out of place, so uncharacteristic of all the other stories of jealousy and violence that had filled my head since this whole bloody business of Tristram and Isolde began. It seemed, in spite of all I had heard of regarding Gaheris and Margause, Gawain and Lamorak, Arthur and Mordred, Mark and Tristram and Isolde, that human beings were at least capable of forgiveness and nobility even when it might be least expected. And I couldn't help wondering aloud, "What would make a man do that kind of thing, when nature might have urged him toward violence and toward revenge?"

"You remember Sir William's shield? The motto *Veritas*—'truth'—blazoned on it?"

"Of course I do," I replied.

"Truth is the highest thing a man may keep," came the muffled proclamation from an unexpected source—it was Brother Thaddeus in the other bed, his face still turned toward the wall. Apparently he had been listening in on the conversation. Not that he would have been able to avoid hearing, it's true, since we were chattering almost right above his bed. Dinadan, cheered by the old monk's platitude, glanced in his direction saying "A timely observation, good brother," and went on with renewed vigor: "Sir Sagramore talked to Sir William a few days later, running into him somewhere in town, and put it to him directly. 'How could you have come into that tavern so calmly, and handled the situation with such composure? I would have burst in, sword swinging, and beheaded the bitch and her paramour then and there!' But Sir William shook his head, at least the way Sagramore told it, and he says 'No. I had plighted her my troth, and that is a vow not lightly undertaken. Truth is a man's identity, it is his core and his integrity. Without it what is he? No better than a beast. But we were made for higher things. My truth means my fidelity. The woman may change. The woman's affections may not be constant. She may become something I never anticipated, and our life something far different that I had envisioned. But truth is permanent. Fidelity doesn't mean *I will remain true until you change*. Truth is truth. This is where integrity lies. This is where honor lies. It is the same as an oath to my liege lord. I am bound by honor to uphold that oath. That is truth. A man's word must be his bond, or what are we? Barbarians at the gate?'

"And that, my dear Merlin, is why I say that we can trust what Sir William of Caen tells us. He lives and dies by that motto on his crest. For him truth is not an option. It is the only conceivable course of action." Dinadan finally let out a tense breath, and added, "I suppose that's what makes him so damned boring.

"But enough of Sir William. If what he says helps us find these villains, so much the better." At that Brother Thaddeus gave out a low moan, as if on cue. "People are getting hurt. Innocent people, like these poor monks who only tried to protect me. This has got to stop—you boys need to stop whoever is behind these attacks, and soon too. I mean, today!"

"I only wish you were with us," I began. "Or Captain Jacques. I for one am feeling pretty vulnerable with just the two of us, and our weapons locked up in the palace."

"Well, from what I've heard, I think the abbot may have something to say about that when you meet with him. But tell me, are you any closer to finding the culprit?"

Merlin was never one to jump to hasty conclusions, but he did cautiously suggest, "I think we are now very close. There are two things we need to know that I think you may be able to clarify for us. First of all, what can you tell us about Sir Andred? You were with Tristram in the court of King Mark in Cornwall. We know that Andred came here from his home country of Cornwall. What was, or what is, his connection to the court?"

Dinadan hmmphed and said thoughtfully, "Andred is a sullen, taciturn, unfriendly lump of brawn who lets his sword and lance do his talking. He's got a lot of muscle there, mostly between his ears, and he could give Tristram a run for it whenever they jousted. I wouldn't be very surprised if he turned out to be behind this whole thing, though he must have had an accomplice if he's the culprit, because I don't see how he would know about the poisons. He's not exactly a healer. But even though he's from Cornwall, he isn't connected with the Cornish court, at least not now. I do remember him being sort of a hanger-on when Tristram and I first came to Mark's kingdom, but that was, what, ten years ago? Anyway, he disappeared after maybe a year and wasn't heard from again there, at least as far as I know. I was pretty surprised that he turned up here, and as Kaherdin's cousin to boot. But I suppose I shouldn't be too surprised. The Bretons and the Cornish are related, after all."

"So, he had a connection with the Cornish king, but not a close one, and it was some years ago," Merlin summarized.

"That doesn't mean he couldn't be the murderer," I asserted. "It just means it's less likely that King Mark put him up to it."

"That's certainly true," Dinadan said, adding "Of course, the more I see of him, the more I feel it's less and less likely he has a brain in his head either. What's the other thing you wanted to ask me about? Hurry up, boys, can't you see what a busy man I am? My calendar is really full today."

"The city watch," Merlin said. 'We touched on this when you were singing Sir William's praise. Who controls it?"

"Why, Kaherdin of course. Who else?"

"Who else indeed, "Merlin muttered thoughtfully. "But does he give them their orders directly, or do they go through someone else, as we conjectured before?"

"Oh, I imagine he tells one of his minions what to do, and they relay it to the guards. Why?"

"Why?" Merlin echoed, surprised. "Sir William made that evident, and it's obvious why he's looking into it. Clearly they haven't been doing their job the past few nights, have they? No one at all on the streets at night, except for villains and murderers. What sort of town is run this way? If this kind of thing happened in Caerleon, the king would have heads rolling along the upper bailey of Camelot."

"I don't know," Dinadan scowled, taking in the full weight of Merlin's words. "But what you're saying agrees pretty much with the direction Sir William's thinking was going: that it was Kaherdin who deliberately kept the watch from patrolling this section of the city for the past two nights in order to give that hired band of ruffians the opportunity to kill us? And Captain Jacques?"

"Someone did," I put in.

"I still maintain that there is no way that Sir Kaherdin would have harmed Sir Tristram. When I say he loved Tristram I am not speaking lightly or metaphorically."

"Perhaps he would not have harmed Sir Tristram, but he could have held back the watch for another reason," Merlin said slowly.

"Perhaps he is trying to protect the person who actually was behind the murder."

"Well why would he do that," I asked. "Unless…," I suddenly had a sickening thought. "Unless it is his sister?"

"I cannot say that it would surprise me a great deal if Isolde had one of her white hands in this, but the actual killer had to have been one of Kaherdin's guard."

"Which brings us back to Sir Andred," I concluded.

Merlin shrugged. He noticed that Brother Aaron had appeared again in the doorway. "I think it's time we set off. We need to stop by the abbot's office before leaving. But then we must confront Lord Kaherdin and his staff. There can be no more delays. You will be all right if we leave you again? They are taking good care of you here, and you are improving?"

Dinadan chuckled. "The food could be better. I joked about the abbot and his fat swan, but in fact the monks here are mostly on pretty ascetic fare. Or at least that's what they feed their guests! But Master Oswald is a wonder with his herbs and such. I'm already feeling stronger, and it seems that my wounds are mending nicely. No, don't worry about me. Go off and catch these bastards so we can go home to Camelot, will you?"

"You have my word," Merlin concluded, and stepped off to join Brother Aaron. I looked around for the dog before I left, and noticed that she had slipped over to the bed where Brother Thaddeus had turned his broken body to the wall, and was nuzzling the old monk's neck. Surprised, he raised his head for a moment, and the dog lunged at his face with her tongue, turning up her mouth in what I could swear was a real smile. Brother Thaddeus's tense face relaxed and he sat up, stroking the dog's long, smooth head with his unslung arm, and whispering bemused greetings in the borzoi's ear. With that, she turned and trotted toward me, ready to head out the door, and a calmed Brother Thaddeus waved goodbye to her with his good hand.

"Well," Merlin murmured as we stepped into the dorter's hallway. "That dog is beginning to grow on me."

CHAPTER TWELVE
HAWKING

Moving through the cloister, Brother Aaron walked us down the steps and out of the dorter, where the monks had their cells. Off the cloister was the chapter house, where the monks met together and where, I noticed, they kept a small library in the corner. On the other side of the cloister was the refectory, where the brothers took their meals. Next to the refectory was the kitchen and, a few steps from there, the abbot's quarters in a separate building. Brother Aaron took us into the foyer, a waiting area for those who came to see the abbot. Here two small wooden chairs welcomed us, and we sat in them as Brother Aaron knocked on the door to the abbot's private inner office. After poking his head in, Aaron stepped back from the door and told us, "They're ready for you now, if you'd care to go in."

"They?" I wondered aloud. But I didn't have long to wonder. When we stepped into the inner office, two particularly manly looking monks stood on either side of the abbot, who sat behind a small wooden writing desk facing us as we entered. Two more wooden chairs were set up for us facing the desk, but we remained standing for the moment, all the time eyeing the abbot.

He was a beefy specimen, with a large round face and magnificent jowls that waggled when he moved his head from side to side. His pale blue eyes looked at us without expression, and so I was having difficulty deciding whether he was friend or foe. The other two monks looked solemn, but I marked that down to worry over what had happened the previous night, and not to animosity toward us.

The room was sparsely decorated, but was certainly less ascetic than the other monks' cells in the dorter. A door in the rear of the office led, I assumed, to the abbot's private chambers, but judging from the size of the building as it had appeared from the outside, I knew those quarters could not be particularly large or luxurious. The office did have one tapestry hanging from the rear wall, which depicted Judas Maccabeus cleansing the Temple from the abomination of pagan worship. I had the feeling that this abbot was of the same bent as those Jews of old, especially remembering his reported performance of the previous evening.

"I am Abbot Urban," the portly monk began in his sonorous baritone. "Please," he gestured toward the wooden chairs, "Make yourselves comfortable," and we sat down. The chairs were *not* particularly comfortable, as it turned out. The dog lay down on the floor to my right, and I had the briefest sense that she was far more comfortable than I was.

"Father Abbot," Merlin began. "I am Merlin, a representative from Logres, from the court of Camelot. This is my assistant, Gildas, squire to the king's own nephew. Please accept our deepest sympathies for last night's incident. I understand that the brigands were searching for me and my companions. I am grateful to you for your protection of Sir Dinadan, and I regret whatever role we have had in bringing trouble to this house."

Abbot Urban's eyes closed and he held up his hands in an exculpatory gesture. "Please," he began, "You are not the ones at fault here. I appreciate your courtesy, but the villains responsible for this deed are the ones who performed it. And I have cursed them with bell, book and candle. But I mean to do more. Show them what we intend, brothers."

The two big-shouldered monks behind him revealed to us, hidden in the folds of their robes, heavy short swords that they both carried. Merlin's considerable eyebrows shot up fairly quickly as the abbot continued, "We intend to guard this abbey tonight as if it were a castle keep, and will continue to do so until these curs and the villain who holds their leashes are brought to justice." It may have been my imagination, but I thought for a moment I heard a muffled but indignant growl from the dog, as if she did not appreciate the abbot's metaphor.

"Brother Michael and Brother Gabriel are former knights, who joined our order after half a lifetime of warfare. They are well versed in matters of defense, and we will have some surprises in store for anyone who thinks of attacking this house of God tonight." Abbot Urban's face had waxed crimson as his ire rose. "The audacity of these men—to profane the temple of the living God and to violate the sanctuary of His divine house! Their actions are unconscionable, and as abbot of these premises I will not tolerate it. It will not happen again.

"But," he continued, calming himself somewhat, "I asked you here for two reasons. One is to give you my blessing and encouragement in your hunting down of the ones behind all of this murder and mayhem. If there is anything that anyone at this abbey can do to assist you in this quest, do not hesitate to ask. We are ready."

"I wish we had come to you earlier," Merlin sighed. "Much damage may have been prevented. But you can assist us a great deal by continuing your care for Sir Dinadan. I know that under Brother Oswald's nursing he is improving by the hour. But I have one question that might help a bit: I understand that these two fellows, Brother Michael and Brother Gabriel, went this morning to complain to Lord Kaherdin about the attacks last night. Can they tell me what success they met with?"

Abbot Urban looked up, deferring to his two subordinates. Brother Michael, the one on the abbot's right, with a square, rock-like jaw, steel-grey eyes and a dark brown tonsure tinged with grey, was the one to speak. "Lord Kaherdin was livid when he heard our story. He shouted that no abbey in his territory would be insulted this way without a price being paid. And he called for Sir Andred immediately, told him to take a dozen men and scour the city streets. Of course, there was nothing to find in broad daylight, so the scouring was fruitless."

"And did you ask him why there had been no city guard in this part of town the past two nights?"

Brother Gabriel, whose neck looked to be about the circumference of his head, lowered his eyes, glancing to the side, and answered, "We did not ask. We thought that his willingness to send the troops out this morning was enough, and he did promise that he would issue orders that the city guard should be particularly zealous in patrolling our area of the city for the next several nights."

"If we can take any comfort in that," the abbot said sardonically, under his breath.

"But Father Abbot," I interjected. "You said there were two reasons you had asked to speak with us. What was the second?"

The abbot's jowls shook slightly and I realized he was chuckling to himself. He glanced up at Brother Michael and nodded. "Show them," he said.

Michael leaned down and, from behind the writing desk, produced a small wooden chest that we recognized immediately. "Our sea chest!" I exclaimed. As Michael set it down before us. I jumped up to open the chest and there, among our change of clothes and other items, were our own swords.

"We spoke with Sir Dinadan earlier, and learned how you had been without your weapons and personal belongings since arriving here in Saint-Malo, and how you felt in danger if you returned to the palace because it seemed likely that the murderer you were tracking was there. Dinadan also told us that the chest was in Captain Jacques' room, and so when Brother Michael and Brother Gabriel went to the palace this morning, they were able to gain permission to rescue your chest from its prison and bring it to you."

"God's tonsure," Merlin exclaimed with good humor. "This is unexpected, and very welcome. For we leave here to enter the belly of the beast—we must confront Lord Kaherdin and his courtiers, and doing so unarmed when we're about to reveal a murderer did not seem advisable. This will make us far more confident."

"Or at least less ridiculous," I murmured, strapping on my scabbard and sheathing my sword.

"Lord Abbot," Merlin said, belting on his own sword, "with your permission, we take leave of you now to fulfill our duty to our king and to set these matters right if we can."

"With my permission and my blessing," boomed Abbot Urban,

who stood up and, holding up the fingers of his beefy right hand, intoned the prayer "*In nomine Patris, et Filii, et Spiritus Sancti*, may your way be blessed and your quest find its successful end. Go with God's speed. *Amen*."

***

We entered the small wooded area to the east of the city, across the quay and on the Saint Servan side of the River Rance. It was now well past none and nearing compline, and the shadows of the chestnut and hickory trees were lengthening. Having left our sea chest with the abbot, requesting that the monks store it in the infirmary with Sir Dinadan, we had made our way to the palace, only to find that Lord Kaherdin was not there. Sir Andred and Melias were absent as well, and even Sir William of Caen seemed to be off. A contingent of the guard was performing its drill in the town square, and after some time Merlin was able to get the attention of the unit commander, who told us that Kaherdin and several members of the court were out hawking, and that they typically availed themselves of the wooded area near Saint Servan when they engaged in that sport. And so we had traipsed this far on foot, hoping to find them all in one place and confront them with what evidence we had. I remarked that it did not seem that we had much, but Merlin listed the items for me as we walked: "First, that Tristram was certainly killed by a lance and not by a Viking spear. Second, that whoever killed Tristram was also behind the murder of Captain Jacques, who had recognized one of the villains in the marauding band as a member of the court party. Third, one of the king's closest advisers had been overheard on the ship bringing La Belle Isolde to Brittany describing his knowledge of the poison that killed her lover. Fourth, that whoever this person was, he was in a position of enough power and influence to prevent the city guard from being present where it was vitally needed over the past few nights. It was evidence that narrowed down the suspects to a precious few: Melias, Andred, and Kaherdin himself—or his sister wielding power behind the scenes."

"So you no longer suspect Sir William?"

Merlin shook his head. "He seems an unlikely candidate. He would not have had the power to control the City Guard, and while he may have been aboard the ship that brought La Belle Isolde to this country, he is not likely to have been described by Captain Jacques as one of Kaherdin's closest advisors. I'm not saying he could not still prove an accomplice, but he's certainly not the chief mover of these events. And besides," he shrugged, "Sir Dinadan's opinion may be good for something after all."

Among the trees, we heard voices coming from off to our left, and knew it must be the court party. Walking through the lengthening shadows of those trees, I heard quite clearly and unmistakably the song of a nightingale, warming up, it seemed, for the darkness that would be falling before long.

In a moment, we stumbled into a clearing, and found ourselves in the company of a good number of Lord Kaherdin's court. There was the commander himself, mounted on a muscled destrier and gaily dressed in a bright blue riding tunic, green hose, and brown boots, and wearing a red cap with a feather in it. On a white horse to his right sat Melias the squire, attired quite similarly, almost a mirror image of his master, even down to the feathered cap. Sir Andred, in dull brown breaches and tunic, rode a serviceable bay stallion. Sir William was present, with three other knights—members of the guard whose names I hadn't learned—as well as the eccentric Sir Neville. To my surprise, the lady Isolde of the White Hands was also along for the sport, riding a small brown palfrey and holding out her left forearm on which stood a hooded bird. With the lady Isolde was the poor girl who served as her lady-in-waiting, riding a small grey mare and looking as miserable as ever. We stopped to take the scene in, and the cautious dog backed off a bit, nervous apparently, or so I thought initially, in the presence of all these horses.

The entire party turned as one to look at us as we entered the clearing. "My lord Kaherdin," Merlin began, but received only a tense "hush!" in answer. Sir Kaherdin, his left hand covered with a leather gauntlet like his sister's, pointed straight up, and Merlin and I followed his gaze to see a white speck in the sky that seemed to be diving straight down. In mid-air we saw the powerful white bird strike a single seagull that had flown in from the shore. The falcon's talons grasped the other bird in an iron grip while her powerful curved beak broke the neck of the hapless gull without pausing in her flight. Finally, she flew down with her quarry in her beak, landing back on Kaherdin's arm, where she proudly displayed her prey. As the nearest to him, Melias sat astride his horse watching Kaherdin with undisguised admiration. Carefully, Kaherdin reattached her creance, the bird's short leather leash, to her left leg. He then placed the small leather hood over the great white hawk's eyes. Finally, he took the dead seagull from the falcon's beak and handed it to Sir William, who had come up behind to assist Sir Kaherdin. The dog, watching all of this, cocked her head with interest at the bird's hunting prowess.

"Now," Kaherdin said. "You caught us in the middle of hawking. My sister was about to unleash her own gyrfalcon. What is it you want, old man? You've done your investigating and what? You're here to report that you've found nothing, that everything I told you was true, and that you're ready to return to King Arthur to report that the deaths of Tristram and his paramour were just as originally reported, and that all is well in Saint-Malo?"

"No, my lord," Merlin answered patiently. "I'm afraid that is not the case."

Lord Kaherdin stared down on us with imperious disdain, his eyes displaying annoyance and frustration. Sir Andred looked equally perturbed, though Melias was still watching only Kaherdin.

"Well what is it, then?" Kaherdin demanded. "You've come to tell us something, find your tongue old man and stop wasting my time!"

"My lord, I think you are unlikely to find this a waste of your time. Let me say first of all that our investigations have led us to a number of conclusions. The most important piece is this: that Sir Tristram was not killed by a Norseman's spear."

"What balderdash is this, you daft old man? He was wounded in the battle. We all saw."

"That you did not. None of you, by your own testimony, saw the blow that actually wounded him. Did you?" Kaherdin was silent. Sir Andred looked uncomfortable. The other soldiers looked at one another and shook their heads.

"The wound in Tristram's leg was incompatible with the kind of blade used in Viking spears. The wound was clearly made by a rounded point: the kind used in the making of lances, borne by your own knights into battle."

The audible gasp that accompanied Merlin's revelation lasted only a few seconds before the shrill voice of Isolde of the White Hands burst out. "Are you saying that one of my brother's own men killed my husband? Who is it? I'll have him flayed!" Either she was a marvelous dissembler, I thought, or my theory that she had persuaded one of the knights to murder her husband was untenable.

"I'm afraid it's true, Madame," Merlin said, though Sir Andred let out a hearty scoff. "Furthermore, we are certain that whoever is behind Tristram's murder also set a band of villains after us, who wounded Sir Dinadan and attacked the Monastery of Saint Vincent last evening." At this, Andred looked at Kaherdin with a sudden glimmer of understanding in his eyes. "Furthermore, this same culprit compounded his villainy by the cold-blooded murder of Captain Jacques yesterday morning on the street beside the abbey…"

This seemed too much for the squire Melias, who rolled his cropped head about in frustration and cried out, "This is ludicrous! Everything that happens you seem to want to lay at the same door!"

"All stories are the same story," I muttered under my breath, glancing down at the dog standing alert at my right, who had inexplicably begun to growl rather noticeably as she glared ahead at the knot of mounted courtiers in the center of the clearing.

"Murdered Captain Jacques, I say," Merlin continued, unperturbed, "Because the captain had recognized one of the killer's accomplices among the brigands who attacked us. And murdered him just as he was about to give evidence that would expose the killer's guilt. Evidence he overheard on the ship that brought Isolde of Cornwall to this land."

At that, in a smooth unhurried motion, Sir Andred removed his sword from his scabbard and pointed it at Merlin. Startled, I fumbled a moment with my own, but drew it as well, ready to defend the old mage with my life—if that should prove absolutely necessary. "Enough of these subtleties," Andred rasped in his gravelly voice.

"Tell us what you know." Merlin looked up at him. The dog growled even more loudly, and began to bare her teeth. We all stared at each other for what seemed like minutes but must have been only a moment or two. In the silence I heard again the clear song of the nightingale.

Melias moved so fast that his intent did not even register with me. He yanked on his reins to pull his horse's head around, and kicked at his mount's flanks to set him galloping as quickly as possible, hoping to outrun anyone trying to ride after him and so make a getaway.

But the dog, whose eyes had been steadily focused on him, moved more quickly than Melias, and started much faster than the horse. She was in full stride within her first two steps and, stretching her long legs to their fullest extent, she caught the horse before it had gone ten yards. Using the full strength of her powerful hind legs, she leaped high over the horse's flanks, striking the startled Melias full force with her front paws and knocking him sideways off the horse. He hit the ground hard and was momentarily paralyzed, while the dog, baring rows of long sharp teeth, stood over him, growling and darting teeth-first at his exposed throat.

The rest of us had finally started moving. I got to the fallen squire first, and, sheathing my sword, held on to the borzoi's leash to prevent her from tearing Melias' throat out before he had a chance to confess. Sir Andred was right behind me, replacing the dog's teeth with his own sword at Melias' neck. Merlin continued his litany of charges as if nothing had happened: "Captain Jacques overheard Melias talking about the poison that killed Tristram in a way that only the killer would have known. I believe Sir Andred can testify to that."

"I can," Andred growled through his teeth. "He did so, and I didn't really understand it until now."

"As for the dog," Merlin concluded, "She was with her master Jacques when he was murdered. She has very clearly just testified as to who it was she saw murder him."

"Killer! Killer! Killer!" Isolde began to wail. Her white gyrfalcon was hopping about on her gauntleted arm in feathered confusion. "Oh put him on the rack! Draw and quarter him! Disembowel him! The monster has killed my Tristram!" And those were real tears flowing down her cheeks—probably, I thought, the first real tears she had shed in this whole affair. Now that it was over, her façade of indifference was crumbling. Her miserable lady-in-waiting was trying unsuccessfully to console her, but at least Isolde was allowing the poor girl to give her that attention.

Kaherdin had sat still through all of this, his visage a translucent white from the shock of the realization that his squire had in fact murdered his best friend. Now his face began to change color until it nearly glowed red with ire.

"You!" He exploded at the cornered Melias, and Sir Andred, with two of the other knights yanked the shaken youth to his feet and roughly pinned his arms behind his back. "My own squire, the one I trusted with every idea, every secret, every facet of my life, would turn on me and kill Tristram? Tristram, who you knew was the image of my own best self?"

"Tristram, whom you loved! Yes, your precious Tristram. You thought of nothing but *him. He* must be the one you shared your secret self with. *He* must marry your sister, so that you could love him through her. No wonder you were so outraged when he wouldn't sleep with her. It was always Tristram. What about *me*?" There was a pleading quaver in Melias's voice and the tears now filled his own eyes. "I was there all the time! I was loyal and true. I cherished my time as your squire. But you never saw *me*. You only saw Tristram. Well your precious Tristram is gone now, isn't he? *Now* who do you see?" His voice rose to a shriek with his last words, until Andred, annoyed with the ranting and, I assumed, uncomfortable with the revelations pouring out, struck Melias across the mouth with a brawny right fist, effectively silencing the former squire. Except for the sobbing.

The lord Kaherdin, now dealing with shock after shock, looked down his face reddening again. Whether it was from discomfiture or wrath, or perhaps both, I could not say. But when he raised his head again, his face appeared stern and inflexible. "Take this murderer out of my sight and put him in the dungeon. Isolde, we *will* set him on the rack, until we know the details of his crimes and the names of every one of the ruffians who assisted him."

"I have one right here," came a voice from behind him, and we all turned to see Sir William of Caen, his sword drawn and pointed directly at the throat of Sir Neville of Acre, whom he had backed against the trunk of a tree. "I have suspected for some time that Sir Neville was the creature of your Melias. But it was not until I heard from Sir Dinadan about the glint in the face of one of the night rioters that I became certain. He would have fled himself when he saw Melias bolt on his horse, but I had been watching him this entire time, and drew upon him then. Arrest this vile knight as well, my liege, and we shall have their stories together, and the names of all their cursed accomplices."

"So it shall be," Lord Kaherdin ordered with a wave of his hand bidding them all begone. Sir Andred and Sir William marched Melias and his coconspirator off, followed by the rest of the soldiers leading their horses. Then Kaherdin rode to Isolde's palfrey, held her by the ungauntleted hand, and the two of them began to ride off, each with a falcon on one arm and a valued sibling's hand in the other. She leaned over to rest her head for a moment on his shoulder. They stopped momentarily before Merlin, and Kaherdin said, "Stop and see me tomorrow. We'll discuss these matters more fully. I swear I will have out of these villains every scrap of evidence they can give before I put them to death." And they rode out of the clearing, followed at last by the harassed young lady in waiting. Looking down at me as she trotted gently by, she looked me in the eyes, turned the corner of her mouth up, and winked at me. And then she was gone.

I chuckled a bit as visions of the lady Rosemounde danced through my mind, and then turned my attention back to the dog. I held her by her collar and told her, "Good girl! You did a good job!" and then I squatted down so that my face was at the same level as hers, and allowed her to nuzzle me and lick my chin and nose with her wet, pink tongue. Tilting my head slightly toward Merlin standing above me, I said with determined finality, "I am never letting this dog go."

The old necromancer laughed. "God's jawbone, why would you want to?"

I turned back to the dog and stroked the sides of her long, narrow head with both hands. "You are the best," I told her. "You definitely deserve a name—something more than just 'Girl,' at least. So let me see: you're smart, you're loyal where you've placed your love. You're brave and aren't about to let anybody push you around or get away with anything…and, let's see," I considered as she tried to pull the sword out of my scabbard again, as if it was her own toy. "You also think you're in charge, don't you?" I stroked her silky head again and smiled to myself as the name came to me in a flash. "I'm going to call you Guinevere."

CHAPTER THIRTEEN
THE RETURN

Ten days later, Merlin and I stood in the lord Kaherdin's public chamber again, this time with only Sir Andred at the commander's side. In addition to hearing the latest word about the questioning of the squire Melias, we were also seeking Kaherdin's leave to return to Camelot. Our task was done, and Brother Oswald had told us the day before that Sir Dinadan was now well enough to travel without much danger of his wound bursting. The *Rosemounde* still lay in the harbor, ready to take us on our return journey, bearing the good news of her sister's innocence to the real Rosemounde and to the queen. As for the other Guinevere, she was spending the day in the kennels with some of her old friends before taking ship with us for her new home in Logres.

"There was no difficulty getting him to confess," Kaherdin was saying. "Essentially, he already had when you confronted him. He obtained the snake venom with which he poisoned his spear some weeks before the Viking raid, so he had plotted Tristram's murder well ahead of time. He saw his moment in the skirmish and struck from behind, while all our attention was on the enemy. And if that was not cold-blooded enough, he determined to kill Captain Jacques, even though he had no idea what kind of evidence the captain had, or even if it would implicate him. He simply could not take the chance, he said, and so that morning he followed him from the palace, approached him at the abbey gate, and in the middle of a friendly exchange slit the captain's throat in one quick movement, once he was certain there was no one around. He did not count on the sharp senses and the loyalty of the dog. After a bit more persuasion from our inquisitor, he seemed to remember the names of every one of that band of brigands who attacked you and the abbey. With Sir Neville's corroboration, which took much less persuasion, we have lost no time in rounding them up and they are now Melias's companions in our dungeon—as, I suspect, he will be theirs on the gallows. His only motive, as far as we can determine? Jealousy, and unrequited love."

"The unrequited love of a catamite," Sir Andred spat.

"Yes. Yes, there is that," Kaherdin said absently, his eyes watching the floor in front of us and his lips pursed. "At any rate, the case is closed. Sir Neville admitted to acting as Melias's accomplice, largely for hire, though it appears that, world-traveler though he was, he had in fact been born in Cornwall, and he may have assumed he was doing a service to the king of his home country by helping Melias with his schemes. Sentence has not yet been passed on him or on his hired ruffians. Unlike Melias, they did not in fact kill anyone. But it was not for lack of trying, and I do not anticipate mercy in their future. Melias has been sentenced to be beheaded at dawn the day after tomorrow, if you care to witness that event."

"No, no," Merlin answered quickly. "We have no need or desire to see that. We really do hope to be on our way back to Camelot by this time tomorrow. I am assuming that the good ship *Rosemounde* is still at our disposal, and that it will be fitted and manned tomorrow in time for us to sail with the tide?"

"Indeed," the commander answered. "She is ready, and only awaits your pleasure to be on her way. I expect that she will be bringing my father back from Logres on her return, since I am sure that his business with King Arthur is concluded by now. So we will take care of both needs with a single round trip."

"My lord," Merlin continued, "We are very grateful for this. And there is one other item that I want you to be aware of: in our interview with the lady Brangwen a few days ago, I made her the promise that we would bring her back to Logres with us, thus facilitating her return to Cornwall, if that was her wish. She was eager to accept the offer, and so I wanted to let you know we would have one more passenger aboard."

"Excellent!" Kaherdin exclaimed. "That relieves me of an extra burden. I was wondering what we were going to do with her, or whom we should send her to. Without her mistress, this certainly has not seemed to be the place for her. I'm more than happy to have you take her off my hands."

The mention of the faithful Brangwen gave me the opportunity to bring up a point that had been disturbing me for the entire conversation. "One more question, my lord, if I may," I began. "What has Melias said about Isolde of Ireland? Has he revealed how he poisoned her on board the ship that brought her and Lady Brangwen here?"

Kaherdin's eyes looked straight ahead and his face assumed a stony blankness. "No," he answered simply, then added, "We have not pressed the point. But he was asked, and merely answered that he knew nothing of any poisoning of that woman. He had nothing against her, he said. Only Sir Tristram."

"We assume he is lying," Sir Andred added—loquaciously, for him.

"But why?" I pressed the point. "Why would he lie? He's already guilty of two murders, plus the attempted murder of Sir Dinadan and the sacrilege of attacking a church. Why deny this last crime?"

Kaherdin shrugged. "It is always possible he's not lying. Maybe she really did die of a broken heart."

I glanced at Merlin, and he shook his head imperceptibly, so I dropped the subject. But it continued to eat at me. I felt we had not yet concluded our business here.

"We will be off, then," Merlin told the commander, and gave a slight bow. "We want to visit the lady Brangwen and Sir Dinadan at the abbey to make sure they are quite ready to sail tomorrow. We thank you again for your hospitality and your help, and will convey your loyal greetings to our liege, King Arthur."

"Do that," Kaherdin pronounced rotely as we turned for the door, adding "Godspeed, gentlemen." But after a moment called after us, "Gildas!"

I was taken aback, since he had never before used my name. I turned and said, "My lord?"

Kaherdin's eyes would not meet mine, but glanced furtively to the side as he said quietly, "Greet my sister for me as well, will you? The lady Rosemounde?"

I smiled and bowed to him. "With pleasure, my lord. Farewell."

***

Merlin and I walked in silence for some time. It was difficult to speak anyway in the town square while walking down the market street with the fruit and vegetable peddlers and other hawkers calling out their wares.

"Wine here! From the best vineyards in the neighborhood!"

"Chestnuts! Chestnuts here!"

"I have apples! Juicy red apples! Finest in Brittany!"

"Gloves made to order right here! From real goatskin! Get them while they last!"

I was thinking back over the two weeks we had been in Saint-Malo. We had found a murderer. I had acquired a dog. We had made a new friend and lost him in Captain Jacques. I thought back to the captain's funeral, conducted by Abbot Urban himself in the Cathedral of Saint Vincent three days earlier. It was a solemn occasion for which the lord Kaherdin, the lady Isolde, and all the court had turned up, but also Claude and Nancy from the Cock and Bull, holding a grieving Meg between them. It was a sad farewell, but one that I was glad we had been able to attend, to give me some closure in the matter of the captain.

I was still seeking for closure in other areas, and when it was finally quiet enough, I chose the moment to pester Merlin with my thoughts.

"So," I began. "The wolf with horns?"

"Cuckoldry, my lad, as you so astutely pointed out earlier. You just had the wrong notion of who was being cuckolded. As it happened, Melias took on the role of the jealous husband, and Tristram provided the horns."

"I suppose," I agreed. "So Captain Jacques was right all along—it's like his story of the nightingale. It was all about love and jealousy."

"It's always about love and jealousy," Merlin replied.

"All the stories are the same story," we said in unison, and I laughed at the coincidence. "And the dog turning on its master? I suppose it must have referred to the borzoi, though I'm not sure how she could be said to have 'turned.' Unless, as you said, it's metaphorical. Melias certainly turned on his master. Maybe he was like a dog."

Merlin shrugged. "It's possible," he said, but he didn't sound convinced. And I wasn't either.

"And I suppose you're going to tell me you knew it was Melias all along, right? You just didn't tell me because..."

"I wanted you to figure it out for yourself. I can't do all the thinking around here, boy!" Merlin chided good naturedly. "No, I admit that in the beginning I did not suspect him at all. And even later, I couldn't be sure. His relationship with Kaherdin was suspicious to me as our investigation progressed, however, I will say that. And all the subsequent evidence kept pointing toward him. I knew, for instance, that as Kaherdin's acting clerk, he had to be the one to relay his orders to the city guard, and so would have the easiest time manipulating those orders to make sure that the guard would not appear anywhere near the place he had sent his band of thugs to attack us or harass the abbey. Yes, it was always Melias."

"You let me think it was Andred..."

"Only to see whether you could convince me he was a strong candidate. I admit his connection with Cornwall was an issue, but it does not seem to have been a factor in the murder. He was never Melias's accomplice."

We continued to walk until we had nearly reached the doors of the cathedral. We were expecting Brother Aaron to meet us there and usher us to the lady Brangwen's makeshift closet, since we had sent word the previous day that we wished to visit the faithful lady shortly after terce the next morning, and that hour had now passed.

But we still hadn't talked about what was really bothering me. "But what about La Belle Isolde?" I demanded. "Did Melias kill her or not? Will we ever know? And don't tell me you buy Kaherdin's story of her dying of a broken heart. You already told me that never happens."

"It doesn't."

"Well then how did Isolde die?" I asked as we entered the cathedral doors, and the fussy Brother Aaron came toward us wringing his hands.

"Something tells me we're about to find out," Merlin said.

***

"God be praised that you are here," the youth began. "I wasn't sure what to do. She wanted me to bring her the herbs from the infirmary. I thought no harm. But now I cannot vouch for her safety. I have left her but I think I need to go back. Or you do. I don't know what she will do."

Merlin looked into Brother Aaron's round, cherub-like face and saw the same thing I saw—his visage wan, his brown eyes pooling with tears, his brown curls sagging. "You have given her herbs? What herbs?"

"Well, aconiste for one…"

"Wolf's bane?" Merlin answered quickly. He looked up toward the lady's room. "Go now. Find Brother Oswald and tell him what has happened. There may still be time."

Hesitating, Brother Aaron raised his face as if to speak again, but Merlin turned his body physically and gave him a gentle shove. "Go now!" He said. "There is no time to lose."

Then, "Come on, Gildas! With me!" And we vaulted the steps that led to the clerestory level, and ran along the floor until we had reached the faithful Brangwen's closet. Merlin burst through the door without ceremony.

The lady Brangwen sat comfortably. She wore a simple yet elegant long dress of royal blue, with sleeves that hung down fashionably nearly to the floor. Her wealth of red hair flowed unhampered over her shoulders, and she held a silver wine cup in her hand. In his haste and fear, Merlin forgot all courtesy and shouted at her, "God's eyelids, woman, do not drink that!"

She looked at him with all the calm of a sage, and in that sultry voice intoned quite simply, "Silly wizard. I already have." And with a languid gesture she turned he cup over, revealing that it was empty.

"Oh, my lady," Merlin sagged with the weight of defeat. "Why? This was not necessary."

"So *you* say," she answered. "Tell me: when did you first suspect me, old man?"

Merlin's face became stoic. It seemed there was nothing that could be done now to save her. "I knew it had to be you as soon as I realized you were the only one on that ship with enough knowledge of herbs to have mixed the poison that killed your mistress. Her illness made it easy for you to slip something into her seasick potion. You had the means, motive, and opportunity."

"Motive?" She raised the dark brows over her fiery green eyes. "What do you know of a motive?"

"Our earlier conversation made it more than clear that you resented your lady enough to cause a great bitterness in your heart. I could not be sure at first whether that bitterness was deep enough to incite you to commit murder. But no one else could have done it."

"Deep enough? You have no way of knowing what it is like to be a barren woman in a noble family. To have no hope of marriage and so to have but one option: to *serve*. To serve a woman of nobler birth. To hear *her* beauty praised. To have *her* marriage anticipated and planned and negotiated as if it's the most important thing in the world. To devote yourself completely to her and her interests, only to have her ask you—*order* you, the effect is the same—to give your virginity to a man you have never met for the sole purpose of concealing her own adultery? Is that enough motive, do you think? Could that bitterness be deep enough?"

Merlin closed his eyes. "Resentment, yes. Bitterness, yes. It is not difficult to understand, even to sympathize. Now please my lady, it may not be too late." At that moment, Brother Aaron appeared at the door with Master Oswald in tow. The young monk was glowing with perspiration on his forehead and his tonsured scalp. His lower lip was quivering uncontrollably and his eyes sparkled with tears. Master Oswald pushed through the door and tried to rush toward the lady, but she quickly produced a dagger she had concealed in her free hand, and held it to her throat.

"Stay away!" She warned. "Or I will make my death much swifter!"

The older monk stopped, but pleaded, "My lady! Please, allow me to purge the poison from you. Odds are you may live yet!"

"Live? For what? To be brought back to Cornwall and put to death by law for murdering the queen?" Brangwen laughed mirthlessly. "You still don't understand, any of you. King Mark was my first lover. He was my only lover. I hated the thought of him at first, but he treated me with tenderness and respect when he believed that I was his wife. When it was revealed to him that it was me and not Isolde he had been making love with, he changed. Changed for the better, if you want to know. He never truly loved Isolde. He told me so. He loved only me. But he needed to keep up the façade of Isolde as queen. His honor demanded it, his alliance with Ireland demanded it, his status with King Arthur demanded it. But it was me he loved. Me, not her, do you understand? And I grew to love him. When that idiot Tristram took me away and stashed me in that convent, it was all I could do not to despair. Thank God he finally came here, to be with his bosom chum Kaherdin and that other, foolish Isolde. I could return to Cornwall, be with my Mark, and all was well. Until the gallant Kaherdin arrived with that wretched summons."

Without warning, Lady Brangwen doubled over when a sudden spasm of pain surged through her, as the poison began its inevitable consequence. "My lady, please…" Master Oswald begged.

"No!" Brangwen cried. "Let the poison work! That summons came, and my perfect lady sprang immediately into action. She must leave at once. She must go to rescue her beloved. Never mind that this was in the middle of court where her husband the king must of necessity maintain his honor. Never mind that they were both married to someone else. She must needs fly to the arms of her dying Tristram. Well that was more than I could bear. I could accept her using me, her humiliation and abuse of me, but not the deliberate dishonoring of her husband before his own court. I vowed that was the last time she would ever hurt him. And it was." Brangwen doubled over again, her face contorted with agony. She coughed into her hand, and when she took the hand away it was covered with blood. I looked over at Master Oswald, and he had relaxed into a defeated crouch. He knew it was too late to do anything for her now.

"But why the poison?" I cried out, unable to hold back any longer. "Surely King Mark would have protected you…"

"Surely he would not!" She growled through gritted teeth, all the allure of her voice now gone. "He would have to bow to the law, to the pressure of the court. The murderer of the queen of Cornwall could not be allowed to escape unpunished. It would undermine the whole social structure. I must be condemned, and he must preside over my execution. I would not put him through that torment. Not while I had the means to prevent it."

"But why return to Cornwall at all?" I pleaded, apparently the only one in the room not now resigned to her death. "Why not stay here? Or come to Camelot?"

"Anywhere in Arthur's empire would return me to Cornwall under arms, to stand trial. No, this was the only way…the only way…" And that was all the strength she had. She collapsed onto the floor. Master Oswald was upon her quickly, feeling for a pulse, but finding none, he looked up and shook his head.

Brother Aaron pushed by me and fell to his knees as Master Oswald backed away. Cradling Brangwen's head in his lap, the young monk howled as the tears rolled down his chin and onto her frozen face. As his shoulders shook with uncontrolled sobs, he reminded me of nothing more than Captain Jacques' dog the morning we found his body. The faithful Brangwen may have had only one lover in her life, but he was not the only one who had loved her.

***

Two days later, Merlin and I stood on the deck of the *Rosemounde* leaning over the rail and looking into the sea's spray misting around our bow as we cut through it, occasionally glancing to the right as we passed by Mont Saint Michel. Sir Dinadan, barely able to walk, had been carried aboard and laid in a cot in the ship's castle. Guinevere had at first been very curious about the ship and all that it carried, but once we left port and the deck began rocking under her, she began to wail with fear and astonishment. She had already been sick once on the deck, a fact that did not endear her to the ship's crew, and so she was avoiding them and was now curled up at my feet, giving the occasional moan, and I stroked her occasionally to reassure her that this too would pass.

Below decks in the cargo hold a simple wooden coffin had been stored, cradling the remains of the lady Brangwen. True to his word, Merlin was bringing her back to Logres, from which, in compliance with her wishes, she would be sent on to Cornwall.

The lord Kaherdin had been kind enough to delay the ship's departure another day so that Lady Brangwen could be casketed and her body taken aboard. But it was the kindness of the monks of Saint Vincent's Abbey that had made our smooth departure possible. Abbot Urban had set the abbey's carpenter to making Brangwen's coffin right away. He had also given her the last rites, though in so doing he knew he was violating Church policy, under which a suicide was considered damned, beyond hope of redemption. But as Urban had said, it was not up to him—or even the Church—to decide the fate of Brangwen's soul, and extending her the last rites could not possibly do any harm, to her or anyone else.

It was also Urban who had solved two of our other knotty problems. Sir Dinadan was as yet in no condition to ride a horse, as the jostling was likely to burst his semi-healed wounds and undo all the good that Master Oswald's ministrations had achieved. So Abbot Urban proposed that we visit the new Cistercian monastery that he said lay just south of the harbor at Southampton, where the ship was to land. The monastery was a large and busy one, he told us, and a hub of communication between various parts of Logres. He knew the abbot there, Abbot Hugh, and assured us that the monks would lend us a cart with which to transport Dinadan back to Camelot. The brothers would also, he was confident, take the responsibility of seeing that Brangwen's remains reached King Mark's court in Cornwall. In his own hand he wrote out an introduction and request to those effects, addressed to the Abbot Hugh at the Abbey Church of Saint Mary in Beaulieu, Hampshire, then sealed the parchment with wax and his signet ring. Merlin was all but overwhelmed at the abbot's kindness as he took the parchment and placed it securely in an inner pocket of his cloak, but Abbot Urban waved off any effusive thanks.

"It is I who should be thanking you," he said, his jowls waggling as he shook his substantial head. "It was through your efforts that the sacrilege of our abbey's defilement was repaid. The culprits will never abuse us again, or any other religious institution—or other law abiding citizens. You have our gratitude, and will always be welcome here at Saint Vincent's."

With the help of those powerful former knights, Brother Gabriel and Brother Michael, we brought the coffin up from the abbey and loaded it into the hold, and then carried Sir Dinadan into the ship as well, over his loud protest that he was quite able to walk that distance. Merlin forbade it, saying he was not about to have our departure set back again because of some relapse brought about by Dinadan's stubborn insistence on walking. And now at last we were on our way, looking to make land at Southampton sometime around sext the next day. And by the following day, we should be back in Camelot. I was bursting to get there and to see Rosemounde once again, and to tell my lady all the news about her family in Brittany, and about how I, with a little help from Merlin, had solved the case of Tristram and Isolde's murders, and that her siblings were not involved.

"And so," I said to Merlin as we leaned over the rail. "The case is solved. And it seems there were two murderers after all."

"Yes," the old man mused. "Through pure coincidence, apparently, two separate plots aimed at killing Tristram and Isolde, happened to come together at one and the same time and place."

"Coincidence? Or was it some kind of fated end?"

"What, are you suggesting divine retribution or some such rubbish! Poppycock, boy!" Merlin burst out. "Random events occur randomly. Sometimes two related random events occur in conjunction with one another. Among the millions of random events that occur every day, a few related events are bound to occur together, but that doesn't make them supernaturally related. That's the kind of thinking that makes for superstition, you Cornish dunce."

"And superstition is the chief religious occupation of our time," I admitted. "But that's not exactly what I meant. Tristram and Isolde hurt a lot of people. They made a lot of enemies. Doesn't it seem fated that some of those offenses would come home to roost eventually?"

"I'll give you that," Merlin conceded. "Although Tristram's death turned out to be the result of an infatuation he was completely unaware of, as far as we know. He had become the object of jealousy for a misguided catamite."

There were a number of aspects of this case that puzzled me, that I simply could not assimilate, and this was one of them. And aside from the simple fact of Melias' infatuation, I was somewhat shocked the day before when I discovered that, after long consultation with his sister Isolde and with Abbot Urban, Lord Kaherdin had come to the private decision to commute Melias' sentence from public execution to lifelong exile from Brittany and from all the lands of Arthur's empire—a decision based on further consideration of Melias' youth and his long service to Kaherdin. While there might be a public outcry against Kaherdin's leniency, the sentence of banishment upon pain of death was sufficient to assuage the anger of the mob who might fear Melias as a public danger. The nature of his crime, Urban had reasoned, and had ultimately convinced Kaherdin, was not likely to make him a danger to anyone else, now that Tristram was dead.

"Well, I simply cannot understand Melias at all," I admitted bending low to stroke Guinevere's soft head as she moaned again at a particularly heavy roll of the ship. "It all seems so…unnatural."

Merlin gave one of his habitual shrugs. "There are more men like Melias than you might suspect, young Gildas. Even, perhaps, among the knights of the Round Table itself. But the love and jealousy displayed in his crime is quite natural, I suppose. It's what we see all the time, from men and women of all types."

"Is it not a sin?"

"What? Obviously the murder he committed is a sin. His sacrilege must be a sin as well. As for the rest, I think I must hold with Abbot Urban's opinion about Lady Brangwen. Who am I to say what is damnable? God made Melias the way he was for some purpose, I'm sure. It's not really my business to decide what that purpose was, or to question God's work."

"Hmmph," I commented, detecting a bit of self-contradiction in the skeptical Merlin I knew so well. "Do you really think that God created Melias in that particular way?"

"I'm as certain as I am of God's purpose in creating anything," Merlin answered cryptically.

"But the commuting of the sentence, Merlin. After he had killed two men, nearly killed Dinadan, and violated the sanctity of the abbey, was it just to allow him to simply go peacefully into exile?"

"Was it just?" the old mage tilted his head to give the matter serious consideration. "Why not? You yourself were willing to extend the lady Brangwen the same opportunity when we stood in her closet, were you not? Why not the same chance for Melias? A man is always better than his worst deed, Gildas. Aye, and a woman too. Melias was a faithful squire, clerk, and servant to Lord Kaherdin, a man he admired and loved. He did not wake up one morning, look in the mirror, and say to himself, 'Today I think I'll be a killer. I'll embrace evil and give myself over to the dark side of my nature.' He justified himself according to his own sense of his worth and his own feeling of love. In exile he will continue to be a far better person than his worst deeds might seem to make him. There may be redemption for him yet."

I thought briefly about what Merlin had said: that a man was better than his worst act. Seeing Mont Saint Michel on our right, I was reminded of what I had learned of King Arthur and his own sins. I couldn't deny that his subsequent life had redeemed his past wrongs, and perhaps there was something in Merlin's argument.

"So once again your dream-prophesy has proven true. The horned wolf was Melias, the 'cuckolded' Melias as you call him. The faithful dog that turned on her master was Brangwen. The *faithful* Brangwen—faithful as a dog," I looked down again at Guinevere at my feet and stroked her one more time. "How ironic that name turned out to be!"

"Oh, I don't know," Merlin responded. "She was incredibly loyal to her lady, even after she had been so notoriously abused. But she was also loyal, fiercely loyal, to her beloved Mark."

"I'm far more sympathetic to the lady Brangwen than to Melias,"

I admitted. "As you say, she was faithful for years. She sacrificed everything for others, whether it was her lady or her beloved king. Even her suicide was an act of self-sacrifice and love. When she killed Isolde it was out of a misguided belief that she was defending the one she loved. But redemption is beyond her."

"We don't know that," Merlin murmured.

"Perhaps not," I said. "I guess I'm not too sure what all we don't know. But I know one thing: love or no love, jealousy or no jealousy, I could never be pushed to the extreme of murdering somebody."

Merlin let out a sigh and muttered softly, "None of us knows that, my boy, until we are in the crucible."

***

Getting to the abbey had been less difficult than I feared. The single-masted cog ship had made good time crossing the Narrow Sea, and in the end had come up the Solent, the narrow strait that separated the Isle of Wight from Hampshire. A few knots before turning into the Southampton Water to dock there, the ship anchored briefly at the mouth of the Beaulieu River Estuary, and the captain sent four sailors with small boat carrying me, Merlin, Dinadan, the dog Guinevere (who seemed excited and overjoyed to be off the ship), and the wooden coffin bearing the faithful Brangwen's remains, rowing upriver to land us at the grounds of the abbey.

Wide gardens surrounded the monastery, and the fields were being worked by the monks themselves. Our boat passed by a number of monks working in the fields, and then passed through a water gate into a fortified complex of buildings. When the rowboat docked, five of the monks had come down to meet us, and had helped us carry Brangwen's casket up to the cloister south of the great church, which from here looked to be more than a hundred meters long. Two other monks, perceiving Dinadan's weakened condition, walked him up the bank and toward the monastery. Merlin and I thanked the four sailors and followed the Cistercians toward the cloister, while Guinevere, happy to feel solid ground under her paws again, ran in circles around us. The monks themselves, however, had not spoken to us, but communicated only by signs. As Dinadan walked slowly, leaning on his two escorts, and I dragged our sea chest behind me, Merlin had explained that these Cistercian monks, the newest order in Christendom, often maintained a rule of silence between prime and compline, the better, I supposed, to commune quietly with the inner voice of the Holy Spirit.

We had soon arrived at the abbot's quarters, where we were greeted warmly by Abbot Hugh, particularly when he learned we had been sent to him by Abbot Urban in Saint-Malo. The abbot apparently was not subject to the rule of silence—at least not when it came to conversing with visitors. At any rate, it was soon agreed that we would spend the night at the abbey, and would be loaned two horses and a cart in the morning to convey ourselves to Camelot with Dinadan lying in the back of the cart. Travelers heading west stopped at the abbey quite often, we were told, and Abbot Hugh promised to assume the responsibility of conveying Lady Brangwen to Cornwall. Finally, the abbot had invited us to sup in the monastery's refectory, which lay just a bit farther along the cloister walk. He had promised us simple but nourishing fare, but had warned us that the monks serving our supper would not be allowed to speak with us.

So it was that the three of us—well, four, counting Guinevere—were making our way along the cloister, Dinadan now leaning on Merlin's arm for support. Two monks passed us going the other way in their bright white habits with the black scapulars. They nodded in silence and we nodded back. As we walked I looked around at the architecture of the abbey—simple white stone with the new pointed Gothic style arches, but without any decoration of any kind. The walls were bare everywhere.

I was looking up at some of those arches when I very nearly ran directly into a young man who was walking across the cloister with another Cistercian. He was younger than me, probably about fifteen years of age, but he was taller and more muscular. He, too, was dressed in white, but it was no religious habit that he wore, only a light tunic with tan hose and black boots. I begged his pardon for the near collision, at which he and the monk both nodded silently and moved on. But for a brief moment, I looked into his face and was taken aback. The wavy brown hair. The pale blue eyes. The aquiline nose. The square jaw like granite. Only he was some twenty years younger.

"Merlin," I cried. "That boy…it's…"

"Lancelot!" Sir Dinadan cried, his face looking as astonished as I felt.

Merlin pursed his lips. "I knew about this lad. I did not know he was here, though I knew he was being raised by monks."

"He's Lancelot's son?" I asked, though the question seemed naïve. And then, after a moment's thought, I added, "Does the queen know?"

"You have just seen Galahad," Merlin told us. "Sir Lancelot sired him some fifteen years ago after a night with Elaine, the daughter of King Pelles of Corbenic."

"Who?" I asked, thunderstruck. "Why would he do such a thing?"

"He was tricked into it. King Pelles arranged it because of a long standing prophecy."

"Prophecy?" Dinadan echoed. "What kind of prophecy would persuade a man to use his daughter like that?"

"The prophecy that she would become the mother of the purest of all knights, whose life would be devoted to the quest for the world's most important relic. But this could only happen if the greatest knight in the world was the child's father."

"And how did they arrange to have Lancelot father the child?" I wanted to know.

"By telling him that Queen Guinevere was awaiting him in a dark closet in the castle. He was also told that he should bring no light to the chamber and that he must remain silent so as not to disturb anyone else."

"This is eerily like Brangwen's tricking of King Mark," I decided. "Again, all stories are the same story. What is this great relic?"

"You'll find out soon enough, young Gildas," Merlin said. "The boy is nearly full-grown now. Before long he will be in Camelot."

"No doubt to be welcomed warmly by Queen Guinevere," Dinadan put in. "This great quest intrigues me, though. Perhaps I'll seek to go on it myself."

"Perhaps you will," Merlin said, unconvinced, as we found our way into the refectory.

We sat down at one of the long wooden tables where the monks had their meals, and were soon brought a large plate of bread and cheese and glasses of ale by an unspeaking monk in a white habit. I had just broken off a piece of bread and was about to put it in my mouth when the bread and my jaw dropped simultaneously. Sir Palomides had just walked into the room.

"Palomides!" Dinadan called. "Thank God, somebody who will talk to us!"

"My friends, you've returned!"

"Apparently," Dinadan continued. "We know why we're here. What on earth brings you to this out-of-the-way place?"

Sir Palomides sat with us and, when the silent monk had brought him his own portion of cheese and bread, he explained: "The king has sent me here to arrange for Duke Hoel and his party to stay overnight at the abbey before boarding their ship for Brittany in three days' time. He wanted to send a knight to show his respect for the abbot, and he wanted Duke Hoel to see the abbey because the king has endowed it himself. And so we are met! I will be able to ride with you back to Camelot in the morning. It seems fated, does it not?"

Merlin looked at me askance, raising his great eyebrows, and I gave him a half-smile, remembering his earlier lecture on coincidence. Palomides, however, had something more pressing on his mind: "But my friends, all courtesy aside, I am dying to know: what did you discover about the deaths of my beloved Isolde and my great rival, Sir Tristram? Was Sir Tristram indeed murdered?"

Dinadan and I looked over at Merlin, who glanced at us, raised his eyebrows, let out a deep sigh, and began.

He told the whole story as Sir Palomides listened in rapt attention. He described how Tristram's wounds could not have been caused by Viking weapons, but only by someone from his own side. He talked about the murder of Captain Jacques and the attacks on ourselves and the abbey. Finally he related how the faithful Brangwen had poisoned her own mistress on the ship coming from Cornwall. All this while, I passed the time by secretly feeding Guinevere pieces of cheese and bites of bread as she lay quietly under the table. "It's a long and sordid story," Merlin finally concluded. "But it is the truth of the matter."

The story of Sir Neville's golden teeth had piqued Sir Palomides' interest, and he commented, "Yes, in my country I have seen some of the gentry affect this fashion of the gold teeth. Strange that a Frankish crusader—or rather, as you say, a Cornish one—would decide to copy it, but who can say why people do what they do? But this story of yours makes me uneasy." Now it was Sir Palomides' turn to sigh. He pursed his lips and blew out a deep breath. His eyes grew wide in an expression of disbelief, then his brow furrowed and he shook his head. "No," he stated firmly. "I will not accept this explanation. This story may consist of facts, if you say so, but it is not truth. My great rival cannot have been killed in this way. More importantly, my beloved lady cannot have been turned upon by her faithful servant. La Belle Isolde must die of a broken heart. That is where the poetic truth resides."

"Palomides," Sir Dinadan retorted. "Did the sun boil your brains back in the desert where you grew up, you crazy Saracen? You've got the truth and you've got fairy tales. What can you do but accept it?"

"I do not accept it," Palomides insisted. "I will write the story of Tristram and Isolde in verse, and I will tell the story my way. Look, I can think of a beginning already. It should go something like this:

Attend, my lords and ladies dear
Unto my words, and you shall hear
A tale of unequaled woe
Of Tristram's life and love and death,
His call for Isolde with his dying breath,
And how she saw him lying low,
And fell down, fainting dead away—
Dead of a broken heart, all the people say.

I'll have to clean up some of the meter, you understand, but that will be the general direction of my verse. You spread your story, old man, and I will circulate my poem, and let us see which version of the tale people remember after some years, shall we?"

"All right, have it your way," Merlin grumbled. "I must needs report the truth—the facts—to the king and queen. What foolish romantics end up believing, I have no control over."

Sir Palomides smiled, his wide smile revealing teeth that shone a brilliant white against his dark skin. "It is finally the poet who has control, is it not? Surely you agree with me, young Gildas? There is some poet in you, no? Oh yes, for you have written your own poems, for your lovely Rosemounde, eh?"

I felt myself coloring. Since we had left Brittany, the eagerness I felt at being able to meet with Rosemounde, to be able to reveal to her that her brother and sister were innocent of wrongdoing in the Tristram and Isolde affair, even to bring her greetings from her long estranged brother at his request, these things had made me impatient to get here, all the more impatient at spending another night on the road before returning to Camelot and Rosemounde. All of these things my blush, I feared, displayed to the world.

But a strange look came suddenly over Sir Palomides' face. His brow furrowed again and the corners of his mouth turned down, and he looked away from me, to the floor at my left.

"Oh dear," he said. "I was so caught up with my own concerns about my sainted beloved that I almost forgot. You have been away from Camelot these past two weeks. You will not have heard about the wedding."

"Wedding?" Dinadan responded. "So we missed some merriment, did we? One of the knights tie the knot?"

"Indeed," Palomides answered, still not meeting my eye. "The king's nephew, the newly knighted Sir Mordred."

"Mordred!" Dinadan exclaimed. "Who on earth would ever marry *that* sourpuss? There's a woman who's got a miserable time ahead of her, wouldn't you say?"

Palomides did not respond. "The lady…" he began, "the lady was given away by her father. It was a political match worked out between King Arthur and the lady's father." I was not sure why, but a wedge of hot emotion had begun to well up from my bowels and into my chest, attacking the back of my neck and then, just as quickly, draining all the blood from my face. I could see Merlin glancing at me askance from under his lowered brows. Palomides went relentlessly on. "Her father had come for the induction on Pentecost and then stayed to negotiate the marriage treaty with the king, and it was decided that, since he was already in Camelot, the nuptials should be celebrated immediately, before the duke could return to Brittany. As I said, I've come here to negotiate Duke Hoel's accommodation for his trip home."

"You're saying..." I rasped, "My lady Rosemounde has married *Sir Mordred*?"

Palomides was still for a moment, and then silently nodded. "It is finished," he said.

The room went dark, though there was fire behind my eyes. My head was spinning and I tried to hold it between my knees to keep from passing out. My blessed lady, gone from me. Yoked for life to that...that...that brute of a human being, a person with no grace, no joy, no courtesy, no love in him. I found myself wishing, and not for the last time, that King Arthur had been successful in his attempt to exterminate the child before he became a man, if that's what you could call him. Nothing in my life would ever be the same. But I can tell you this: I truly wanted to kill him. And I would have there and then had the means and opportunity been present. For I surely had the motive. Oh Lord, I had the motive indeed.

EPILOGUE
SAINT DUNSTAN'S ABBEY

The old monk was quiet now. After a few moments, the six young novices realized that there would be nothing more to the story, and a few of them began to object.

"What? Is that all?" cried the youngest of them, his blond curls bouncing indignantly about his tonsure. "You can't leave us hanging like that!"

The red-headed youth flashed burning green eyes at Brother Gildas, complaining, "Surely there is more to tell than this! Surely this marriage of Lady Rosemounde and Sir Mordred was broken, or annulled, or something. The story cannot end this way."

"I'm afraid *this* story does," the aged monk responded. He leaned back in his seat along the wall of the monastery's chapter house, where the others had gathered to hear him hold forth.

Brother Gildas, forty years a Benedictine monk of Saint Dunstan's Abbey in Hereford, near the Welsh border, enjoyed regaling the young initiates during the hour between vespers and compline. Officially, the monks were expected to spend this time in meditation and study. But both the prior and abbot turned a blind eye on Brother Gildas's storytelling sessions, figuring, after all, that his stories were instructive, in their own way, and besides, both prior and abbot had been novices under Brother Gildas's tutelage themselves some twenty years earlier.

"Surely you will tell us about that marriage another day?" Brother Nennius suggested. Nennius of Wales, who had been hearing Brother

Gildas's stories longer than any of the younger monks present, was always the most curious of his audience, and always pressed for more details, as if he were memorizing the stories to tell them himself one day. Gildas found nothing wrong in that. He himself was two generations removed from these novices, and King Arthur had been another generation older. If Brother Nennius told these stories to youths young enough to be his own grandchildren many years hence, did that not suit Brother Gildas's purpose? He kept Arthur, Queen Guinevere, Merlin, Sir Lancelot, Sir Gawain and Gareth and Dinadan and yes, even Tristram alive in more than just name, and if he could keep the lady Rosemounde alive, his life may have some wider purpose after all, beyond singing the lord's service hourly for two score winters within these stark but by now comfortable and homely walls. In the end, he thought, Sir Palomides was right: it was the poets, the storytellers, who kept the spirit alive, and who always had the last word.

"Another time, yes. We'll talk about it another time," the old monk agreed.

"But tell us, at least, whether that marriage turned out to be a wise or happy one," the blond youth pleaded.

Gildas shook his head. "Not wise. Not happy. And it was not only my own biased view that saw it that way. But there is no time today. Compline is drawing on, and it will be dark soon."

The monk with the considerable ears, which made him look like a great bird about to take off, added, "I want to know more about Sir Galahad, too. You will tell us about the quest of the Grail sometime, Brother?"

"Yes, yes," Brother Gildas agreed, his old eyes looking tired, his hands, palms down, suggesting that he had had enough of such requests for now. "Everyone wants to know about the Holy Grail. Another day, another day."

"I…I h-have heard this st…st…story of T-t-Tristram and Isolde befo…before," began Brother Notker, the dark-eyed monk they called the Stammerer. "I am sure Isolde d-died of a b-b-broken h-heart."

Brother Gildas closed his eyes. "Another romantic," he muttered to himself. "Sir Palomides wins again."

"But what happened when you finally met with Lady Rosemounde, after you returned to Camelot? How did you face that interview?" Asked the handsome, blue-eyed youth with the dark wavy hair surrounding his fresh tonsure.

The aged monk sighed and rubbed his eyes with his right hand, hanging his head. This story had been most difficult to tell, since it had ended with one of his life's most trying moments. Finally he revealed, "I never had that interview. I did not meet with Rosemounde. Merlin told the story to the queen and, I assume, the lady Rosemounde. When I got back to Camelot, I spent the first few nights with Merlin and my dog in his cave, away from anyone but him, and he knew not to speak to me about it. When I felt I could be among people again, I returned to Sir Gareth, and lost myself in the work of being his squire. Finally a royal command came down: I was to come to the queen for an audience."

"Did she chide you again for your obsession with the woman you could not have?" Nennius wanted to know. Sometimes there was a little too much thought behind his questions, Gildas reflected, but answered honestly, "No. Not this time. She knew that I had lost my beloved, that she was now beyond all hope, and spoke only words of comfort and sympathy. She even offered to marry me off to one of her other ladies in waiting, if I so chose. But I did not so choose. Those others were not my Rosemounde, and if I could not have her, I did not want to take another wife as a consolation prize. I had learned the folly of that through my interview with Isolde of the White Hands, thank you, and wanted no such situation for myself. In fact, it was at that point that I first began to think about life as a monk. The kindnesses of people like Master Oswald, Abbot Urban, and Abbot Hugh had made me think there may be some good to be done in the world after all, although the case of Brother Aaron made it clear to me that the monastic habit could not shield me from the love, temptation, and grief of the outside world. But I was still many years from finally putting on the habit."

"Brother Gildas," the red-headed novice asked. "Was anything more ever heard of Melias?"

"Nothing for many years. I did hear a rumor once that he had died in the Holy Land, battling the infidels as part of a crusading army. I have no notion whether that is true or not, but it gives me some hope that he found something to give his life some meaning at last."

"What about Sir Dinadan?" Inquired brother Big-ears. "His wounds healed all right, I take it?"

"Oh yes, and we spent many good times together...until the Grail. He did eventually have the chance to take part in that quest, as he wished."

"What about Guinevere?" asked the young blond novice.

"Guinevere?" The old monk scratched his dry tonsured scalp. "Why, she remained queen, of course, until the end, until Arthur's table finally fell..."

"No, no," the blond monk colored visibly. "I meant the dog."

The aged monk smiled for the first time since the end of his story. "Oh, Gwenny! Yes, she stayed with me. I kept her in the kennels, with the hunting hounds, when I couldn't have her at my side, and she loved to go on the hunt. But she also just liked to be with me, and she was my companion for many years before she finally died. I buried her outside the kennels at Camelot, so she could watch the dogs go out to the hunt, if it's not too heretical to think that kind of thing. She loved me better than any person I've ever come in contact with in my life. If I can see her again in heaven, I would say that God had finally made the pain of living worthwhile."

The bells rang, calling the abbey to compline, and the seven monks got up and began their walk down the cloister toward the abbey church to sing the service. Brother Gildas, using his advanced age as an excuse, brought up the rear of the group, but Brother Nennius fell back to walk at the old monk's side. "Speaking of the pain of living," he said quietly to Brother Gildas, so that none of the other novices could hear. "When did you see the lady Rosemounde again? Or *did* you ever?"

"Not for many months," Brother Gildas revealed. "Perhaps it was years, I do not recall precisely. She went to live on her husband's estate in Orkney, though she did finally return to Camelot under the queen's protection, but that was much later. And she was much altered."

"But still your beloved?" Nennius asked.

"Still my only love," Brother Gildas answered, his eyes filling.

He had told a small untruth, Brother Gildas thought to himself shuffling now in silence along the cloister. He had seen Rosemounde. He had seen her every day of his life, in his mind's eye, even as he saw her now, at more than four decades' distance. Her face shone before him in all its youthful beauty, her eyes sparkling mischievously, the corners of her mouth drawn up in her knowing smirk, her brown hair cascading free over her shoulders.

But through his misting eyes he also saw the grim, dark features of Sir Mordred, and his ancient blood raged within him. For the things the bastard had done to Rosemounde—for the things he had done to his father Arthur—for the things he had done to Camelot in general, Brother Gildas was absolutely certain he could have committed murder. That knowledge, when he let himself dwell on his hatred, made his life bleak and empty as the sea. He had prayed, sincerely prayed, over the years for God to lift him out of this sin, but he always returned to it, and he returned to it now. But that, he said to himself as if he were still addressing his band of novices, was a different story, and would be told at a different time. All he could think of right now, as he began to finger the rosary that hung from his belt, were the twin poles of his hatred and his love. His was, he had to admit to himself, just another story of love and jealousy. "All stories are the same story," he mumbled to himself as he shuffled along.

In one of the trees within the cloister, he thought he heard the song of a nightingale.

CAST OF CHARACTERS

Aaron: Brother Aaron is a very young monk attached to the Cathedral of Saint Vincent of Saragossa. He is assigned to wait upon the Lady Brangwen when she stays in the cathedral, and develops a strong attraction to the older woman.

Agravain of Orkney: Sir Agravain is a nephew of King Arthur, one of the brothers of Gawain and Gareth.

Andred: Sir Andred is cousin and close adviser to Kaherdin, lord of Saint-Malo. A native of Cornwall, Andred is a grim and tight-lipped knight, loyal to Kaherdin and suspicious of outsiders and jealous of his master's rights.

Arthur: King of Logres, holding sovereignty as well over Ireland, Scandinavia, Scotland, Wales, and Cornwall, Brittany, Normandy, and all of Gaul. And he is claimant to the emperor's throne in Rome. He is the son of Uther Pendragon and Ygraine, former Countess of Cornwall.

Bleoberis: Sir Bleoberis is not known for any of his individual feats of arms, but is a reliable knight of the Round Table and a member of the group of knights that forms Sir Lancelot's usual entourage.

Brangwen: Known as "the faithful Brangwen," she is lady-in-waiting to La Belle Isolde. She is known to be devoted to her mistress, even to the point of duping Isolde's husband King Mark in the marriage bed. The lady Brangwen is known to be a skilled herbalist and healer like her mistress, and is reputed to have concocted the love potion that drew Tristram and Isolde together.

Claude: Proprietor of the Cock and Bull Inn, and ally to Captain Jacques.

Dinadan: Sir Dinadan was Sir Tristram's closest companion. He is a skilled knight but better known for his sharp tongue than his prowess. He eagerly joins Merlin and Gildas in investigating Tristram's suspicious death.

Florent of Orkney: Eldest son of Sir Gawain, recently knighted by King Arthur. Florent was accused of rape in the previous novel, but was saved by the testimony of Nimue, who married him and took him to live in the palace of the Lady of the Lake.

Gaheris of Orkney: Sir Gaheris is son of King Lot of Orkney and Queen Margause—whom he is known to have beheaded when he found her in bed with Sir Lamorak. Gaheris resembles his younger brother Sir Gareth in coloring, but not in temperament.

Galahad: Son of Sir Lancelot and the lady Elaine of Corbenic Castle, daughter of King Pelles. He will become vitally important in the story of the Grail quest.

Gareth of Orkney: Knight of the Round Table and younger brother to Sir Gawain, Sir Gaheris, and Sir Agravain, and half-brother to Mordred. He is son of King Lot of Orkney and Margause, the daughter of Ygraine and Duke Gorlois of Cornwall and so Arthur's half–sister, which makes him King Arthur's nephew. Gildas is squire to Sir Gareth.

Gawain of Orkney: Sir Gawain is Arthur's nephew and heir apparent. He is son of King Lot of Orkney and Arthur's half-sister Margause, and the older brother of Sir Gareth, Sir Gaheris, Sir Agravain, and Mordred, and father of Sir Florent and Lovel, his new squire.

Gildas of Cornwall: Son of a Cornish armor-maker, squire to Sir Gareth, former page to Queen Guinevere. Gildas narrates the story and is Merlin's assistant in his investigations.

Guinevere: Queen of Logres, and married to King Arthur. Gildas was formerly a page in her household. She is the daughter of Leodegrance, king of Cameliard, an early ally of Arthur's. Her long-standing affair with Sir Lancelot, Arthur's chief knight, is a perilous secret in the court.

Hoel: Duke of Brittany, and Arthur's vassal and close ally from the beginning of his reign. He is the father of Lady Rosemounde. He is also the father of Isolde of the White Hands and her brother, Kaherdin.

Hugh: Abbot of the new Cistercian abbey at Beaulieu, stopover for Merlin, Dinadan, and Gildas on their return from Saint-Malo, where Galahad is being fostered.

Isolde: La Belle Isolde is the daughter of the king and queen of Ireland, and was queen of Cornwall, married to King Mark. A famous healer and herbalist, she once saved the life of Sir Tristram with her potions. She was also Tristram's secret lover, and died upon seeing his dead body.

Isolde of the White Hands: Isolde of the White Hands is Sir Tristram's wife in Brittany. He married her essentially because she had the same name as his beloved, but he never consummated the marriage. As the daughter of Duke Hoel, she is half-sister to Gildas's love, the Lady Rosemounde, and full sister to Kaherdin.

Jacques: Captain Jacques is commander of Kaherdin's Breton guard. He is an honest knight, solid in a fight, loyal to Kaherdin and Duke Hoel, and a lively companion. He does enjoy frequenting the taverns of Saint-Malo, telling stories, and traveling with a tall, boisterous Borzoi hound.

Kaherdin: Lord of the fortress city of Saint-Malo in Brittany and the natural son of Duke Hoel, Kaherdin commands the troops of this port city and reports to his father as his liege lord. An arrogant and Spartan warrior, Kaherdin was also a close friend of Sir Tristram, and convinced Tristram to marry his sister, Isolde of the White Hands.

Kay: Sir Kay is King Arthur's seneschal, which means he is in charge of the king's household He was Arthur's foster-brother when they were boys, and Arthur promised Kay's father Sir Ector that there would always be a place for Kay in his court.

Lady of the Lake: Queen of Faerie, a being of great mystical power. She is responsible for giving the sword Excalibur to King Arthur. She lives in an enchanted palace north of Camelot on a lake named for her.

Lamorak de Galis: Sir Lamorak is one of the three great knights of Arthur's table. He was the son of King Pelinore, who killed King Lot and thus began a feud with the house of Orkney. Sir Gaheris caught Sir Lamorak in bed with his mother Margause and let him escape, but Gawain, Gaheris, and Agravain killed Sir Lamorak later in ambush.

Lancelot: Sir Lancelot is the greatest knight of Arthur's table, and is the secret lover of Queen Guinevere. He is the son of King Ban of Benwick, and his close kinsmen—Sir Bors, Sir Hector, and Sir Lionel—form a powerful bloc of Round Table knights. He himself knighted Sir Perceval, and he is therefore Perceval's mentor and champion at Arthur's court.

Lot: King Lot of Orkney was an enemy of Arthur's who would not accept the fifteen-year old boy as king of Logres. With an alliance of other kings, he made war on Arthur to get him off the throne, but was ultimately defeated and killed. He was married to Arthur's half-sister Margause, and was the father of Gawain, Gaheris, Agravain, and Gareth.

Lovel of Orkney: Sir Gawain's second son, and his new squire, replacing Sir Florent.

Margause: Mother of Gawain and his brothers, Margause was the wife of King Lot of Orkney and was one of Arthur's half-sisters, daughter of his mother Ygraine and Duke Gorlois of Cornwall. Not known for her high moral standards, Margause was killed by her own son Sir Gaheris when he caught her in bed with Sir Lamorak.

Mark: Mark is King of Cornwall, and was married to La Belle Isolde. He was also the uncle of Sir Tristram, who was his wife's lover. King Mark gained the Cornish throne as the result of heroic action in Arthur's war with Ireland, but has been known to seek vengeance on Sir Tristram before. He is also Gildas's own lord and king, and vassal to King Arthur.

Meg: Serving-wench at the Cock and Bull Inn, with a great affection for Captain Jacques.

Melias: Melias is son of the Count of Poutou and squire to Sir Kaherdin. He is one of Kaherdin's close advisors, and greatly admires Kaherdin, for whom he also performs clerkly duties as a kind of secretary.

Merlin: Arthur's chief adviser in his early days, Merlin helped Arthur solidify his realm, win the war against King Lot and his allies and the war with Ireland. Rumored to have magical powers and to be able to see the future, Merlin is essentially just a more logical and scientific thinker than most of his contemporaries. His hopeless love for Nimue, the damsel of the lake, regularly sends him into fits of depression, particularly now that she has embraced Sir Florent as her lover.

Mordred: Mordred is the youngest brother of Sir Gawain and Sir Gareth, the youngest child of Arthur's half-sister Margause. He becomes Sir Mordred in this book. But his parentage is doubtful:

he does not resemble any of his brothers, and his birth and early childhood are shrouded in secrecy.

Morgan le Fay: Queen of Gore, wife of King Uriens and mother of Sir Ywain, Morgan is King Arthur's half-sister, the daughter of his mother Ygraine and Gorlois, Duke of Cornwall.

Neville of Acre: Sir Neville is one of the Lord Kaherdin's knights at Saint-Malo. The mysterious and unorthodox Sir Neville had been a crusading knight prior to taking service with Kaherdin, and so is worldly with a great deal of experience in matters of war.

Nimue: Lady-in-waiting to the Lady of the Lake, Nimue lives in the Lady's mystical palace and never ages. Her beauty enchanted Merlin, who remains in love with her though she has definitively rejected him.

Oswald: Brother Oswald (or "Master" Oswald) is a monk attached to the Cathedral of Saint Vincent of Saragossa in Saint-Malo. He was the attending physician at the deaths of Sir Tristram and of Queen Isolde, and can therefore give the most accurate accounting of the death scene.

Palomides: Sir Palomides is a Moorish knight who has joined the Round Table and become a Christian. He was Sir Tristram's great rival for the love of Isolde, and is known as a composer of love poems. He is also fascinated by cooking with the spices of his native lands.

Perceval de Galis: A new knight recently arrived at Camelot, Perceval is the brother of Sir Lamorak and so the son of King Pelinore, who killed King Lot and thus began a feud with the house of Orkney. Perceval has renounced any such feuds, and, championed by Sir Lancelot, is devoted to chivalry and ready to become a knight of the Round Table.

Robin Kempe: Captain of the King's Guard and of the Royal

Archers, Robin spends a good deal of time on guard in the barbican of Camelot, when he isn't training his archers. One of Robin's favorite pastimes is goading Gildas of Cornwall, for whom he has a good deal of affection.

Roger: Roger is the chief cook of Camelot.

Rosemounde of Brittany: Lady Rosemounde is the seventeen-year-old lady-in-waiting to Queen Guinevere who is the object of Gildas's deepest affections. She is daughter of Duke Hoel of Britany, and therefore is obligated to make a politically advantageous marriage. Her half-sister is Isolde of the White Hands, whose reputation she is concerned with protecting.

Safer: Sir Safer, a Moorish knight, is brother to Sir Palomides and his closest companion and confidante.

Sagramore: Sir Sagramore, now deceased, was nephew to the Emperor of Constantinople. Formerly a companion of Sir Tristram's, he was implicated in King Mark's plot to destroy Tristram in the previous novel.

Thomas: Young sandy-haired squire to Sir Ywain, Thomas is one of Gildas of Cornwall's closer friends.

Tristram: Sir Tristram was nephew to King Mark of Cornwall, and in love with his uncle's queen, La Belle Isolde. He was married to Isolde of the White Hands, a noblewoman of Brittany—daughter of Duke Hoel, sister of the lord Kaherdin, and half-sister to Rosemounde of Brittany. He was well-known as one of the three greatest knights of the Round Table.

Urban: Abbot of the Marmoutier monastery of Saint Vincent in Saint-Malo, which protects the Lady Brangwen after her mistress's death, and houses Brother Oswald, physician who attended on the dying Sir Tristram.

Vivien: Lady Vivien is one of Queen Guinevere's ladies-in-waiting. She is French by birth, has green eyes, and enjoys romances, poetry, and gossip.

William of Caen: Sir William of Caen is a knight in the service of Lord Kaherdin. He is a strait-laced, chivalrous knight, who believes in following all the rules of courtesy and keeping himself sober and uncorrupted.

Ywain: Sir Ywain, known as the "Knight of the Lion" because he often goes on adventures with his pet lion, is another nephew of King Arthur, the son of King Uriens and Morgan la Fay, Arthur's half-sister through his mother Ygraine. Sir Ywain is devoted to his cousins Sir Gawain and Sir Gareth.

ABOUT THE AUTHOR

Jay Ruud is a retired professor of medieval literature at the University of Central Arkansas. In addition to *Fatal Feast* and *The Knight's Riddle*, the first two books in this series of Merlin mysteries, he is the author of *"Many a Song and Many a Leccherous Lay": Tradition and Individuality in Chaucer's Lyric Poetry* (1992), the *Encyclopedia of Medieval Literature* (2006), *A Critical Companion to Dante* (2008), and *A Critical Companion to Tolkien* (2011). He taught taught at UCA for fourteen years, prior to which he was Dean of the College of Arts and Sciences at Northern State University in South Dakota. He has a Ph.D. in Medieval Literature from the University of Wisconsin-Milwaukee.

CPSIA information can be obtained
at www.ICGtesting.com
Printed in the USA
FFOW03n1330190318
45725364-46576FF